★

Frantically I went through the rest of the drawers even though in all the years I'd owned the gun, I'd always kept it in the same place. *No gun.* I dumped all the drawers out onto the bed. Still no gun. It had been there the night Flynn had interrogated me. I'd taken it out and sniffed the barrel. Put it back.

Flynn.

I'd told him I hadn't taken it out of the chest of drawers in my bedroom for at least a year. He would know exactly where it was. *"At least you got some guy on fire investigating,"* Stuart had said, *"willing to do anything, no matter how sleazy, to get his man or woman."*

Goddamn it. *"If you think of anything else call me day or night,"* Flynn had said as he'd handed me his card. I got my purse, unzipped the inner pouch and found it. I punched in the home number.

There was a click. "Flynn here."

"You dirty rat, you took my gun," I said.

★

DEAD FOR THE WINTER

BETSY THORNTON

WORLDWIDE®

TORONTO • NEW YORK • LONDON
AMSTERDAM • PARIS • SYDNEY • HAMBURG
STOCKHOLM • ATHENS • TOKYO • MILAN
MADRID • WARSAW • BUDAPEST • AUCKLAND

DEAD FOR THE WINTER

A Worldwide Mystery/January 2006

First published by St. Martin's Press, LLC

ISBN 0-373-26551-4

Grateful acknowledgment is made for permission to print an excerpt from the following: "Fern Hill" by Dylan Thomas, from *The Poems of Dylan Thomas,* Copyright © 1945 by The Trustees for the copyrights of Dylan Thomas. Reprinted by permission of New Directions Publishing Corp.

All characters in this book are fictitious, and any resemblance to actual persons, living or dead, is purely coincidental.

Printed in U.S.A.

For Patrick

PROLOGUE

HE STOOD LOOKING OUT through the back window of his workshop. Dotted with mesquite bushes and scrub oak, the damp red desert stretched for maybe a quarter mile down to the cottonwoods that lined the river. The leaves of the cottonwoods were just beginning to turn yellow. Green tinged with gold. Beautiful, but he didn't notice.

It had rained for the last two days. Two and a half hours ago, Heather had walked down to the river; he knew it was two and a half hours because he'd been checking his watch every half hour. She'd gone there to do some watercolor sketches and to look for tadpoles. Why wasn't she back? He knew how she worked, so quickly, deftly, maybe five minutes a sketch. Two and a half hours was more than sixty sketches.

Wasn't it too late for tadpoles?

He looked at his watch again, then walked over to his workbench and stared at the board he'd been sanding, part of some shelving for the McGees. Fifteen minutes. He would sand for fifteen minutes, then he would go back to the window. Thirteen minutes later he walked back and looked out again. Nothing had changed, except for a big old jackrabbit, hopping through the mesquite.

There was no reason why he couldn't walk down to the river himself. Maybe take a jar, in case there *were* tadpoles. She'd found some last year, brought them home, built a little environment for them in a shallow bowl with rocks and watched as they grew legs. Then one morning they were all gone, hopped away to their death. Little black shriveled corpses had littered the house for months.

"Hi," he would say. "I needed a break."

But pride held him back. His mind swarmed with nasty thoughts; the phone calls, a few months ago. He'd go out on some job at night and try to call her and the phone, always busy. She wasn't a woman to gab on the phone to her friends, not even her best friend Diana. Who then? Who had she been talking to?

Then suddenly, in the midst of his thoughts about that interminable busy signal, he saw her coming through a break in the trees. Not alone. Damien was with her. That little phony. *I knew it,* he thought. *Goddamnit.* He kicked at a block of wood and sent it skittering across the floor.

Heather was wearing faded jeans, a size too big, a blue T-shirt, and her silly galoshes, also too big. Damien was in black; always in black, so *pretentious*. He couldn't hear what they were saying, of course, but they were laughing about something. Damien was carrying her watercolor stuff. They looked so relaxed, easy with each other, they might have been brother and sister.

Maybe that was all it was, brother and sister. But if it were something else—Heather, in some really weird way, Heather was so *innocent*. He knew how easily these things happened; knew the whole routine so well. The ritual.

God knows what he might have found them doing if he'd gone down there. He clenched his jaw. For a moment he wished he had and caught them, then everything would be out in the open. Simple. He walked back to his workbench.

He was fine-sanding the board's edge when they reached the building; he heard their voices coming round the side. Still laughing, *what was the joke?*

"Sweetie pie!" called Heather, as she came in the door.

He looked up as if surprised, putting down the sanding block. *Sweetie pie.* Her hair was matted from the damp so her ears stuck out, her face flushed pink with happiness.

"You should have come along!" Her voice was vibrant, filled with excitement. "It's so *beautiful* down there!"

"No kidding!" He smiled welcomingly. "Damien! How you doing?" Hearty voice. "You guys find any tadpoles?"

"Not one," said Damien.

He looked at Damien, sizing him up. Vain as a teenage girl in those black clothes. He smiled again, disarmingly, to put Damien off guard.

I'll kill him.

ONE

CRAIG TALKED NONSTOP the whole hour and a half from his place in Cochise County, where I'd picked him up, all the way to Tucson International Airport.

"I think the main problem is my soul. I mean people like you and me, we don't think of ourselves as religious so we don't use that word too much, you know? Soul. Still, we've got one, I know that, and someone like you, Chloe, a normal person, well, your soul is basically okay, maybe not great all the time, but okay. Mine has been stagnating."

I circled the parking lot, looking for a space. They were renovating the airport, and nothing seemed to be in the right place. It was hard to concentrate with Craig talking.

"I think the reason I've been feeling so diminished lately," he went on, "is because the soul is spiritual, and I've been treating it with chemicals. Where's that at? Treating the most precious thing we have with chemicals. In a way it's an insult to God—the Life Force, Higher Power, whatever you want to call it."

I said warningly, "I hope you brought your prescriptions." Ahead I thought I saw an empty slot, but, damn, there was a motorcycle in it. "You did, didn't you?"

"*Of course* I did," said Craig with mock patience. "Have a little faith, Chloe. Not that they've been that helpful lately. But this South American thing is going to work, I can sense it. I'll be meeting real people, poor people, people living on the edge of life just barely surviving. Have you ever thought about how that would affect *you*, Chloe? Have you?"

"Have I *what?*" Damn, I'd gone down this row just a moment ago.

"Thought about how living on the edge of life would affect you." His voice rose. "I mean, *really* thought about it."

My head felt like it was in a vise. "Not *now*. Stop, okay? Just for a minute. I'm trying to park and I can't focus."

"What do you need to focus for? Either there's a space or there isn't."

"So, there isn't." I stopped the car. "Listen, you're going to have to get out here. This is fairly close. The last thing we need is for you to miss your plane."

"Okay, okay, *okay*." He opened the door, reached in the back and pulled out his backpack, all he would need to spend six months with poor people.

I leaned over from the driver's seat to kiss him goodbye. Our heads bumped.

"Have a wonderful trip," I said.

"Wait. I just remembered."

"What?"

"You said you need a bookcase in your living room. In that funny space where nothing fits."

"Craig, *go.*"

"I got the name of a carpenter for you. He lives in Prophecy and he's good—more than good. He's an artist really. And he's reasonable too. I wrote it down." He patted his pockets. "Where the hell—"

"Don't worry," I said, the anxiety of the punctual gripping my okay soul. "I'll figure something out. You're late. Just *go.*"

"Found it!" He smiled happily and thrust a piece of paper at me. It fluttered to the floor. I leaned down and picked it up.

"I'm off. Bye," he said. "I'll write when I can. At least a postcard from Manaus, if they have a post office."

I watched him walk away, a tall tanned man with a brilliant smile. He'd been my boyfriend for more than a year. I watched until he reached the entrance and vanished inside.

Then I put Radiohead in the CD player, *The Bends,* started up the car again, and drove out of the parking lot. Over Tucson, the autumn sky was a clear luminous blue. There were palm trees everywhere. Ahh. No more Craig for six months. My basically okay soul seemed to slowly expand and drift upward, into that blue friendly sky.

I LIVE IN OLD DUDLEY, which used to be the biggest town in Cochise County; a copper-mining town, complete with bars, churches, a big hotel, and even an opera house. The mines went bust some thirty years ago but it's still the county seat. The little wooden mining shacks straggle every which way up the sides of the steep hills, picturesque enough to have attracted a whole new set of people, New Agers: artists, craftspeople and wannabes, massage therapists, aging hippies, retirees, and the certifiably crazy, all living as well as possible on limited funds, trust funds, early retirement funds, and funny money.

In no time a funky miner's shack that had once sold for five thousand dollars when the mines closed down went to fifty thousand unrenovated, a hundred thousand or more fixed up. Me, I moved here from New York before the boom because I inherited a house. I work as a victim advocate at the county attorney's office.

A couple of weeks after Craig left I called the carpenter he'd recommended. His name was Terry Barnett and he lived in Prophecy, a small settlement fifteen miles away near the San Pedro River. It had taken in the arty, hippie, New Age overflow from Old Dudley when the real estate boom hit.

I liked Terry's voice on the phone, relaxed and easygoing, and we made an appointment. About a week later an old red pickup pulled up next to my Geo in the driveway Craig had paved with bricks for me, and parked right on top of the oil spots from Craig's leaky truck.

I watched through the kitchen window as a slender man in his forties got out. He had light brown curly hair, longish and thinning a little, gold wire-rimmed glasses. An ordinary-looking man; not tall, not short, wearing jeans and a white T-shirt with a logo so faded you couldn't tell what it was anymore. He was whistling but stopped when I opened the door.

"You must be Chloe." He smiled. It wasn't a Craig smile, all fireworks and complicated emotions, but when he smiled he stopped looking ordinary. Behind the wire-rimmed glasses, his green eyes danced with light. "I'm Terry Barnett."

His hand came out and I shook it. It was warm and dry.

I led him into the living room and showed him the space. It was between two windows, a little too narrow for a standard bookcase. He measured it, then measured it again.

"Twice," he said, conversationally. "You always measure twice. I used to measure three times, as a trick, to slow myself down."

"It's not good to be fast?"

"If you're too fast, you lose your watchfulness." He smiled again. Zing. I felt myself connecting. Fun, fun, fun. I must be desperate. He was the first man who'd been in the house since Craig left.

Not that Craig was completely gone, remnants of him were everywhere. The vegetable garden he'd dug outside, his gardening books on the coffee table, along with a book he'd lent me months ago: *No Mercy—A Journey to the Heart of the Congo*.

"Watchfulness," I said. "Aha. A Zen carpenter."

"Golly gee." Terry ducked his head boyishly, looking embarrassed. "You're interested in Zen?"

There was something really appealing about him, charming. I laughed and kicked at the coffee table Craig had made from old sautillo tile. "My brother's a Buddhist, he even lives in a monastery—Karme Choling, in Vermont."

"No kidding."

"It really saved him," I said.

Terry sat companionably on Craig's favorite chair by one

of the windows, not in a hurry about anything, and looked at me with interest. "How's that?"

"Oh, he was a wild kid, he went to prison for a year in Michigan, when he was nineteen." I couldn't believe I was telling him this. "Possession of marijuana, Michigan had really tough drug laws. And then…he was different when he got out. Kind of, I don't know—frantically phony? Until the Buddhism."

"Prison." Terry's eyes were warm, concerned. "That's really tough. Nineteen years old. The things we do when we're young. We're all casualties of our youth, in some ways."

Or just casualties, I thought, thinking of Craig. "You're not from around here, are you?" I said, guiltily changing the subject.

"The Midwest." He rolled his eyes. "O-hi-o. Not where you'd want to spend the rest of your life, but it was a great place to be a kid." He pushed his glasses farther up on his nose and added a little wistfully, "You should see it in spring; all those lawns like green velvet, closest thing to paradise."

"You miss it."

He shook his head. "Can't take the winters. I used to like the cold, I lived in Boulder, Colorado, till seven years ago. My mom got sick. My dad was already dead, so I went back to Ohio and looked after her. It was winter then. Snow falling outside, all day, all night, while I watched her dying."

His green eyes dimmed a little. Then he shook his head, almost apologetically. "That was the hardest thing I've ever done. I sat by her bed and we planned her funeral. It kind of kept her going. When we got done with that, we planned mine."

"Your funeral?"

"Yeah. I've got the plot all bought and paid for. I promised her I'd be buried in the old Presbyterian cemetery right next to her and my dad, so she wouldn't be too lonely."

I was impressed. Most men wouldn't have the emotional what?—*composure?*—to tell a story like that. "I'm sorry," I said.

"Anyway, after that I needed to get away from all those winters. So I figured the Southwest. I was in Tucson, twenty years ago, with my brother Fred and I liked it then."

"What was in Tucson twenty years ago?"

"As it turned out, nothing." He laughed. "We were chasing a phantom."

"Like what? A dream of the Wild West?"

"She was a dream all right." He made a face. "It's a long story. Talk about being casualties of our youth. I guess it was hearing about your brother, I even mentioned it. I haven't spoken to Fred in years. We're pretty much permanently estranged."

I loved both my brothers with a passion, Danny who was still alive, James, who was dead. "That's so sad."

For a moment Terry looked off into space, as if remembering. "I don't know, Fred missed the boat somewhere. Sort of weirdly needy, as if nothing was ever enough for him." He shrugged. "Anyway—" He stood up reluctantly. "On to business. You want to paint the bookcase or keep it the natural wood?"

"Wood, I think."

"Good choice. I've got some samples in the truck," he said, "if you want to come look? I was thinking if you want natural wood we can stain it, cherry would be good. For wood, I think you'll like the maple, not as grainy as oak, more subtle."

I followed him out to the old red truck parked on top of Craig's oil stains. Fall had hung on and on this year. It was halfway to December, and still balmy in midafternoon. Orange Mexican sunflowers planted by Craig lined the driveway, watching my every move. I ignored them.

Leaves had drifted into the truck bed while we were inside. They lay among some pale wooden boards, a brilliant yellow.

"Look at that!" said Terry. His face shone like a kid's with a new computer game and he struck me then as a person infinitely easy to be around. "Beautiful, aren't they."

"Yes," I said.

He took some of the boards, one-by-fours cut short, out of the truck and showed them to me, his hands caressing the wood, as if each piece were a treasure. "This is the maple. See how fine the grain is?"

I touched it. "Yes, I do see. I'll trust your judgment."

"Maple then, stained cherry. Well, I guess we're all done." He put the wood back. "I should go."

But he stayed, leaning against the truck. That was fine by me. He was the most attractive man I'd met in years. He looked up at the sky. "Nice day."

I looked up too. The sun on my eyelashes put halos on everything.

"You ever have things you want to forget come back to you," said Terry suddenly. "And then you can't get them out of your head?"

I laughed. "All the time."

For a moment he paused, our eyes met. Then, "I really have to go," he said. He took out his keys and put his hand on the door handle. "You're so easy to talk to. We should talk some more sometime."

"Sure," I said.

WOULD WE HAVE TALKED some more? Maybe not, if I hadn't gone to Sierra Vista that weekend. If Larry hadn't gotten the flu. If it hadn't been raining. Sierra Vista is twenty-five miles away, now the biggest town in Cochise County, and it had recently built a real mall. Larry is a gay friend of mine and we like to go there, sit on the benches and watch the people go by, while Larry analyzes their appalling fashion choices.

I went anyway, by myself, in the rain, and browsed Dillard's. I bought three pairs of panty hose for work and then went and sat on a bench in the false light near the food court.

"Busted," someone said, "at the mall."

I looked up and there was Terry, basically an Old Dudley kind of person even though he lived in Prophecy. Old Dudley people affected to scorn malls. He wore another faded T-shirt, blue this time, and his curly hair was damp. Too manly, no doubt, to own an umbrella. A smile flowed over my face like warm water. I couldn't help myself.

"What do you mean, busted," I said. "You're here too."

"Sears," he said. *"Tools."*

"Ah."

He sat down, stretching out his legs. "I've got an idea," he said. In the mall light his eyes were amazingly green. I wondered if he wore tinted contacts. He was close enough I could smell the wet denim of his Levi's.

"What's that?" I asked belatedly.

"It's lunchtime, I'm hungry, and the food here really sucks. I don't want to risk my truck's crummy brakes all the way home till the rain lets up. But it can make it to this Thai restaurant just down the road."

We ran though the rain to the old red truck, everything inside it damp and smelling of motor oil, wipers hiss-hissing as we drove out of the mall parking lot onto the highway.

The restaurant was jammed with people; Sierra Vista people, strangers, not like in Old Dudley where everyone always looks familiar. We sat cocooned in a back booth near a window that was all steamed up, laughing a lot at nothing. It was so noisy we could hardly hear each other but it didn't matter. We talked about—oh, my job, Terry's theories about art, but all I really remember was the cozy warmth and the tastes of coconut and lemongrass.

Terry dropped me off at my car, back at the mall. "That was really fun," he said. "I was thinking about going to Agua Prieta tomorrow evening. Have dinner over there, across the line. Like to come along?"

I smiled, I nodded. "Yes."

LARRY CALLED ME that night. "How was the mall?" he asked.

"Super-duper," I said. "And I went to that Thai place for lunch. It was great. We'll have to go there sometime."

"Aha." Larry coughed. He coughed some more, then got it under control. "You can't fool me. Something fabulous happened, didn't it? I can hear it in your voice. You met someone. Who?"

"Never mind."

"You shameless hussy. Poor old Craig. Suffering with the peons, and you're having *fun*."

"It's his own fault," I said.

"You have to tell me *everything*."

I would have, but he coughed again, great racking coughs. I held the phone away from my ear. When he finally stopped, I said, "You're too sick. Go to bed. Call me when you're better."

What if I had told Larry? It could have been different. Everything. Maybe.

TWO

AGUA PRIETA IS IN Mexico, twenty-five miles south down Highway 80, across from Douglas, Arizona. Terry took me to a shabby little seafood restaurant off the main drag, where we were the only gringos in the place. The flaking plaster walls were hung with fraying nets and chipped plaster swordfish and the scratchy sound system played "Don't Rock the Boat" complete with nautical sound effects over and over and over.

I ordered shrimp, *camarones rancheros,* and Terry had shrimp too, *al ajillo.*

"I brought you something," Terry said.

"Oh?"

He handed it to me. "It's half a black walnut. Ohio's full of black walnut trees. My father used to polish the nuts up, kind of a hobby."

The walnut was still warm from being in his pocket; a half circle of wood, polished to a rich wine sheen, etched with black squiggly lines. I turned it over in my hand. Inscribed in tiny letters on the flat part of the circle was my name: Chloe. "Oh, my goodness. Thank you," I said. "It's so beautiful. Your father made it? Shouldn't you hang on to it?"

He smiled his warm smile. "I give a few away, to special people. You're so easy to talk to."

I flushed. Things were taking a turn, accelerating. "You're pretty easy yourself."

He pushed his plate away. I'd eaten all my shrimp, he'd only had half of his. "And I bet you're good at keeping secrets."

"Do you have one?" I looked him in the eyes. It seemed the right time, the right place, to go a little deeper.

He looked embarrassed. There was a little loaded silence. The waiter drifted by and dropped the bill on the table.

Terry stood up and grabbed the bill. "Let's get out of here."

We left and strolled down unevenly paved sidewalks to the town square, sat on a wrought-iron bench. Pole lights shone down on the sycamore trees, on yellow leaves lying in drifts around the bandstand. A crescent moon hung overhead. Although a little chilly, it was a fine clear night. Families were out with their kids, couples held hands. When you go across the line, even in the border towns, you're so clearly in another country; more exotic and mysterious than the U.S.A.

For a while, not talking, we watched the people promenading round the square. I held the walnut half, rubbing its smooth surface. "You've got a secret?" I said at last.

"I didn't say that."

"Not in so many words."

"Listen, Chloe, I—oh, *hell.*" He looked at me, then looked away quickly. "I don't want to spoil the evening."

"It's that bad? Maybe talking will make you feel better," I said lightly, so carelessly. "In my job, I'm used to secrets; sad ones, bad ones, they roll right off me."

He paused. "It's—well, it's kind of hard to explain. Basically, I guess, I think I've screwed up. I mean really screwed up big time."

"Oh?"

"You know how you get some crazy idea in your head and it leads to another idea and another, and pretty soon, you can't get all these crazy ideas out of your head?"

"You said something like that before. I think it's called 'obsession.'"

"Obsession. Whew." He ran his fingers through his hair. "Yeah. Maybe so."

"So what are you obsessing about?"

He hesitated. "Remember I told you how my brother Fred and I came out here to Tucson, twenty years ago? Chasing a phantom?"

"I remember."

"The phantom was a woman, actually, April. Her name was April."

"April."

"April Matasky." He smiled. "She spelled it with a *y* not an *i*. M-A-T-A-S-K-Y. I used to kid her about being Polish. Well, it starts back then with her."

"Didn't you—this was twenty years ago and you're *still* obsessing?"

He nodded. "Something will set me off and I start going over it all and then I do stupid things that I really regret when it's too late."

"Stupid things like screw up big time?"

"Yeah." He hesitated, looking shamefaced. "April." He paused. "She was a free spirit and it made her—I don't know— *dangerous*. Just her being so free in herself made other people—" He stopped, sighed, and for a while he looked out across the square at nothing.

"Look," he said finally, "I have to be honest with you about something."

"Please do," I said. I felt a twinge, a flicker of anxiety, I wasn't sure why. A leaf fell slowly from a sycamore nearby. I watched as it fell and fell and fell. "Honest about what?"

"We really clicked, you and me, right from the beginning. I don't know Craig too well, but he said you're his girlfriend. He's going to be gone for a long time, so I thought you might enjoy going out, just, you know, for dinner."

Was that what this was about? Guilt about seeing someone else's girlfriend? "I do enjoy going out," I said reassuringly. "As for being his girlfriend, that's up in the air at the moment."

"I didn't know what it was," he said. "I can see now how

we could be close and I feel sort of bad, like I've been using you."

Using me. That wasn't what I'd expected him to say. Suddenly I knew I didn't want to hear what he might tell me next. In denial, I drifted for a moment, looking across the square at the deserted bandstand, lonely under the pole lights. Summers, there would be concerts.

"Don't tell me," I said finally. "You're married or something."

"Not something, just married."

I was stunned but I should have known. I should have checked him out. I should have asked, so simple. *Shit. Shit, shit, shit.* "I have to admit I would have liked this full disclosure a little earlier," I said. "Does your wife know you're here now?"

"She's out of town, she went down into Mexico with a friend of hers."

I was pissed. Of course I was. Who wouldn't be. Or maybe I shouldn't be. It wasn't like I never socialized, never went anywhere with a man unless it was a romance. But this had never been like going to the mall with Larry and, besides, Larry was gay.

Temporarily paralyzed by what?—good manners?—I wanted to say something but nothing came into my mind. I moved down the bench, a little away from Terry, feeling my body tense up. We sat for a while in silence. Two people having a fight; that was how we probably looked.

Across the square, someone, a gringo like us, waved at Terry, who didn't seem to notice. The man waved again and came closer. He was very tall, skeletally thin, with a black beard.

"Is that someone you know?" I asked.

"Yes." Terry sounded reluctant. He gave a desultory wave and half turned on the bench, away from the man. "I don't want to encourage him. He's really boring."

Then I caught on. Oh. Of course. He didn't want to be seen with me by someone he knew. Someone who might tell his wife. Terry had probably been leading up to some long complaint about her. Well, I didn't want to hear it.

"You know," I said, "this whole thing was a crummy idea. I think I'd like to go home now."

WE DROVE BACK to Dudley. In the car, we chatted like two polite strangers. And whatever it was he'd needed to talk about pretty much went by the wayside.

He parked in my driveway and I started to get out.

"Wait," he said.

I paused.

"Look, we were getting along so well. And I honestly do need to talk to someone."

"Maybe I'm not the best someone."

He groaned and rested his head on the steering wheel. "You know, I go along trying to do the right things, most of the time. I try hard.

Then somehow I screw up. I didn't have bad intentions toward you. I really didn't. I'm truly sorry."

Actually, I believed him. He sounded genuinely like a man in pain. He struck me as more than just temporarily lonely because his wife was out of town. His loneliness seemed more profound than that.

"You don't have to apologize," I said. "I probably overreacted."

"No. I should have told you right away. But it was so nice being around you, someone who wasn't mad at me."

"Well, you fixed that," I said.

I wouldn't have been so annoyed if I hadn't really liked him. If he needed to talk so much, why didn't he confide in his wife? Even if she was down in Mexico, she could check in. Unless she was mad at him. Right, Chloe, blame his wife.

I sensed myself heading for a slippery slope.

"I don't take responsibility for my own actions," Terry said despairingly. "Then I try to drag you in."

Such drama. The poor guy needed a hug, or at least a reassuring pat on the hand. You idiot, Chloe, what are you thinking?

"I'm sorry for whatever your problem is," I said, "but good night."

I got out of the car fast, opened my door, went inside, and closed it behind me. As I heard him back out, I realized I was still holding the walnut half. Shit. I opened a drawer in my kitchen—the junk drawer where I kept dried—out shoe polish, expired coupons, bits of string, keys that unlocked nothing-and tossed it in.

BUT IT WASN'T over yet, not quite. I never lock my doors and I came home from work a couple of weeks later to find Terry's bookcase in my living room and the bill on the kitchen counter with his card. He hadn't called to tell me it was done, just took a chance and dropped it off. It was probably better that way. I *knew* it was better that way.

The bookcase was almost too beautiful to fill with books; dovetailed perfectly and the muted grain of the wood, the maple stained cherry, glowing like satin. The card he'd left was a plain card, and he'd written on it with a calligraphic pen, the strokes bold and distinctive:

Terry Barnett
Carpenter
Box 1583
Prophecy, Arizona
555-3235

I took out my checkbook, to pay him, right away. I wondered if his wife did the accounts, lots of them did. I imagined her, dour-faced, a little bitchy maybe, *mad at him;* opening the envelope, seeing the check, Chloe Newcombe, tossing it in a pile for him to endorse. The phone rang.

I checked my caller ID and recognized the number for Safe Haven, the domestic-violence shelter in Sierra Vista.

"Hello?"

"Chloe. It's Evangeline."

Oh, God, speaking of wives—Evangeline Nolan.

Our first meeting was at a pretrial hearing in justice court over in Sierra Vista. Her husband Chip had been charged with criminal damage and threatening and intimidating. He'd systemically broken almost every dish in the house after she told him she wanted to move out. "What's the big deal?" he'd kept saying at the hearing; a blond guy with a crew cut, boyish. "They were my dishes. I paid for them."

This was correct. The prosecutor dropped the criminal damage charges, Chip pled to threatening and intimidating, got probation and two weeks in jail suspended. He was ordered to stay away from Evangeline.

Now she'd taken to calling me at work with long and repetitious complaints. Somehow she'd gotten hold of my home number and begun calling me there too. Now she called and called, almost every day. *Now you listen to me, Evangeline,* I wanted to say, *I've got my problems too. This guy I met, he—*

"Hello, Evangeline," I said wearily.

I PUNCHED IN Larry's number.

"Larry," I said when he answered. "Oh, *Larry.*"

"Uh-oh. What?"

"The guy I ran into at the mall? We went to that Thai place?"

"He's married."

"Shit. How'd you know that?"

"What else could it be?" He paused. "Poor thing. How bad is it?"

"Scale of one to ten? Four. Oh, maybe five." More like seven, but I have my pride.

"You want my advice?" Larry said. "Stay away. Cool down. It's not worth it."

BUT I DID SEE Terry one more time, two or three weeks later, at the Rooster's Attic, a big antiques and collectibles store just outside Old Dudley. I'd gone there to browse and was just headed out the door when someone said, "Chloe?"

There he was, standing beside an old blue Volvo parked next to my Geo. Not completely cooled down, my heart made corny little thumps, you can't control these things. I hadn't seen him inside but the place was like a big barn, piled high with basically junk.

"Hi," I said breezily, not really looking at him. "You got my check? The bookcase is beautiful."

"I feel so shitty about everything," he said forlornly.

"Don't. It's okay."

"Really?" His tone was skeptical.

"Really." I stared past him, into the middle distance beyond his shoulder.

Larry was right, it wasn't worth it. It was a shame if he was in a bad marriage but he had to face up to that directly and deal with it. He had to grow up and take charge of his life. Or maybe he would get lucky like me and his wife would decide to go to South America for six months. At that moment I felt myself forgiving him. We're all weak.

I came toward him and we hugged. The day was chilly, and he was wearing a blue sweater covered with fuzzy little balls. They tickled my chin. We hugged several seconds longer than strictly friends would. But like I said, we're all weak.

Then I stepped back. For the first time I really looked at him.

Behind the gold wire-rims his green eyes seemed burdened, exhausted: a man in over his head and struggling to stay afloat.

He turned, opened the door of the blue Volvo, and got inside. "Bye, Chloe," he said.

"Terry," I began. "Are you okay?"

But the door of the Volvo slammed shut, cutting him off from my concern. He started the car and drove away.

THREE

SWEET, SWEET HEATHER, he thought. But what had she done to her hair? Cut herself bangs. They were way too long, but he wouldn't tell her. Funny Heather. She stood in the glassed-in porch, among the geraniums she grew so profusely. She only liked the red ones, not the white or the pink. She was on her way out, wearing jeans—too big—a long-sleeved black T-shirt, and the leather vest she'd painted herself with stars and a crescent moon that dripped roses. The January evening was chilly.

"Don't you need a coat?" he said.

She shook her head. "The heater works."

"You should take one anyway," he said. "What if the car breaks down?" He wanted to keep her around a little longer. Afraid, he thought, I'm afraid where she might be going and afraid to be alone with myself.

"It won't," she said. "Sure you don't want to come along?"

He shook his head. "Too tired. I was up too late, finishing that job for the Meekses. I really got into it and I couldn't stop. You know how I get."

"I know." She looked concerned. "But you've been working too hard lately, you *know* it. You get so wired up you can't even sleep. You need to take a break sometimes."

But it wasn't that, the working too hard, that made him so he couldn't sleep, it was the worry.

"Besides," said Heather, "it might be fun." He could feel her itching to go but controlling the urge. "A poetry reading at the Cranny." Her mouth twitched. "What could be more delightful."

Almost anything, he thought. He leaned down and brushed at sawdust on his jeans. "Will Damien be reading?" he asked, more to see if Damien would be there, than because he cared even remotely about Damien's lame and useless poetry.

I'll kill him.

She shrugged. "Who knows?"

"I'm just not up for it. I wouldn't be any fun." He paused. "You know how you hate me when I'm no fun."

She rolled her eyes and brushed at her bangs. Such silly bangs. She never cared if things were silly or not, just did what pleased her. And yet she was basically so defenseless. Didn't Damien realize that? He wanted to protect her, didn't know how.

"I'll do a little cleanup in the shop," he told her. "Then I'll crash."

"Fall asleep on the cot, probably." She pouted. The pout said, I'll come home to a cold bed, without you in it. Not a real pout but a compliment.

Did she mean it?

She turned away, and opened the porch door. "Well, ciao."

So defenseless, and those ridiculous bangs. She would be cold, with just the vest over the T-shirt. And the heater took a while to warm up. "Sure you don't want to take a coat?"

"Don't *worry*."

"Ciao then," he said.

He watched her get in the car, drive away. The taillights got smaller and smaller, then vanished. One of these days he would like to follow her, see if she went where she said she was going, but tonight he really was tired. And Damien probably would be reading. Even though Damien was just a kid, she had more fun with Damien than she did with him. Maybe that was all it was, fun.

It would be nice if he didn't have to kill him.

He turned tiredly and walked through the house and out the back door to the shop. The night was cold, colder than usual for Arizona. He thought again of Heather without a coat. In the distance, maybe a quarter of a mile away, he could see lights on in a house, though his neighbors' house, the Blofelds', was dark. He breathed in deeply. Somebody was burning mesquite in their woodstove. He loved the smell of mesquite. He'd gotten where he could identify woods by the smell of their burning.

What have I done? The thought drifted up in his mind and he staved it off by thinking about Ohio.

Back in Ohio when he was a boy, it got seriously cold. They'd had a big fireplace, and they hadn't burned mesquite, mostly oak. He almost thought of his mother, but staved that off as well—too painful. Better to think of hanging out with his best friend, Mike O'Reilly. The two of them had given his brother Fred such a hard time.

Poor old Fred. Even though Fred was doing a lot better than he was financially, in fact, was actually a big success to their father's way of thinking, he always thought, *Poor old Fred.* But maybe Fred was okay now, with all his success, so why feel sorry for him? Because he didn't have someone like Heather? That made him smile.

But then he felt worse.

He went inside the shop and flicked on the light; it had once been a kind of barn, not a back East barn but it had high ceilings. The little potbellied cast-iron stove was still hot. He'd finished a cabinet for Howard Meeks and his wife late the night before, it had to be two a.m. at least, and he'd delivered it this afternoon. The Meekses were religious nuts, probably they'd fill it up with tracts and Bibles.

Tools were scattered along the workbench, the floor covered with sawdust. Even though he was tired, he picked up the broom and swept the larger pieces into a pile in the middle of the floor. He couldn't stop thinking about Heather.

She was happy, wasn't she? From time to time things went off course between them. *My fault,* he thought, *but I'd rather be with her than anyone else in the world.* Years of marriage, and he still wasn't sure what she was thinking.

What have I done? Are we still safe, Heather and me?

He looked for the dustpan and found it under the workbench. He'd need the shop vac for the finer stuff, but didn't see it. She must have borrowed it and he didn't feel like going back to the house and tracking it down. Too tired. Worry had sapped his energy.

Maybe a little nap would be good. He went over to the cot at the back of the shop. It was all made up, pillow plumped. He was touched. She must have come in while he was delivering the cabinet and changed the sheets. He pulled off his boots, kept his down vest on and pulled back the wool army blanket. The sheets had a faint detergent smell, sickly sweet, because the washing machine, as Heather had told him a million times, wasn't rinsing very well.

He lay down. The sheets were cool, but not unpleasant. He was asleep almost at once. A deep sleep. Maybe it was dreamless, or maybe he dreamed of Heather, or of being a boy in Ohio, of poor old Fred. Or maybe his worries surfaced again and woke him later. If he heard the sounds outside, rustling movements, he might have thought it was an animal. Heather's orange cat Pi-Pi or a jackrabbit, maybe a javelina, nosing around.

Or Heather herself, come home.

FOUR

IT WAS JANUARY IN THE HIGH desert and cold. Not cold like it used to be when I lived in New York, but cold enough to be uncomfortable in my house without central heating. It was close to ten p.m. and I was down for the night, wearing thermal pj's and chenille socks, the electric blanket on high. One-postcard-from-Brasília-Craig was still in South America, *Hi, Chloe, keeping warm? I am.*

The phone rang. Oh, please, God, not Evangeline. I checked my caller ID—unavailable.

"Hello?"

"Chloe? Lori Bishop." Lori is a Victim Witness volunteer over in Sierra Vista, a practical businesswoman who runs a dog-grooming service, the Pink Poodle, but right now she sounded a little panicked.

"Ah," I said. Even though I'm employed by the county attorney's office, a paid day job, in a pinch I go out on calls to victims at night with the volunteers. "What's up?"

"Stacy's on the schedule with me but she has the flu and I can't seem to reach anyone else. We got a call-out, a death notification, in Prophecy."

"No kidding," I said. "Prophecy."

"It's halfway between Dudley and Sierra Vista so I thought maybe—"

"We could meet there," I finished. "Sure. I can do that." One of my chenille socks was lost in the bottom of the bed. I threw back the covers and hit the cold floor half barefoot. "Prophecy," I said again.

"Guess who's the investigator," said Lori. "Flynn."

"Flynn?" I said. "Supernarc?" His first name was Brian, but everyone called him Flynn. His picture had been on the front page of the *Sierra Vista Review* a few months ago, standing victorious on a mountain of confiscated marijuana. "What's he got to do with this?"

"He was rotated out of narcotics," said Lori. "I guess he got a little too famous. This looks like an accident but, you know, they always send an investigator anyway, just in case."

I grabbed the black sweats I'd been wearing an hour earlier and finally asked the question. "So who's dead?"

"His name is, umm, here it is—Terry Barnett."

I tripped, one leg through the sweats, and sat down abruptly on the bed. *"Who?"*

"Terry Barnett."

"Oh, no." Flash: Terry, hair damp, Levi's damp, green eyes. *Busted at the mall.* "Oh, my God," I said. "Are you sure?"

"That's the name they gave me. Why? You know him?"

"I do. Yes. He built a bookcase for me." I could see him now, measuring the space. Not once, but twice. It used to be three times.

"His wife wasn't home when Flynn called me but she's bound to come home sooner or later. Do you know her too?"

"No," I said. "I don't even know her name." He'd never said it, not once.

"Heather. Heather Stephens."

"Stephens?" I said. "Not Barnett?"

"Flynn said 'Stephens' and Flynn said 'wife.' That's all I can tell you. So…" Lori hesitated. "You want to pass?"

I should pass, I knew it. But then who would go with Lori? Besides, I was seized with an avid and voyeuristic compulsion to meet Terry's wife. Heather Stephens.

"No, I'll go. But what happened?"

"There was a fire in his shop, Flynn said. Looks like he died of smoke inhalation."

God, what a waste. What a terrible waste.

"You okay?" Lori asked. "Sure you can handle this?"

"Yes."

I put my feelings on hold, as best I could, and unbuttoned my pajama top, slid it off, *brrr*.

"If the wife gets back there before us," Lori went on, "Flynn said he'll do the actual notification, but he wants us there, you know, to look after her."

Did I have enough gas in the car? Had I charged my cell phone lately? Shit, shit. Awkwardly, still holding the phone, I put on a bra, *brr*, and black sweatshirt. I wondered if I could find the black gloves left over from when I lived in New York.

"Here's how you get there," said Lori. "Ready?"

Shit, a pen. "No," I said. "Hold on."

TERRY, HIS GREEN EYES exhausted the last time I'd seen him. I'd been carrying him around in the back of my mind, like unfinished business. Thinking dumb thoughts like probably his wife was a heartless shrew who he stayed with out of inertia; that people get divorced; that everything changes. And from time to time I still wondered what it was he'd wanted to tell me on the bench in the town square in Mexico, something about a woman he'd known twenty years ago named April, who was a free spirit.

It was a Tuesday night. My street was quiet. My neighbor Lourdes had gone to Safford to visit relatives and Bill, my other neighbor, had been spending all his time at his new redheaded girlfriend's house. Tiny flecks of snow swirled around the streetlights as I backed the car out of the driveway and headed down the steep hill. At least it wasn't icy yet. And the snow didn't look like it would stick.

I passed darkened houses. Everyone in Dudley was either asleep or frozen stiff. The steering wheel was a plastic icicle and I hadn't found the New York gloves. At least I did have enough gas. The heater kicked in just out of town at the traffic circle that leads to Highway 92.

I drove slowly, numbly, feeling upset about Terry, and sad, almost tender. A guy in a bad marriage who'd lost control of his life. I might have let him talk a little more if I hadn't been a heartless egomaniac.

More tiny flecks of snow danced in my headlights as they drifted across the black highway. No moon or stars and no houses for miles and miles and ten miles to go to the turnoff at signpost 29. I was utterly alone.

I thought again of the careful way Terry had measured for the bookcase. Thought of the Buddhist term my brother Danny used so often. Terry had used it too. Watchfulness. A fire in his workshop? Terry, what happened to your watchfulness?

A rhyme from a childhood poem went through my head. To stave off ghosts, I recited some lines out loud, "'I listened, I opened, I looked to left and right, but naught there was a-stirring in the still dark night.'"

A couple of miles from where signpost 29 would be, I saw the lights of another car, coming toward me. It turned. Probably Lori. I passed the signpost and turned too, went by a little store, dark except for red and green neon lights in the windows. There must be a curve ahead, I couldn't see any taillights. I sensed rather than saw houses, mostly dark, then a couple with lights still on. After the curve, I saw the blue and red of police lights flashing, and a fire truck; an old blue Volvo and Terry's red truck, where he'd carried the wood samples, littered with yellow leaves.

Look at that. Beautiful, aren't they?
Jesus, I thought, *can I handle this?*

THE SMELL OF SMOKE was thick in the air, and another smell too, the smell of water. Over to my left was a cluster of firemen and a deputy but I headed for Lori, chubby and blond, wearing a fuchsia down jacket over powder-blue sweats. She stood with Flynn, the investigator, and another man, tall and thin, wearing pink-rimmed plastic glasses and a brown knit cap, but it was Flynn, in his forties with a strong jaw and long narrow creases down his cheeks, wearing a dark brown leather jacket, who caught my eye.

Or rather, his eyes, dark and shallow, trapped mine. "You the Chloe we been waiting for?"

I looked away first. "I'm the Chloe," I said.

"The wife's inside." Flynn the supernarc's dark hair was cut short as a storm trooper's. His eyes roamed around, as if a gang of drug lords might be lurking somewhere out there in the dark.

"Did she see him?" I took a breath. "Terry?"

Flynn shook his head. "The body's already been transported. Howard Measley here IDed him."

"Howard *Meeks*," said the other man. He blinked. Behind the pink plastic-rimmed glasses, his eyes looked like a bunny rabbit's. He was holding a Bible. "Terrible thing. Those wood-burning stoves, they ain't safe at all."

"Heather Stephens," I said. "The wife. How'd she take it?"

"She didn't," Flynn said flatly.

"What do you mean?"

"I mean she blanked out. Said she was going to make a pot of coffee."

"Sir?" Howard Meeks pushed the plastic glasses up on his nose and brandished the Bible as if to subdue vampires, or maybe just Flynn.

Flynn's roaming eyes settled on the book. "The EMTs found some sort of religious pamphlet on the floor near the deceased. That yours?"

"Most likely it's the one I gave Terry just the other day," said Howard Meeks. "The one on Brother Louis."

"You the Barnetts' minister?"

"Well, not a minister at all, strictly speaking," said Howard.

"I'm Pentecostal, praise the Lord. And there's certain times when the need for faith comes up real strong." His voice heated up. "Might be that time for Heather. I'll just go inside with these—"

"Sorry," Flynn cut in. "Not unless you're actually her minister. Look, man, I'm a God-mother-country man myself, but people can get funny that way."

My eyes met Lori's. Hers were blue and round and deceptively naive.

"Ladies," said Flynn, looking at us impatiently. "Get on in there. Make sure she's okay."

I followed Lori through the open gate in a weathered cedar fence, into a grassy yard with a flagstone path down the middle that led to a glassed-in porch. The door was wide open. There was something funny about the back of Lori's head.

"Lori," I hissed. "You've got a roller in your hair."

"Mother of *God*." She pulled it out, put it in her pocket. She giggled nervously.

"Careful," I said. "Flynn delivered the death notification. God."

"I think he took some sensitivity training, when he got rotated." Lori knocked on the door which was open. "I *hope*." She knocked again.

"It's just an outside door," I said. Taking charge made me feel better. "There's another one inside."

It, too, was open. Open to the cold, as if whoever had gone in last had forgotten to close it. In the dark, I smelled geraniums. There was a light on but far inside the house.

"Hello?" said Lori again. "Is she elderly? She might be hard of hearing."

"No, she's not *elderly*," I said, thinking of Terry.

"Mrs. Stephens!" shouted Lori.

"In the kitchen!" called a woman's voice. "In back!"

I closed the door behind me to keep out the cold, and we followed the light down a hall, past a door to a darkened living room, wood and ferns, then another door to the kitchen. On a wall through the doorway a large painting glowed with rich tones of brown and red and explosive little suns of gold and silver like some Russian icon, unearthed from a tomb; *beautiful.*

A long oak table, sautillo tile floor, ancient time-colored bottles on the windowsills, Mickey Mouse clock over the sink, with the second hand swooping round and round. All the cabinet doors were open but the room appeared to be empty.

It wasn't till we stepped through the doorway that I saw her, leaning against the counter by a Mr. Coffee machine and an open can of coffee. A small woman, late thirties—early forties, in baggy jeans, boots, and a leather vest. She was holding a coffeepot, a dazed look on her face.

"Heather?" My voice sounded weird, gravelly.

She nodded, brushing aside bangs that were too long with her free hand. I saw blunt-cut nails, a leather bracelet. You couldn't call her pretty—her nose was a little too long, her mouse-brown hair cropped jagged as if she'd done it herself, her wide mouth colorless, skin pale and unadorned. She resembled an androgynous little elf.

"We're with Victim Witness," I said, thinking uncharitably that Terry would be the star in this marriage and this mouse person would be the background; the assistant handling the props. "I'm Chloe and this is Lori. We're here to help if you need us."

"Terry always made the coffee," she said, looking as if she might cry. "I don't know how."

"I know those Mr. Coffee machines," said Lori efficiently. "Use 'em all the time. You fill that pot with water and I'll do the rest."

Heather Stephens turned obediently to the sink. On the back of her leather vest were stars and a silver crescent moon, cascading roses.

"That's a beautiful painting," I said, pointing to the wall, working on contact, as Lori spooned coffee. "Is it a local art-ist?"

"It's me." Heather stood with the pot, head bent like a child, staring at the faucets. "And it's not a painting, it's a collage." Her voice was without affect.

I stared at it. Up close I saw the bottle caps. The silver and gold suns were bottle caps, flattened out, the browns and reds, beer bottle labels. But it was still beautiful, which, for some reason, I found faintly annoying.

Trying again, I blurted out unthinkingly, "Terry did some work for me last fall. A bookcase. He did a wonderful job."

She turned, and looked at me. She really needed to trim those bangs, they mingled with her eyelashes. She brushed at them again. "What was your name?"

I shouldn't have come. What if she knew about me and Terry? What if some night he'd gone into confessional mode, told her? But there was nothing to tell. Some people wouldn't see it that way.

"Chloe," I said and held my breath.

But Heather only nodded, her eyes remote. "I was in Dudley," she said, "at a poetry reading, at the Cranny. I wanted Terry to come along. But he was too tired. He must have been asleep—" She bit her lip. "When I got back, they'd already taken him away." She didn't turn on the water but stood with her back to the sink still holding the coffeepot. "I didn't even get to say goodbye."

"That would be important," I said carefully. "I'm so sorry."

"I mean, how do I even know it was really him?" Her voice rose, coming to life. "Because that Bible-thumper Howard Meeks says so?"

"How well does he know Terry?" I asked.

"*Years.* He's known us for years. He was the first one at the door when we moved in, with his *pamphlets.* But Howard could have, you know"—her wide mouth twitched—"been blinded by the Lord." She gave a high-pitched giggle, just on the verge of out of control.

I felt myself on the verge of a giggle too. I willed myself into calm. "Take a few deep breaths," I said. "You're in shock."

"Maybe a glass of water?" said Lori, by the Mr. Coffee.

Heather looked at me, her face stark in its sorrow. "God. Oh, *Terry*." Her eyes filmed with tears. "Does smoke inhalation *hurt?*"

"I don't know." My voice trembled just a little. "It might be like going to sleep."

"Heather!" someone called. "Are you there? Heather, honey? It's us! Brandon. And Helen!"

Heather rolled her eyes. "The *Blofelds*." She looked down at the coffeepot she was holding. "My eternal neighbors."

"Do you want them to go away?" I said. "I can—"

"No, it's okay." Her mouth twitched, like she might start to giggle again. "Nothing can stop the Blofelds anyway."

An elderly couple entered the room, hands flapping, faces blurred, jostling each other in their hurry to get to Heather. Flynn was just behind.

"Sir," he was saying. "Ma'am! I have to clear the room." Why was Flynn clearing the room? "Everyone has to leave. I need to get a statement from Mrs. Stephens."

The Blofelds engulfed Heather. She stepped back.

I eyeballed Flynn, took him aside. "Can't it wait?"

"No it can't. Let me do my job."

"Can't you see she's in shock?"

Flynn's dark eyes flicked off mine. Till now, a narcotics man, he wasn't used to victim advocates. Under his tight control, I sensed impatience, the need to get on with it: kick down doors, get the suspects prone on the floor, go, go, go.

"These are ordinary law-abiding citizens here," I said pointedly. "At least let me stay. I can help."

"Okay, okay. You, but nobody else." He jerked his head at Lori. "She goes. I want everyone else out too. *Now*."

The kitchen seemed full of people talking and in the center, as if in the eye of a hurricane, calm and quiet, was mouse-brown Heather, still holding the coffeepot. The leather bracelet slid down her arm as she raised the glass pot high over her head. She dropped it. It hit the tiled floor with a crash and shattered into a hundred little pieces.

FIVE

"MY GOD," SAID HEATHER. "I don't know why I did that but it felt good." She was trembling.

We were alone in the kitchen now, me and Flynn and Heather. Sometimes it calms people just to touch them. But I didn't have an instinct for it with her.

The tiled floor was littered with glass. The room had the haunted feeling rooms have after a big party when the guests have just left. Flynn was a medium-sized man, but his presence towered in that room, taking more than his share of space.

"Ma'am, I need to get a statement," he said to Heather. "Why don't you sit down."

Mickey Mouse grinned idiotically at nothing. Flynn loomed under the kitchen lights. Heather backed away a little, glass crunching under her boots, but she didn't sit down.

"Or stand. It's all the same to me." Flynn's face was expressionless. He handed her a form. "I'd like you to fill this out. Just write down where you were tonight." He put it on the table.

Heather ignored it, still defiant. "I was at a poetry reading. Over in Dudley."

"Look, we don't have to butt heads here. Make it easy on yourself." Flynn's voice was calm and controlled as if he'd just stepped into his element. "Names, times, addresses. It'd be a lot easier, sitting down."

"All right, all *right*." She sat, pulled the form to her across the pine table. Then she looked around. "Pen?"

Flynn handed her one.

She took it but she didn't start to write. "I don't see why I have to do this now."

Why indeed. Smoke inhalation, why would it matter where Heather was?

With an air of concession, Flynn sat down. He leaned toward her across the table. "Humor me," he said.

Doing my job as helper while Heather wrote, I found a broom and dustpan, swept up the broken glass. I dumped the shards into the trash, then I closed all the cabinet doors. They were simple cabinets, maple-stained cherry, just like my bookcase. I knew Terry had made them. The doors closed perfectly, at a touch, as though he were guiding them. For a second I could feel his presence everywhere, saw him standing in my living room, green eyes dancing behind his gold wire-rims.

Married to this close-to-forty but immature, childish mousebrown person.

When I was done I sat down at the far end of the table.

Heather looked up. "Thank you," she said. She pushed the statement over to Flynn. "That's it. Can I be alone now?" She looked at me impatiently. "Could you tell him? I can't think, when I have to keep responding and responding." Her long bangs tickled her eyelashes but she didn't brush them away. Her fatigue was palpable. "And besides, I have to go to work tomorrow."

Work tomorrow. I almost wanted to laugh. "They'd probably understand," I said, "if you took some time off." I said to Flynn, "Are you done now?"

"Not quite." Under the bright overhead light, his shallow eyes were pouched in little puffs of flesh, his chin stubbled with dark hairs.

"Anything unusual going on with Terry?" he asked Heather. "Anything at all you can think of out of the ordinary?"

"Well—" She hesitated. "He's been tired. Not sleeping well, like he's worried."

Flynn pounced. "Worried. What about?"

"Nothing." She blinked a couple of times, nervously, like a little tic. "I don't *know*. And so what, anyway? What difference does it make?" She put her head down on the table.

"Stay with me here, Heather," said Flynn. "He fighting with anyone? Neighborhood feuds, that kind of thing? Maybe he did a carpentry job for somebody and they weren't too happy with it and things kind of escalated?"

She raised her head. "Terry doesn't make enemies. He's one of those people, his whole life people have liked him." She stopped. "What are you saying? The fire—you think someone set it?"

"I got a call from the EMTs who transported the body."

I flinched at the word "body." "He has a name," I said pointedly.

Flynn ignored me, completely focused on Heather.

"And?" She stood up, swaying slightly. She clutched the back of her chair for support. *"What did the EMTs say?"*

"Either you or Terry own a gun?" Flynn persisted. "Maybe he kept one in his shop?"

"No. We don't own a gun. Either of us. Why?"

"Ma'am, sit down, please," said Flynn.

Heather sat back down.

"Your husband didn't die of smoke inhalation," Flynn said. "He was shot."

Shot. Menace filled the room as I tried to take it in.

"How could he be shot?" Heather's voice rose, thick with anxiety. "There'd be *blood*. They would have known—the EMTs—"

"Not always," interrupted Flynn. "A bullet can go in clean, not come out."

"You're telling me someone *killed* Terry?" Heather blinked. *"Murdered* him?" Little muscles trembled in her cheeks. She wrapped her arms around her body. "Oh my God, oh my God, oh my God," she said. *"No."*

She got up and left the room.

Flynn looked at me. For a second I was mesmerized by his face, so unreadable, the barrier just under the surface of his eyes, blocking all emotion; almost a form of intimidation in its own right. "Isn't this where you kick in?"

"You got your statement," I said defiantly. "The victim comes first, from my point of view. She told you where she was. Her husband was murdered. How much do you expect anyone to take? Can I tell her you're done for now? I mean," I added bitingly, "it's not like you found a meth lab in the backyard."

I thought I saw a glimmer, the merest glimmer, of light in Flynn's eyes, but maybe not. His hands came up and he rubbed his face. "Okay, okay. You made your point."

I stood up and went after Heather.

I found her in the living room full of ferns, sitting on the couch in the half dark, holding a large orange cat.

"Heather?" I sat on the other end of the couch. "Are you all right?"

"No. Why would I be all right?" She bent over the cat, rubbing her face in its fur. "Murdered. Oh, Pi-Pi," she crooned forlornly. "Poor old Pi-Pi." She looked at me over the twitching ears of the cat. "That investigator makes me nervous."

"He's that kind of guy," I said. "I've made him promise to leave you alone for tonight. Let's talk about you, Heather. You mentioned work?"

She nodded. "Cochise College—elder hostel. I teach a nine o'clock art class."

"Maybe someone can call them."

"No. I'm going to work. I *want* to." She looked at me curiously, "Chloe? That's your name? You said you knew Terry."

My neck muscles tensed up. "He did some carpentry for me last fall. A bookcase."

"A bookcase," she repeated. Then she laughed. It sounded odd, eerie in the half-dark room.

"It's entirely up to you," I rushed on, to hush up the sound, and besides, I was tired, "but at some point you might feel like talking to a counselor. I can drop off a list of them for you."

"A *counselor?*" She squeezed the cat, so tight it scratched out and leaped from the couch. "I'd rather be dead."

I certainly wasn't going to argue. "Then there's relatives," I said efficiently. "Doesn't Terry have a—"

"Never mind. *Please.* I can handle it. Everything." She licked at the scratch on her wrist. "Listen, if you really want to help. The Blofelds, my neighbors? They were just here? Could you call them, 555-3210, and see—see if their grandson's home yet. His name's Damien. Ask if he can come over and be with me."

"I'll be glad to."

I CALLED THE BLOFELDS and a woman said Damien would be over in a few minutes. Heather had vanished. I was exhausted and there seemed to be nothing left that she would let me do anyway. Flynn had gone out back, with a deputy; I saw their flashlights probing the dark as I left the house and got in my car, thinking about Terry; worried, not sleeping, Heather had said, she didn't know why. He'd been worried in November too, something about a woman named April, twenty years ago. He might have told *me* why, but I hadn't let him.

I started the car and was pulling away when I saw Heather, standing to one side of the house; little and stalwart without a jacket in the cold, hands in the back pockets of her baggy jeans, watching Flynn and the deputy probing the dark on the worst night of her life and I hadn't really helped her at all. What had I done? Or more to the point, not done.

Too late, shame hit me.

I drove toward home down the chilly highway, little pictures of Heather popping into my mind; dazed with the coffeepot, head bent over the kitchen faucet, face stark in its sorrow, holding the cat. The mouse-brown person. She deserved much better, but that was who I'd wanted her to be, wasn't it, a mouse-brown person Terry couldn't quite bring himself to leave.

I could have handled things a lot better, especially in the living room. I'd been—what? Not cold exactly but perfunctory. Just doing my job. Badly. A heartless idiot. I punched on the CD player, hard, turned the volume up high as Radiohead sang about "Fake Plastic Trees," but it didn't drown out the shame, it stayed with me all the way back to Dudley.

SIX

THE NEXT MORNING I drove out to Cochise College, parked my Geo near a prefab metal-looking building where the office had told me the elder hostel class was held, and got out. A nasty little wind nipped irritably at the bare young trees by the parking lot. It had taken me longer than I'd planned to get here, and now it was just after nine. Heather's class would already have started. Fighting the wind, I opened the door and went inside. Fluorescent lights shone off the beige linoleum tile of a long bright hall, doors open to empty classrooms.

Judging from the numbers, Heather's class was near the end. If she was even there. I walked down the hall and stopped.

Inside a room, a group of senior citizens in aprons stood around long tables covered with paper; a couple of men, more women, frozen in place, holding objects aloft like daggers. Near me, a large white-haired woman had a whisk broom; a grizzled man beside her, a kitchen sponge; a tiny Hispanic granny, a peacock feather.

Heather, in paint-smeared jeans and T-shirt, big sunglasses, stood in front of the group, arms raised like a conductor. "And a one and a two and a three—go!" she said.

The room came alive in a frenzy of zestful movement. The large white-haired woman dabbed her whisk broom rhythmically, the grizzled man plunged with the sponge, the Hispanic granny swooshed her feather delicately, eyes half closed.

Heather pranced round the table, cheering them on. Her jeans were a little too short, revealing black high-top sneakers with red plaid laces. The sunglasses and the fact that parts of her unruly bangs were standing straight up like antennae, gave her the appearance of an exotic insect.

"Fabulous, Ethel!" she said. "Marvin," she cajoled, "try it with less paint! *Yes!*"

I stood at the door of the classroom, counselor list in hand. Because I'd been worrying about Heather all night, it wasn't so much to give her the counselor list—*I'd rather be dead*—that I'd driven out to the college, but just to check on her. I needed to feel better about myself; in some irrational way, I wanted to make sure she'd survived the night in spite of me; had neither been shot to death by Terry's murderer, or by her own hand. And maybe we could arrange to talk after her class, and I'd do a better job this time.

She spotted me then in the doorway and stopped her pacing. I couldn't see her eyes behind the dark glasses, but I had a pretty good idea why she was wearing them. Cried all night probably and still had the gumption, the sheer bravery, to go to work.

"What is it?" she asked.

I held up the unwanted list, suddenly aware of the selfishness of my motives—to make *me* feel better, not Heather. "I brought you this," I mouthed in embarrassment. "Just in case."

"What is it?" she said again.

I hesitated. Something in her voice had stopped the frenzy at the table. The senior citizens were staring at me, wrinkled flushed faces alert, fluorescent light winking off their glasses; whisk brooms, sponges, feathers ready for battle, like a gang of ancient brigands prepared to protect their leader at all costs.

"I'll just leave it at the office," I said.

I CALLED FLYNN from work that afternoon to see where things stood. It was easy to see how in spite of what had happened, Heather would want to go to work, be sheltered by the ancient brigands. But they could hardly move into the house with her.

Did she plan to soldier on so bravely, shielded only by her big sunglasses, while Terry's murderer was still at large?

"Has anyone been charged in the Barnett case?" I asked.

"No, ma'am."

Ma'am, as if I were a member of the general public and a hundred years old as well. I clenched my teeth.

"I knew Terry Barnett," I said, to get that out of the way with Flynn. "He did some carpentry work for me."

"Oh? What kind of guy was he? Short-tempered?"

"I wouldn't think so. He seemed pretty mellow to me. How's the investigation going? Any suspects?"

He ignored the questions. "Did the widow say anything useful to you when you chased after her last night?"

"Flynn, just so you know, advocates don't pass on conversations with victims, unless it's exculpatory. We have confidentiality."

"Feisty little thing. She strike you that way?"

Right, Flynn. Answer a question with a question. "I think she's pretty vulnerable underneath," I said.

"Could be an act."

"Right, *sure.* Jesus, Flynn," I said in exasperation, "if you're thinking of her as a suspect, forget it. You heard her. She didn't even know he'd been shot. And she was asking me about smoke inhalation earlier."

"Sure you should tell me that?"

"What?"

"Her asking about smoke inhalation," he said, needling. "It's not confidential?"

An image of Flynn came to me, the picture in the paper; Flynn victorious on a mountain of marijuana. Smirking, arms folded against his chest. He was probably smirking now.

"Exception to confidentiality, remember?" I said. "Exculpatory statements."

There was a certain sick enjoyment to sparring with Flynn, except it was getting me nowhere. "You're not going to tell me *anything?*" I said, trying to keep the frustration out of my voice.

"Not until there's an arrest." His voice was stoic. "It's an ongoing homicide investigation."

"Listen, *Flynn,*" I said. "She's all alone in that house now. Maybe a deputy could check in from time to time, make sure she's okay."

"Don't know if we have the manpower. We're pretty short-handed."

"Could you *try?*"

"I'll try."

I sighed. "Well, thanks for whatever."

"No *problem.*"

I called Heather after I hung up, wanting to let her know there might be a deputy stopping by, but got no answer, not even a machine. Flynn's voice rang in my ears. Even just thinking about him set off alarm bells—*watch it.*

During the next two days I kept calling Heather, several times until finally someone picked up.

"Hello."

"Heather?" I said.

"No. This is Diana. I'm a friend." She hesitated. "I guess you know about Terry?"

"Yes."

"She's been in such a state, I've been handling her calls. I even had to call Terry's brother to tell *him.* Fred, in Ohio. *That* was fun."

"Ah," I said, remembering. Fred, they hadn't spoken in years.

"You can give me your name and number, but I can't promise she'll get back to you."

"That's okay," I said.

"The funeral's the day after tomorrow, back in Ohio. Heather would have liked him to be buried here, but that was what he wanted."

Buried next to his mother, the plot all paid for. I'd forgotten till now.

"Then Heather will be flying to Ohio?" I asked.

"No." Diana sighed wearily. "It would be too much for her. She planned to but she kept on going and going, you know how she is, and now she's on the verge of collapse. There'll be a memorial service here tomorrow evening. Seven o'clock at the Women's Club in Old Dudley. All of Terry's friends are welcome."

We hung up. Terry's friends. Heather on the verge of collapse. I should go, sit at the back. It seemed like something I should do. It seemed like—

My phone rang.

"Evangeline Nolan," said Gigi, the receptionist.

Oh, God. Back to work. "Hi, Evangeline," I said in as chipper a voice as I could muster. "What's up?"

"Chip's going to kill me," she said, "first chance he gets. Do you know that last summer, he mowed the lawn exactly one time? And he mowed right over a rosebush I'd just planted. He acts like he's so—"

EVANGELINE TALKED for what seemed like hours. When I got home, I unplugged my phone in case she called me back with some new detail about Chip's insensitivity. I nuked a healthy dinner, salted it heavily to make it palatable, and ate in front of the television in the living room. I thought about Terry being buried next to his mother back in Ohio, thought about him sitting with her as she lay dying, planning his own funeral while the snow fell.

Where did that leave Heather? He hadn't been married back then. Well, I couldn't keep trying to assume responsibility for her just because I liked and admired her and felt guilty, let's face it, for briefly lusting after her husband. *Let it go*.

Exhausted, I went to bed. Maybe because I hadn't thought about Craig for a while, I thought of him then, in a dream, in some place that I knew was South America but it looked like Arizona and it was snowing. Craig was wearing big snow-shoes, moving fast. The shoes left tracks in the snow like tomb-stones.

"It looks like you're dying," I said to him. "Are you sure you took your medication?"

He went even faster, leaving me behind, and I ran through the swirling snow till I caught up to him. Even though his back was to me I knew suddenly that he wasn't really Craig but Terry. That was why he was dying. "Bulletproof," said Terry. "I wish I was."

"You have to stop," I said. "It's our fault and now we've got to help Heather, before it's too late."

He turned and grinned at me. He had black stubble all over his chin and his eyes were two black marbles. It wasn't Craig, it wasn't even Terry. "It's never too late," said Flynn.

"No!" I woke with a shout, sitting straight up in bed.

SEVEN

OH, NO. I'D SPENT most of yesterday afternoon on the phone with Evangeline Nolan, and now here she was, way down the street by the courthouse. Through my office window at the county attorney's, I could see her getting out of the black Nissan pickup truck with the purple lightning decals, which wasn't actually hers, but Chip's, her soon-to-be ex-husband. Not *now*. My brain was too fuzzy and unfocussed. Tonight was Terry's memorial service. I was planning to go.

Evangeline's hair was fresh bright red and she wore new stiff jeans, and a tight green stretch blouse. It was right after lunch and the temperature was only fifty degrees, which in southern Arizona is chilly. She looked cold teetering on the asphalt as she climbed the hill in red cowboy boots with two-inch heels. She walked doggedly, head down, as if battling not only the hill, but life and what it had done to her.

Poor Evangeline. She'd parked pretty far away. It would take a while for her to get here in those boots. My phone rang.

"Victim Witness."

"I have a Mr. Barnett here for anyone at Victim Witness," said Gigi, the receptionist. "I'll put him through."

Mr. Barnett? "Hello?" I said.

"Who's this?" said a male voice.

"Chloe Newcombe. I'm the victim advocate for Cochise County. What can I do for you?"

"I'm in Ohio. I got this number from the National Victims Center. They said you might be able to help. That anything I said to you would be confidential."

"Of course," I said.

"My brother was murdered in your county. Terry—" He whooshed out a sigh. "Terry Barnett. I'm Fred Barnett."

My god, Terry's *brother.* Absurdly, my hands were shaking. "Fred. Yes. Yes, of course."

"You know what I'm talking about then."

"In Prophecy. I was there the night he was killed," I blurted out. "To help Heather."

"*Really.* My brother's wife. It's hard to believe, but I've never met her. And she's not even coming to the funeral. So you know her?"

"I only met her briefly." I took a deep breath. "I met your brother last fall. He made a bookcase for me."

"I bet he did a good job too." His voice warmed up, turned hopeful. "Wow. You *knew* Terry?"

"Yes, I did." He sounded nice and I felt guilty as if I were somehow deceiving him.

"I loved him. Terry and I didn't get along sometimes but I always—" His voice kind of broke and he stopped.

"I'm so *sorry,*" I said. Poor guy. Didn't get along sometimes. That was putting it mildly, from what Terry had said. It was so sad. And now it was too late. "Are you okay?"

"Give me a second," he said weakly.

I could hear him blowing his nose, then his voice came back stronger. "I called because I thought you could tell me what's going on in the case. I mean, since I'm his brother, maybe you could tell me more than just the general public."

Not with controlling, smirking Flynn running the show. I felt a little light-headed. "The police are very closemouthed about homicide investigations," I said. "Even to relatives. All I really know is there hasn't been an arrest."

"I kept wishing Terry would decide to come back to Ohio. And then he did, in a coffin. Guess you have to be careful what you wish for. The whole thing's kind of zapped me, like I'm looking at my own life now and saying 'What for?'"

"I'm so sorry," I said again.

"The thing is—I don't know how to say this. Are you sure it's confidential?"

"Absolutely. What did you want to tell me?"

"I got a letter from Terry—a couple of weeks before he was murdered. He said some things in it, that, well—they might be important to the case."

"No kidding. Then I think you need to call law enforcement, right away," I said urgently. "The sooner the better. Detective Flynn. I can give you his number."

He sighed. "It's sensitive stuff. Private. I thought you could get me an update first."

"Psst."

I looked up. "Excuse me just a second," I said. I put my hand over the receiver.

Lucinda, my boss, stood at the door to my office, in full boss regalia: royal-blue suit with big gold buttons, big gold earrings, and three-inch heels. She had a habit of running her fingers through her pageboy salt-and-pepper hair, and as usual it looked like she'd just come in out of the wind.

"Evangeline," she mouthed. "She's out in the lobby. You know how she is. And she wants you." I could hear the impatience in her voice. Lucinda was an okay administrator but victims irritated her.

Damn. To put it bluntly, Evangeline was a real pain, calling the office all the time to vent. She wasn't my favorite person, but I could handle her. Listening to people vent was part of my job.

"What's the call?" Lucinda asked.

"Someone wanting an update on a case," I said.

She reached out her hand for the phone. "I'll take over."

"No," I said, a little too forcefully. "It's okay."

Lucinda was tough, rode right over people's feelings. That was basically why she was running the show. Not only that, she would probably stand there till I finished talking to Fred.

"Fred," I said, "I have to go. Call me tomorrow, *please,* and I'll have the update."

IN THE WAITING ROOM, behind her desk with the phones, Gigi the receptionist gave me a sympathetic little smile and rolled her eyes. Evangeline was standing by the window, her back to the room, looking out. I came up behind her. Over her shoulder I could see her view of the parking lot and the black skeleton trees behind, and the gray sky beyond that. She was probably soaking in all that desolation.

"Hi," I said.

She turned. *"Hi."*

"What's up?"

"I had to come to Dudley to get art supplies, so I brought you a present." She reached into her purse and pulled out some brightly colored yarn wrapped around sticks and handed it to me. "It's one of my god's eyes." Financially strapped, like so many other women getting a divorce with no bankable skills, she was trying to get into the craft business. The god's eye was in shades of black, red, and yellow.

"Well, thanks." I held it up to look at it. It made me sad. Black, red, and yellow are not my favorite colors. "It's beautiful."

Her face lit up, improving her looks considerably. Despite her bright hair she was plain with a hard face, beak of a nose. She dressed sexy so you wouldn't notice.

"I have a favor to ask you," she said. "Chip's gone off to Tucson—his probation officer told me. I want to go back to the house, get some more of my clothes. Half the time I have to wear the same things two days in a row."

I tried not to look impatient. She had bigger problems than that. Her jeans were new, and so was the stretch blouse, I'd seen it at Target last week. Every time I saw her she had a different outfit and she needed to save every penny.

"Come with me, okay?" Her voice was pleading. "I know it's a long drive for you to Huachuca City and back but I'll be quick, I promise."

I hesitated for only a moment. I knew she was lonely, hadn't made new friends since the breakup. She had no one to turn to but people in an office. No one to call at night when things were tough but someone like me who prayed she wouldn't.

"Okay," I said. "Sure. I'll follow you in my car."

Her eyes shone. "You're the best. You really are."

"We'll need to get a deputy," I said.

"No problem," said Evangeline, "I took care of it."

"All right," I said. "Just a sec."

I went back for my purse. Lucinda was in her office, on the phone. "Look," she was saying, "I did not mark a second color choice. I do not want red or any—"

"Ahem," I said.

"Hold on," she said to the phone. She put her hand over the receiver, frowned and raised her eyebrows.

"I'm going to help Evangeline get some stuff from her husband's house," I said. "He's out of town."

"You need to get a deputy."

"It's not a problem. Evangeline took care of it."

EIGHT

SIERRA VISTA IS half an hour from Dudley, and Huachuca City, where Chip lived, is on the far side of that. The trip with Evangeline would take up the rest of the day. I followed her black truck down Highway 80 through the wintry desert, took the bypass around Sierra Vista past the big Wal-Mart shopping center, then onto Highway 90.

The whole time I kept thinking about the phone call from Fred Barnett. They must have made up since I talked to Terry in November if Terry had written him a letter two weeks ago. Something in it, important to the case? I almost didn't see Evangeline's blinker going at the traffic light, noticed it just in time and made the turn.

We were on a residential street, low to low-middle income: cinderblock tract houses interspersed with double-wide trailers. There were no sidewalks and the rutted asphalt of the street faded into dirt and brown crabgrass at the edges. Still, in summer it would probably have some grace, there were sparse trees, empty flower beds.

Several houses down, Evangeline pulled into the drive of a pale green cinderblock. The rosebushes by the driveway had a few faded-pink dead blooms that a careful gardener would have removed. The bushes were small; she'd probably planted them last summer before she moved out. Hadn't she told me Chip mowed over one of them?

There was an improbably large motorboat in the driveway of the house next door. A man in orange mechanic's overalls had the hood up on a battered ancient Oldsmobile. But I didn't see a police car anywhere. Where was the deputy?

Evangeline was out of the pickup and heading up the driveway by the time I pulled over and parked on the street. I wound down my window. "Evangeline!" I shouted. I unfastened the seat belt and opened my door. "Hold on!" I got out and started toward her.

She stopped.

"We need to wait for the deputy," I said. "What time did you tell him?"

"I didn't, actually." In the chill light, her red hair and green blouse looked like neon. Mascara had beaded on her lashes, under her green eye shadow.

"You didn't, what?"

She shrugged, a little embarrassed. "Well…I didn't call one."

"What do you mean, you didn't call one?" The man working on the Oldsmobile had his back to us. I was furious, but I kept my voice low. "Evangeline. You *told* me you called a deputy."

"Oh, Chloe." Her voice was anxious, pleading. "Chip'll have a shit fit if he finds out the cops were here." Still worrying about Chip, I thought, scared, catering to his every need, walking on those eggshells. "He's in *Tucson*. We don't *need* a deputy. It's *okay*."

"No, it's not okay. Wait. Just wait a minute while I call one."

"Can't you see?" Her voice was whiny as if all she ever did was fight and it never got her *anywhere*. "His *car's* not even here. Chloe, all I want to do is get a few clothes from the closet in the bedroom. It'll take two seconds."

"I don't care. I *have* to call a deputy. Don't move. I'm doing it now," I said over my shoulder as I hurried back to my car.

I picked up my cell phone. My hands were numb with cold. This didn't merit a 911 call. Shit. I'd forgotten to bring my resource book. What the hell was the number for the Huachuca City PD?

The man in the coveralls was wiping his hands on a rag.

Somewhere, not far, a dog barked. Hopefully it was chained in a backyard. From my experience people in neighborhoods like this were prone to own Dobermans, Rottweilers, pit bulls, along with a gun in every bedside table.

I was just punching in information when Evangeline turned on her high-heeled cowboy boots and strutted up the driveway. She vanished into the house, leaving the door open. Damn. I was doing her this big favor and she couldn't even wait?

Oh, what did it matter, Chip was in Tucson. I threw the cell phone on the car seat and headed up after her. The dog was still barking and the air smelled smoky as though someone had a woodstove going. Cold, uncomfortable, and angry, I just wasn't focused on this.

Through the open door I heard a loud crash. Great. No deputy, Evangeline in the house, violating her end of the restraining order and destroying Chip's property.

"Evangeline," I shouted.

"No!" she shouted back, from somewhere inside. "Wait! Don't!"

"Don't *what?*" I called, from the driveway.

"Miss?" Out of the corner of my eye, I saw the coverall man throw down his rag, walk toward me. No, run. Why was he running?

"Chip!" Evangeline shouted. *"Chip? No! Don't!"*

Then she screamed. Why was she screaming? Chip. *He's in there*. I ran toward the house, got almost to the door, when I heard fireworks. Bam. Fourth of July was months and months away. And something, a flash of orange, hit me from behind, knocking me down. Another bam. I felt a stabbing pain in my knee as it hit a rock. I lay there dazed on the dead crabgrass that smelled like hay.

LIGHTS REVOLVED ON the two deputy cars and on the ambulance parked outside the green cinderblock house, like a nightmare replay in daylight of the scene at Terry Barnett's. The man in the orange coveralls was talking with a deputy. I sat, crouched low in my car, and waited. My muscles seemed to have atrophied. I felt nothing except an ache in my knee. I rubbed it.

Evangeline had told me she'd called a deputy. I'd told her to wait, I thought blankly. I'd told her and told her and told her.

Across the street, a gray-haired woman wearing black spandex Capri pants, purple fraying lace blouse, and pink sneakers came out of a house, puffing on a cigarette. She meandered toward me, taking her time, working the cigarette as she came.

"The hell's going on?" she asked in a gravelly voice when she finally arrived.

"I think somebody got shot," I said.

"Son of a bitch. I looked out my window and saw his ex, or almost, going in the door." In their pouches of wrinkles her tired eyes looked like they'd seen everything and more than once. "That who got shot? Evangeline?"

"Probably." I swallowed hard, though there was no moisture in my mouth.

"Gumper there tackled you." She nodded toward the man in the coveralls. "Used to be a Green Beret." She chuckled. "He tackled you like in a damn football game. You might be dead, weren't for him."

I looked at Gumper, arms akimbo, black oily hair: my greasy savior. Feeling was coming back, my heart thudding in my chest. I couldn't seem to catch my breath.

The woman took a thoughtful drag on the cigarette. "She went and left him, you know. After he fixed up that house just the way she wanted it. He was a *hard worker*."

Shut up. "Umm," I said.

"And for what?" she nattered on. "She's got his pickup truck, then he had to take his car to the shop this morning. If it's not one thing, it's another."

A deputy came out of the house and walked toward us. He reached my side of the car, his jaw muscles working hard. He was young and fair-haired, blue-eyed, with the kind of work-out muscles that make it impossible to put your arms to your side.

"He shot her," he said. "Two or three times, at least. Then turned the gun on himself. EMTs couldn't do a thing, both dead before we got here. Gumper over there"—he jerked his head "he knows her ma, over in Whetstone. She's pretty elderly. He'll go sit with her, make sure she's okay. Don't go anywhere, till we get a statement." He paused, looking at me. "She a good friend?"

"Not exactly."

"You okay?"

A line of cold sweat formed on my upper lip. "I don't know," I said. For a moment I thought I was going to throw up. I closed my eyes and put my head down on the steering wheel. The world seemed to turn around me slowly, forming a little vortex, and in the center was Evangeline, in red and green neon plastic, purified at last of her suffering.

"He fixed up the house just like she wanted it," the woman repeated. "What'd she want to go and leave him for?"

Her voice seemed unnaturally loud, shocking me back to reality. I opened my eyes.

The woman threw her cigarette on the sidewalk and ground it out with her foot. "She goddamn broke his heart," she said.

NINE

I DROVE TOWARD HOME on automatic pilot, my mind veering away from the scene at the green cinderblock house, thinking I didn't have any more control over my life than Evangeline had. Or any better judgment. And my knee hurt like hell.

Past Sierra Vista on 80, the highway cut through the empty desert. I accelerated to seventy-five, and in the private bubble inside my car, I began to scream. Amazing how hard you can scream and it sounds like nothing at all. And in the midst of the scream I saw Evangeline standing in the waiting room at the county attorney's. An hour to live and I'd begrudged her the new green stretch blouse from Target.

Back home, my house was chilly and winter dark. My knee was throbbing and my throat felt raw from my primal scream session, but I wasn't tired: adrenaline had kicked in, leaving me jittery as a chipmunk. It was too late to go back to work, but not too late for Terry's memorial service.

THE WOMEN'S CLUB is in an old brick building on a hill close to the courthouse. Wanting to be inconspicuous, I got there a little late. I would just slip in and stand at the back, leave early. Cars filled the small parking lot and went all the way down the street. I finally found a slot a block away by the courthouse and walked up, limping a little.

A fortyish woman with blond hair in a long braid was sitting on a low wall under a streetlight in front of the building. She looked familiar.

"Hi," she said when I reached her. She wore some sort of ethnic-looking long black dress and in the yellow glow of the streetlight her face was as pretty as a Pre-Raphaelite fairy-tale princess. "I'm Diana French."

Oh. Diana *French*. So the Diana who'd answered the phone yesterday was *that* Diana. I didn't have time for the art scene in Old Dudley, but Diana French practically ran it: circulated petitions to raise money for arts projects, set up exhibitions, organized a Christmas Cantata in December, filled the window of the natural foods co-op with a family of skeletons for the Mexican Day of the Dead. A little powerhouse.

She didn't look like a powerhouse now, more like all drained out and her eyes were puffy as if she'd been crying. "You're going to the memorial?" she asked.

"Yes."

"I had to get out of there. I've been helping Heather, but it got to be too much."

"How is she?"

"I'm so worried. She—she—"

"What?"

"Oh, it doesn't matter." She looked puzzled. "Have we met before?"

I felt reluctant to identify myself. "I think we talked on the phone."

She nodded blankly.

"I'd better go on in," I said, turning away.

"Don't forget to sign the guest book," she called after me. Dying to know who I was, I bet.

Inside it smelled of something burning. Just past the door on a little wooden table was the guest book, but I ignored it. I went down a short hall to a big room, a stage filled with flowers at one end. Along the wall to the right was a fireplace. A big fire blazing. The room was packed, the chairs all filled and people sitting on the floor. Artsy Old Dudley people in Birkenstocks and clogs, soft faded clothes in black or earth tones.

I recognized a lot of them, by sight if not by name; potters and poets, weavers, seamstresses, painters and sculptors, hangers-on. They tended the art galleries; worked the cash register at the natural foods co-op for peanuts, or more likely pesticide-free cashews and piñon nuts; hung out at the post office and the local coffee shops with seemingly endless time on their hands for socializing. I looked for Heather but didn't see her.

I stood at the back. On the stage, in the spotlight, was a young man dressed in a black velvet shirt with flowing sleeves, tight black leather pants. Features delicate as a girl's, full sensual mouth, long eyelashes that shadowed his cheeks. He was the most—what?—luscious person I'd ever seen, like a young Elvis. Who was he? I'd never seen him around Old Dudley.

He was reading the last part of "Fern Hill."

Oh as I was young and easy in the mercy of his means,
Time held me green and dying
Though I sang in my chains like the sea.

I'd heard "Fern Hill" a million times, but now in my hyped-up state it was as though I'd never heard it before; its emotions felt raw, almost unbearable, as I thought of Terry telling me about the lawns in Ohio, the lawns like green velvet. Tears stung at my eyelids. With an effort I willed them away. Under my skittery energy was bottomless fatigue.

For a long moment, the place was as silent as if everyone were holding their breath. The fire crackled. Then the young man said softly, "That was one of Terry's favorites."

A child wailed, someone else began crying audibly. People shifted and I saw Heather then, sitting up near the stage. Her bangs were gone, tucked under the black scarf she wore around her head. She still had on the sunglasses.

I thought of her, so stalwart outside the house, as she watched Flynn probe the dark. Suffused with regret I looked away, then looked back again. Some power of withheld emotion seemed to make the white oval of her face, punctuated by the sunglasses, a focal point to the room.

The young man left the stage and an older man, white-haired, wearing a Western shirt, not an Old Dudley person, came up from the side, lugging a rocking chair. He set it center stage and stepped back.

"Hello," he said. "I'm Bill McGee and I brought this to show everyone. Had a hell of a time getting it here but I think it's important." He tilted it back and started it rocking. "Look how it glides, so nice and easy. Terry made it for me, two, three years ago. So well made it'll last a hundred years. How many of us can leave something behind that'll last that long?" He looked embarrassed as if he suddenly realized he was on a stage. "I loved him and I'll miss him. That's all I've got to say. I think Howard Meeks wants to say something."

Howard Meeks. The neighbor already at the house when Lori and I showed up. With his Bible. The spotlight shone on the pink plastic-rimmed glasses, making his eyes bright blanks. Without the brown stocking cap, I saw he had pale red hair. He cleared his throat. "I'd like to read from the Scriptures."

Someone near me groaned softly.

"'Jesus said to them,'" Howard Meeks intoned, "'are there not twelve hours in the day? If a man walks by daytime he will not stumble because he sees the light of this world. But if a man walks at night he will stumble because there is no light in it.'"

I turned my head and there was Flynn.

Flynn, in his brown leather jacket over a denim shirt, was leaning against a wall next to a skeletal man, very tall with a black beard—someone I'd seen before and at first I couldn't think where. Then it came rushing back: the same man who had waved at Terry as we sat together on a bench in Agua Prieta, Mexico. He was talking in Flynn's ear and looking at me.

Not tonight. No way. I'd had enough. I backed out the door.

OUTSIDE, IT WAS clear and cold, the sky shot with stars, like bright bullet holes. I took a long deep breath and hobbled down the hill, keys in hand, reached my Geo and unlocked the door.

"Chloe."

I jumped and turned.

"Too damn hot in there," said Flynn. He'd pursued me, silent in his running shoes. Clean shaven, not like in my dream, but eyes like black marbles. "How come you're limping?"

"I fell. Who was that man I saw talking to you in there?"

"Peter French, used to be a cop." Flynn's lower lip curled. "Those ex-cops, some of 'em, they'll drive you crazy. Get all pissed when you won't involve them in investigations, like they got a right."

"*French?* Does he have a wife named Diana?"

"Pretty blonde?"

"Yes."

Flynn nodded and zipped up his leather jacket. "Where you headed?"

"Home. I've had a hard day," I added, meaningfully.

But he didn't take my cue. He must not know about Evangeline. Huachuca City PD had handled it, not the sheriff's department. "I'm really tired," I said. But I wasn't. I was full of unnatural energy, dizzy with it.

"There's coffee at the substation here. I could offer you a cup. You said you knew Terry Barnett, I'd like to talk to you about your impressions."

"And what I was doing with Terry in Mexico last November?" I said, giving up.

Flynn smirked. "That too."

THE FLUORESCENT LIGHT overhead was too bright, emphasizing the starkness of the beige linoleum-tiled floor, beige cinderblock walls, green chalkboard on an easel. Video camera in one corner, tape recorder on the beat-up wooden table. No windows. Even in the daytime, the room would look just the same: so much like every interview room I'd ever read of in a book, or seen in a movie, it couldn't be real.

Nothing seemed real, Strawberry Fields rang in my head like an auditory hallucination. Driving to the substation, all my energy had drained away, leaving me headachy, weepy.

I sat on a white plastic chair at the beat-up table trying to rehearse what I would say to Flynn but the silence in the room jabbered at me. I was on the astral plane. Chip. No. Bam. Bam.

It was almost a relief when Flynn came in the room with two Styrofoam cups. Stubble on his chin already; probably needed to shave every hour. Stone-faced, he put one cup in front of me and sat down with the other.

"Nice place you have here," I jested lamely.

Flynn smirked. "We like it."

Nothing seemed real. Strawberry Fields. Strawberry Fields, forever. I took a sip of the coffee, hoping it would bring me to my senses. It hadn't been freshly made in a long time.

Flynn pulled off the leather jacket, unbuttoned the top button of his blue denim shirt, and jerked around his neck. It occurred to me he was quite good-looking, in the way of every macho jerk I'd ever had a crush on in high school.

"So what were you doing in Mexico with Terry Barnett?" he asked.

My mind was numb. I took another sip of coffee. God, I didn't want to be here. "I met him back in November. He came to my house," I said slowly, "to measure for a bookcase. He asked me to have dinner with him in Agua Prieta." I stopped, tired.

Flynn waited, steepling his fingers as if he were praying. "Didn't bother you he was married?" he said after a while.

"I didn't know." I could have asked, should have. It seemed obvious now. But Craig had gone to South America, I was hot to trot. My hands were shaking a little. I pressed them against the table edge. I didn't want to tell Flynn all this, what a dupe I was or worse. Why did that Peter French guy have to see us? Peter French married to Diana.

"God," I said suddenly. "Does *Heather* know about this?"

"The widow doesn't know beans. About you, I mean. Peter French asked me not to tell her."

And Peter French didn't know my name or he wouldn't have had to point me out to Flynn. "Are you going to?"

"No reason to tell her anything, unless someone's charged."

"After Terry and I had dinner," I said, "we sat in the square. That's when he told me he was married. It pretty much ended things for me right there."

Flynn nodded. "Must have really pissed you off."

"Kind of. But I felt sorry for him too. He said he needed to talk to someone. He seemed lonely."

"Lonely." Flynn tilted his chair back and studied the wall behind me. I thought of all those people at the memorial. It sounded pretty lame. "You do that kind of thing a lot? Go places with Terry Barnett?"

"I just told you. I had dinner with him that night, that's all. Flynn—" I stopped, breathless, exhausted. "It was nothing."

Flynn pressed on, like one of those giant trucks that come up too close behind you on the freeway when you're passing another car. "But you maybe saw him more than once, feeling sorry for him and all."

"Not really," I said. I couldn't think. Strawberry Fields. Bam. Bam. I wanted to go home. This was all so *irrelevant*. I wanted to give in and just cry, right there in front of Flynn, put my head on his denim shoulder. Jeez.

Flynn sighed. He looked tired too, stubbly, battered even, the skin under his eyes bluish. He pulled out a card and a pen from his pocket, and pushed it toward me sadly, as if he'd done his best and it hadn't worked out.

"Chloe, I want you to read this, then sign it, to show you understand what it says."

I looked down. "What? What's this? My *rights?*"

My rights? Why? I couldn't be a *suspect*. I couldn't believe this was happening. Suddenly my fatigue lifted, and everything came into focus: the ugly cinderblock walls, the scarred table. And Flynn, inexorable Flynn. My hands and feet were cold. That wasn't a dream I'd had about him, it was a premonition. I signed the card hurriedly. I already knew my rights. I worked at the county attorney's.

Flynn reached over and turned on the tape recorder, said the date and time and his name. "I'm here at the substation in Dudley with Chloe Newcombe. Chloe, we were talking about you and Terry Barnett. He was at your house to make a bookcase and, other than that, you're saying you had dinner with him once, in Mexico? That's it?"

"Well," I said, "basically."

"Peggy at the Sierra Vista substation?" Flynn leaned across the table at me; loomed, some kind of white combat scar I hadn't noticed before across one eyebrow. "Peggy says she could have sworn she saw you two at that Thai place, close to the mall, over in Sierra Vista. Are you saying she's mistaken?"

"*Wait,*" I protested. No fair. "That was *before.*" My voice rose. "*Before* we went to Mexico, *before* I knew he was married." Too late. I'd blown it. If I hadn't been so tired and cutting corners I'd have realized you don't even half-lie to the cops. Either tell the truth or get a lawyer. No. Guilty people got lawyers.

"I *forgot,*" I said. "It was just a brief encounter, maybe an hour, tops. I ran into him at the mall—my friend Larry—it was completely accidental, then because of the rain—" I stopped. I was babbling.

There was a silence. Then Flynn nodded as if what I'd just said made perfect sense. "Sure." He paused. "Anything else you just forgot?"

"Not really. I mean, like *what?*"

"Like maybe you and him embracing each other one time in front of that junk store outside of Dudley."

I stared at him, flabbergasted. "That doesn't *count.*" God, I was actually whining. "I didn't even know he was there, until

I ran into him outside. It was just a friendly hug and the whole thing probably lasted two minutes." Every time. Someone had been watching every single goddamned time. How could I be so unlucky?

Flynn leaned across the table again. "Chloe, just tell me this—were you having an affair with Terry Barnett?"

"No!" I was almost shouting. I lowered my voice. "That's absolutely everything. I swear it." Jesus Christ. This was a joke. I glanced at the tape recorder. "It was all back in November. Ancient history. The night Terry was murdered I was home in bed with my cat."

And both neighbors gone, Lourdes in Safford, Bill with his redheaded girlfriend. I should have cried, earlier; should have cried on Flynn's denim shoulder and confessed every irrelevant little detail. "This is my private life," I pleaded. "Can't you see it's embarrassing?"

Flynn's eyes skittered off mine. "I can understand how it would be embarrassing," he said unreassuringly. "I have one more question then you can go. You own a gun?"

"Yes. A thirty-eight. Which I haven't taken out of the chest of drawers in my bedroom for at least a year." I looked at him. "You can have it."

"I'll let you know about that. This concludes the interview. It's, uh—" He looked at his watch. "Nine forty-five p.m."

He leaned over, switched off the tape recorder, reached into his pocket. "Here's my card," he said. "You remember anything else you want to share with me, Chloe, call me, anytime, day or night."

Numbly, I took it.

Flynn stood up, victorious over my inert body. "I won't keep you."

TEN

I DROVE HOME FAST, went inside and called my lawyer.

"Stuart," I said when he answered. "It's Chloe."

"Chloe! Want to come over?" He was obviously chewing something; dinner, lunch, breakfast, Stuart had no regular eating habits. "I made a big pot of spaghetti."

Stuart was a criminal defense lawyer, not really my lawyer, but we'd gone out for a while, until I'd gotten tired of his twenty-four-seven workload and his habit of having me to dinner with his clients. If you could call it dinner. We were still friends but I shuddered at the thought of Stuart's, not pasta, but spaghetti.

"No," I said hurriedly. "Listen, I might be in trouble. This guy that was murdered over in Prophecy, Terry Barnett?" My voice quavered. "Flynn's the investigator."

"*Flynn?* What, Barnett was a dealer?"

"No. Flynn got rotated. He *read me my rights*. I knew Terry, he—I—we—we—I didn't know he was married and all these people—"

"Chloe," he interrupted. "Stop. Take a deep breath and then start from the beginning." His voice was soothing; the same voice he probably used for dopers, petty thieves, rapers, and serial homicidists. "Stuart's here. Everything's fine."

I took a deep breath and told him all the things I could think of in only roughly the order they had happened.

"That's it?" he said when I finished. "Anything relevant you left out?"

"Not really."

"Not really, really, or not really like you told Flynn?"

"Don't rub it in. Not really, really."

"Look, okay, you're a client now, you just hired me—send me a dollar in the mail. Now there's lawyer-client privilege. Don't talk to Flynn ever again unless I'm with you. Jesus Christ, Chloe, you should have known that, you work for the county attorney. When he read you your rights, why didn't you call me?"

"It would have made me look guilty."

Stuart clicked his tongue disgustedly. "That's what they want you to think. Now. I always tell my clients, tell me everything, 'cause if you don't, it's sure as hell going to come up later."

"I did tell you everything."

"So what are you so worried about?"

"You tell me. Should I be?"

"No. Don't let Flynn scare you. He's probably overworking everything just to prove himself as a homicide investigator. Besides. One. Everybody lies to the cops. You were embarrassed and protecting your reputation. Two. No one saw you with this Barnett guy after November, early December tops, right? Because you never saw him after that. Right?"

"Right."

"Three, and most important. There's no physical evidence linking you to the crime. Unless a person confesses, they're not going to charge them without physical evidence. Slam dunk no-brainer. I mean, you've never even been to the guy's house."

"Wait," I said. "Shit. I *have* been to his house."

"*What?* Goddamnit, Chloe. I told you, you have to—"

"No," I interrupted. "It was after he was murdered. I went out on the death notification."

"Why the hell'd you do that?" Stuart said in exasperation. "Guy gets murdered I'd stay the hell clear away."

"They didn't *know* it was murder then, they thought smoke inhalation. Lori needed a partner. Shit, I touched all *kinds of things*. But he wasn't killed in the house, he was out back in his workshop. I've never been in there. I don't know why I went on the notification. Kind of to say goodbye or something. God, Stuart, I'm just blowing it and blowing it." In my exhaustion and anxiety I started to cry, blubbering into the phone.

Stuart waited till I stopped then he said, "You've never been to his workshop. I'm not worried, okay? I don't think Flynn will even call you back in for questioning. If he does, let me know and I'll be there. Got that?"

"Yes," I said meekly.

"If you think of any more 'not reallys,' you let me know right away. And I'll tell you one thing, if you told Flynn you owned a thirty-eight and he's not up there already with a warrant to collect it, then your buddy wasn't killed with a thirty-eight."

"Unless someone stole it from me," I said creatively, "and left it at the scene and Flynn's checking the registration right now."

"Worry, worry, worry." Stuart clicked his tongue. "Right now Flynn's probably questioning the guy who did it. You're tired, Chloe. Go to bed. Get a good night's sleep."

Oh, sure. I hung up and went quick to the dresser drawer in my bedroom where I keep the gun. I hardly ever take it out. With dizzying relief, I saw it was still there, nestled under my bras and slips like a coiled snake. I took it out and sniffed the barrel gingerly. No whiff of cordite, as if it had recently been fired, just a faint smell of gun oil. I put it back, undressed, and got into bed.

I couldn't sleep of course. Listening for cars, wondering if Flynn was going to come up here in the dead of night with a search warrant. Was there anything at *all* incriminating I'd forgotten to tell Stuart? Physical evidence. What about those wood samples Terry had had in his truck? Had I touched any that day, when he was showing them to me? What if I had, and he'd taken them home and unloaded them in the shop and they were sitting there now with my fingerprints all over them. *Had* I touched them?

I focused on the scene now, saw only the yellow leaves in Terry's truck, his smile and Craig's orange sunflowers watching as I, with my basically okay soul, flirted with Terry Barnett two weeks, *only two weeks,* after Craig had left. No, maybe three weeks. So what? Guilty as charged, your honor.

And what if, when I'd hugged Terry that day in front of the Rooster's Attic back in November, a hair from my head had gotten caught in that blue sweater covered with those fuzzy balls that tickled? People don't wash sweaters that often. *What if he'd been wearing it the night he was murdered?*

My God, what if O. J. Simpson was actually innocent?

By morning, I was so tired I was ready to believe I probably could have murdered Terry, maybe in a fugue state. Or I'd been satanically ritually abused in my childhood, repressed it, and it had all come out in a murderous rage at Terry which I was repressing now.

It was light outside, had been for some time, I realized, and looked at the clock. Eight-thirty. I got up, drank a lot of coffee, which cured me of some of my wilder thoughts. When I got in the car to go to work, there was the yellow, red, and black god's eye Evangeline had given me lying on the passenger seat. My stomach turned. I put it out of sight in the glove compartment. Full of caffeine, I buzzed down to work at the county attorney's where all the prosecutors lived.

ELEVEN

"OH, POOR CHLOE!" cried Gigi, when i walked in at nine-fifteen. "The woman that got shot? That was her, wasn't it! The woman that was here yesterday!"

I nodded.

"And you're limping."

"I fell," I said stoically.

"How come the deputy didn't stop him?"

"The deputy?"

"The one she called. I heard her, she said she'd called one."

"She lied, unfortunately."

"No." Gigi's mouth opened in a little O while she considered this. "Oh, here, you've got a message." She handed me a slip.

Fred Barnett had called at eight-fifteen. Fred Barnett, *with the letter from Terry, that might be relevant to the case*. "No phone number?" I said. My voice rose shrewishly. "Gigi, why the hell didn't you get his *number?*"

She flinched. "He said he'd call back. Chloe, are you sure you're okay? I mean if you're not, I can hold your calls. I've got one for you right now from—"

"I'll take it," I cut in.

I limped back past Lucinda's empty office. She never arrived at eight like a peon, or nine either. I took the call at my desk. "Hello? This is Chloe."

"Ollie Menton here, from the *Sierra Vista Review*. Heard you were there when the tragedy happened over in Huachuca City. You're lucky to be alive. I wondered if you'd care to comment?"

"No," I said, "I'm sorry. I can't."

"No *problemo,*" said Ollie heartily. "Just thought I'd give it a try."

After he hung up I called Gigi. "No reporters," I said. "Anyone else is fine."

As I hung up I could hear Lucinda, her high heels rat-a-tatting as she came into the outer office.

"Chloe?" She was at my door. Red dress with big black polka dots, lots of big gold jewelry. Her face radiated detached and obligatory concern. "The Evangeline thing. That poor woman. Are you all right?"

"Yes."

"I have to talk to you. Come to my office as soon as you're done with what you're doing."

"I'm done now," I said.

A POSTER OF a little girl crying hung on the wall of Lucinda's office. IT SHOULDN'T HURT TO BE A CHILD. A row of dead coleus plants lined the office window, and on top of a bookcase photographs of her six grandchildren, most of them missing front teeth, grinned at me triumphantly, safe in Lucinda's love.

The rest of the room was a clutter of papers, pamphlets, brochures, and half-finished quarterly reports to the Arizona Criminal Justice Commission and Victims of Crime Act. Most of what Lucinda did was compile reports, give trainings and workshops, make speeches. I wouldn't have had her job for anything. She looked more windblown than usual today, her hair frizzy at the ends and she hadn't gotten her lipstick on straight.

She cleared a stack of papers from her chair and sat down. I stayed standing. "Evangeline," she said. "Horrible. You're *sure* you're all right?" She looked at me shrewdly as if she knew I wasn't.

"Yes."

Lucinda raised her eyebrows skeptically.

"Look," I said. "I didn't see anything. I mean, it was certainly traumatic but not something I can't deal with."

Lucinda sat up straighter in her chair. "Question for you. Why wasn't a deputy there?"

"Because Evangeline told me she'd already called one. You can ask Gigi, she heard her when she said it."

"And?"

"She lied. Chip was supposed to be in Tucson." I rolled my eyes. "She thought he'd be mad if he heard later on there'd been a cop at the house."

Lucinda pursed her lips. "But when you saw there wasn't a deputy, you shouldn't have let her go into the house."

"Lucinda, we were in separate cars. She got there first. It looked okay, Chip's car was gone, but when I saw there wasn't a deputy I told her to wait till I called one. But she went ahead anyway." Suddenly I felt exhausted, explaining and explaining, the same story over and over when I didn't even want to think about it. "It all happened really fast," I added defensively.

"Well, I was on the phone half the night with Melvin Huber," said Lucinda. "Defending you."

I tried to look polite. Melvin was the county attorney and a real horse's ass.

"Melvin wanted to fire you on the spot."

"*What?*" I needed to sit down. I picked up a stack of papers from the only other chair and sat, holding the papers in my lap. "He can't just fire me. *Why?*"

"It's not only this. This was just the last straw."

"What else then?"

Lucinda got up. She went to the door of her office and closed it. There was a certain drama to the way she did it that made me think she was enjoying this whole thing.

She sat back down, leaned toward me. "What's this I hear about you and Terry Barnett?"

Well, of course. How could I have thought in a million

years Lucinda wouldn't hear about it? "He did some carpentry for me last November," I said.

"That's all? That's not what I've been hearing."

Damn. I couldn't even call Stuart. There wasn't anywhere to look in her crowded office except back at her. Just the two of us and she had the power.

"I—we got together a couple of times, nothing...it wasn't any big deal, then he told me he was married. So I didn't see him anymore."

"I see." She nodded her head up and down a few times. "Personally, I wouldn't go out with a man unless I knew who he was." She'd been divorced for years. I didn't know if she even went out with men, because she valued her privacy far more than she valued the privacy of others, I thought bitterly.

"I don't care what you do socially, Chloe." She brushed at a thread on her dress. "I know you're from back East and people do things differently there. It's your life, after all. But—" She paused.

"But?"

"The man is a homicide victim. His whole life is coming under scrutiny. I understand Flynn questioned you last night. Melvin says you might be a *suspect*."

"Jesus Christ, Lucinda. I had nothing whatsoever to do with his murder. I hadn't seen him for mon—*weeks*. Give me a break here."

"I know it's nonsense. I told Melvin that. Over and over. I told you already I *defended* you. But first it's Evangeline, then this, in a space of hours. It's too much. Anyway, we reached a compromise. How much vacation time do you have?"

"All of it. Three weeks."

"Take it. I want you to keep a low profile for a while as far as the county attorney's office is concerned."

"You're firing me."

"I'm not firing you yet. Let's see how this murder investigation goes. Once someone is charged, one problem will be gone. And another thing."

"What?"

"I want you to promise me you'll go see a counselor about this Evangeline thing while you still have your benefits."

"I'll think about it."

Lucinda looked at her watch. "Police training at nine forty-five," she said. "Got to go. You go home."

SHIT. WHAT WERE they going to do without me? Lucinda hated victims. I looked numbly at my desk. I'd never really domesticated my work space. No pictures of loved ones, no fuzzy little animals, no lucky jade plants in Chinese pots. Even the unkillable dichondra plant on my bookshelf belonged to the office. The only thing that was mine in the whole room was the cartoon taped on the wall: two jailbirds, one saying to the other, "I've tried victimless crimes, but I'm a people person."

It wasn't right. Here I was in the middle of things. And Fred Barnett would be calling back.

If I could talk to him, maybe I would be able to pry out of him what was in Terry's letter. If it was useful to the case I could persuade him to tell Flynn. But unless he called back in the next half hour or so I wouldn't be here. He hadn't left a number. I could call directory assistance. Sure. He hadn't even mentioned a town. Fred Barnett, Ohio.

I sat down and swung round to my computer. I'd try a Google search. I tapped some keys but couldn't seem to get online. I called Gigi. "What's with the computers?" I said.

"They're down." She giggled. "Everyone's pissed."

Damn. And I was the last person in America who didn't have a computer at home.

Who killed Terry, and why? I'd met him in a vacuum, had no idea what his life was really like. So what *did* I know? That he'd been worried about something back in November, he'd talked about obsessing, about screwing up, and it all started twenty years ago with a woman named April. He and his brother Fred had chased after her from Ohio all the way to Tucson.

Fred would know all about April. What had Terry said in that letter?

I called Gigi. "Listen," I said, "I have to go. If Fred Barnett calls, give him my home number. You've got it, right?"

"Yes."

I hung up, opened my desk drawer, took a couple of pens and a Post-it note stack and stuck them in my purse. The lowly office worker's revenge.

Then I limped out of the county attorney's like a wounded war veteran, got in my car and drove away in a fog from the place where I'd worked for the last five years. In the flat blue sky the sun shone on the bare branches of the Chinese elms, the cancer trees, the cottonwoods. A trickle of water meandered through the drainage ditch that lined Tombstone Canyon. It was only early February and already the fennel was showing in patches of green.

As I drove it hit me full force: Flynn was closemouthed, but so what. Anyone could have seen me go into the substation with him plus there was Peggy from Sierra Vista who'd seen Terry and me at the Thai restaurant. Lucinda knew already, and it wouldn't be long before everyone in the county attorney's office knew. Then their husbands and wives, parents, children, grandchildren, and distant relatives. It was just too juicy not to get around.

What if Flynn continued to storm about, amassing suspects, but never caught who did it? The rumor would grow as it was passed along, gathering barnacles of misinformation. Years, *years* from now people would still be whispering, "That's Chloe Newcombe, she killed a man and got away with it. You know why? They hushed it all up 'cause she worked for the *county attorney*."

Heather would eventually hear about it too, of course. Hear

that the same woman who had sat with her the night Terry was murdered, dispensing sham comfort, was probably the one who had killed him because they'd been having an affair that had gone wrong somehow. That was worse than all the rest.

In the meantime what was I supposed to do about making a living if I was fired?

BY THE TIME I got home, I was really mad. I would sue the county attorney for firing me without cause. I'd get a large settlement and move somewhere far, far away. I called Stuart and ranted. About Terry, Evangeline, Flynn, losing my job, everything.

"I'm a criminal defense attorney," he said, when I finished. "You want a civil guy, I can give you some names, but you're jumping the gun here. Technically you haven't even been fired yet."

"Yet," I said bitterly. "Technically."

"Maybe never. Calm down. Melvin's just protecting his ass. This will all fade away once they make an arrest."

"*If*," I said. "Flynn is totally wasting his time, going after people like me."

"What do you want?" said Stuart. "A plodder? I've had dealings with Flynn. At least you got some guy on fire investigating, willing to do anything, no matter how sleazy, to get his man or woman."

I shuddered. "What if he decides it's me?"

"Chloe, Chloe."

"I could do a better job than Flynn. I've figured cases out before, ahead of the cops."

"Jesus, Chloe. Don't even go there."

"Why not?"

"Your brain's addled from that woman getting shot. Stop and think. Stay low, and stay out of it. Let Flynn do the investigating, it's his job, not yours. Look, want to come to dinner? I'm making porcupines."

"You're making what?"

"Porcupines. You know, balls of ground beef, tomato sauce, and Minute Rice. The rice sticks out of the balls like quills." He chortled. "Porcupine balls."

"No, thanks."

I hung up. I wasn't vanquished yet, there was still Fred Barnett. He could call any minute. Although what I wanted to do more than anything was call Heather. I wanted to confess, wanted her to understand I hadn't known Terry was married, *that nothing had really happened*. Goddamnit, I wanted *absolution*.

I stayed home all the rest of the day, waiting for Fred's call. At quarter to five, I called the county attorney's.

"Gigi," I said, "didn't Mr. Barnett call back?"

"Oh, Chloe, yeah, he did. But Lucinda was here, she told me to give her all your calls."

I gritted my teeth to keep from yelling at Gigi. "Thanks anyway."

I pushed the off button and threw the phone across the room where it lodged in a large and hideous thorny cactus Craig had given me.

TWELVE

"IF IT'S SERVED ON Lu-Ray, it's a-okay," said my dead brother James. His beautiful blue eyes shone as he set a plate in front of me with a flourish. The plate was palest turquoise and piled with macaroni in bright orange sauce, decorated with a tiny sprig of parsley. He was broke, living in a room the size of a closet in the West Village; it was before he'd moved to L.A. and all he could afford to eat was Kraft macaroni and cheese.

Back then he hadn't come out yet, not even to me, but how many straight guys scoured the thrift stores for Lu-Ray china? Not that I cared—straight or gay, I loved him just the same. Except if he had been straight he wouldn't be dead now, leaving me ambushed by this memory as I stood in the Safeway holding a box of Kraft macaroni and cheese.

Way down at the far end of the aisle, I saw Marilu, one of the legal secretaries at the county attorney's, wearing jeans and perusing the hamburger. I liked Marilu but I hurriedly put the macaroni and cheese in my cart next to the ramen noodles, the broccoli on sale for sixty-nine cents a pound, the cheap Safeway brand cat food and headed away from her toward the checkout, rounded a corner and there was Flynn.

He was in the checkout line holding a carton of orange juice. He didn't even live around here. I didn't know where he lived, in a cave somewhere in the Chiricahua Mountains maybe, where he gnawed on jackrabbit he'd strangled barehanded. I almost wanted to cry. I'd bought a copy of the Sierra Vista Review, the biggest local paper, last night, and it had said there were no leads in the Barnett case. What was Flynn doing—tailing me? I made a sharp turn into the cereal aisle away from him.

IN THE PARK in front of the Mining Museum, they were having a crafts fair. Purple, red, and green tie-dyed T-shirts and skirts, fringed leather bags fluttered in the breeze; silver, turquoise, and malachite jewelry gleamed in the sun. I drove slowly by, on my way home from Safeway.

At the biggest booth Diana French, like a fairy-tale queen in a medley of flowing purple garments, her blond hair tied back with a green scarf, waved her arms at two young men in Rasta braids attempting to hang a hand-painted sign that said natural foods co-op. She looked serene and in charge. But she was married to Peter French. Did that make her my enemy? I felt a headache coming on.

The street was clotted with tourists, the elderly in staid polyester, the young dressed athletically as if sightseeing were a rigorous marathon. They moved like herds of cattle through the streets, jaywalking as they gaped at the nineteenth-century brick buildings, the Western art in the gallery windows.

Without a job, free-floating, I belonged nowhere, neither with the tourists nor the locals. Briefly I yearned for Craig: the good Craig, well medicated and full of things to do. To get him off my mind, I began for the hundredth time to calculate: paychecks ran two weeks behind and, with my three-week vacation, that meant I was good for another five weeks: I could stretch that to last a couple of months. But then what? What if the investigation dragged on for months? There wasn't much in the way of jobs here unless you worked for the county.

Maybe my future lay in tie-dyeing, knitting, jewelry making, or possibly sign painting, with a part-time job at the food co-op. For a little extra cash, I could write poetry and read it aloud for donations at the Quarter Moon Café or the Cranny.

People would come in droves to hear me, the woman who'd killed Terry Barnett and got away with it.

When I got home I took three ibuprofen. Big Foot meowed at me from next to his cat bowl, still full of Safeway brand cat food.

"Come on," I said. "It's not like you're *starving*."

FOR DINNER I HAD salad from my neighbor Bill's garden with the Kraft mac and cheese. I ate about half and then took three more ibuprofen. I was just putting away what was left when there was a knock at the kitchen door. I jumped.

Flynn? Come to read me my rights again? With a warrant this time? I hated Flynn yet I felt almost hopeful as I flicked on the light, looked out the window. A stranger.

A clean-shaven stranger with a good haircut, navy polo shirt under an unzipped navy windbreaker, khaki pants, carrying a briefcase and a newspaper, like a businessman on a commuter train. *Surreal.* What planet was he from?

Then I noticed, several feet behind him, a weedy kid, not yet burnished; nine or ten, baggy enormous pants and turned-around baseball cap.

Reassured, I opened the door.

"Chloe Newcombe?" said the man.

"Yes?"

"We talked on the phone. I'm Fred Barnett."

Fred Barnett, I was astounded. I'd given up being able to talk to him and now here he was. He didn't look anything at all like Terry; had nothing of his lightness. He was darker, bulkier; a little hangdog.

But *why* was he here? I took a step back. "I thought you were in Ohio."

"We flew in this afternoon. This is Sam, my son."

Behind him under the carport light, Sam hunched his shoulders like a gorilla, crossed his eyes and let his mouth fall open.

"I know this is kind of unforgivable," Fred went on hurriedly as if afraid I might slam the door in his face any minute. "Showing up at your house after dinner—I hope it's not *during* dinner. Sam and I checked into the Copper Queen Hotel." He smiled, a little uncertainly, and held up the newspaper he was carrying. It was a copy of the *Sierra Vista Review*. "I bought this to see if there was anything about Terry. Your name's in it."

I hadn't seen tonight's copy. For a second I had a horrible vision; my name in headlines, "Newcombe Chief Suspect in Barnett Case." And Terry's brother here for revenge.

"I thought we might talk," he said.

FRED SAT AT the kitchen counter, while I scanned the paper. Ollie Menton had done an article on domestic violence with Evangeline's murder the centerpiece. Chloe Newcombe, a victim's advocate, was on the scene but would not comment. Damn Ollie, that little shit. It would just remind Melvin. *So what was Fred doing here?*

"And?" I said cautiously when I finished.

"It must have been rough. And this bossy woman in your office said you'd gone on vacation." He looked at me meaningfully. "When I saw that article, I figured that was why."

"This cat likes me!" said Sam. He lay down on the floor and tickled Big Foot under the chin. "What's his name?"

"Big Foot."

"Haw haw!"

"Doesn't he have school?" I said to get Fred's mind off my circumstances.

Fred shrugged. "Travel's educational and a little time off won't hurt him. He's a smart kid, IQ tests right off the scale."

"Dad," Sam protested, from the floor. "It does *not!*"

Fred ignored him. "He gets his brains from my ex-wife. She's on a trip right now so Sam came with me. Myself, I'm just a shopkeeper, but kind of on a larger scale. Sporting goods. We started small but now we just about cover the whole Midwest region."

Sam got up, prowled, picking up my last banana from a bowl on the counter, setting it down.

"Hungry?" I said.

"He just ate," said Fred.

"Take the banana," I told Sam. "It's pretty squishy though."

"Terry got the real brains in our family," Fred said sadly. "And now he's dead. Ah, *Jeez*. I still can't believe it." His face kind of crumpled and he lowered his head onto the palm of his hand. "Sorry. They came back again. They do that all the time, little pictures."

Macaroni and cheese on Lu-Ray china. "Little pictures," I said, warming to him.

He looked up. His eyes were mournful, brown to Terry's green; dog eyes to Terry's cat's. What were the words Terry had used to describe his brother? *"Weirdly needy."* Well, then so was I, still mourning for my brother James.

"Yeah," he said. "Pictures of me, Terry, and Mike O'Reilly."

"Who's Mike O'Reilly?"

"Terry's best friend—all through elementary, high school. Best friends after that too, college and beyond." He sighed. "Till Terry moved down here and got married."

"You must have seen Heather," I said. "I've been worried about her. Is she doing okay?"

Fred looked blank.

Behind me, Sam belched loudly. He belched two more times. "I can belch the first line of 'The Star-Spangled Banner,'" he said.

"And on the phone," I said, "you mentioned a letter."

"Want to hear?" said Sam loudly.

"Could he maybe go in another room?" said Fred. "So we can talk."

"There's a TV in the living room," I said. "There should be a *Simpsons* rerun on about now."

"I HAVEN'T CONTACTED Heather," said Fred.

"Why not?"

"Because—" He paused. Under the kitchen lights his face looked washed out, tired. "Look, I don't want to go to the police just yet. But I'm a stranger and I don't know where to turn, that's why I'm here. I need an objective confidential opinion."

"About what?"

"I think Heather might have killed my brother."

"Haw, haw, haw," said Sam from the living room. "That Bart!"

I stared at Fred, stunned. Thank God he hadn't gone to see Heather yet, she didn't need someone like him, strung out on grief and, I could see now, hyperparanoid. I'd spent years talking to victims and what they often needed most was someone, anyone, to blame. We don't have a criminal justice system just to protect the innocent from the accused, but also to protect the accused from the innocent.

"She did not," I said. "No *way*." I laughed. "You are so wrong. She doesn't even own a gun and she has a solid alibi. She was at a poetry reading here in town, lots of people must have seen her."

"So? That doesn't mean anything," Fred went on doggedly. "She could have been in cahoots with someone else. A boyfriend, maybe. And Terry and I inherited a couple hundred thousand each from my parents, they were old school, saved it and sat on it. There's no will, she gets it all."

It was absurd. Heather struck me as someone who could make do in a hovel. I stood up and went to the refrigerator for something to do, to hide my anger. If it hadn't been for the sound of *The Simpsons* and Sam laughing from the other room, I would have thrown Fred out then and there. I opened the refrigerator door and stared inside blankly.

But it wasn't Fred's fault, he hadn't met Heather, felt the pain she was in that night in her kitchen.

I closed the refrigerator door. "Look," I said, "you want a confidential objective opinion? I know you're very upset about losing your brother and you have a right to be, but these accusations are totally unfounded."

"You haven't seen the letter."

I blinked. The letter. What could it say?

Fred picked up his briefcase from the floor, flipped it open, and pulled out a manila envelope. He took out a sheet of paper and pushed it across the counter. "I didn't bring the whole thing, just a copy of the last page. I highlighted the important part."

The words under the yellow highlighter jumped out at me.

I love Heather very much, she's the most wonderful, innately talented person I've ever met. But the thing is— how do I say this? I just don't trust her. If you'd only come down here to visit, I think you'd see what I mean. Or maybe I'm crazy. If I am, I need you to tell me. Help me out here and come soon.

I looked up at Fred.

"Is that ominous or what?" he said eagerly.

His eagerness bothered me. I stared down at the letter again. Why would Terry say he didn't trust Heather? The lines of words were bland, computer generated, except for the signature, just like on Terry's card: bold and extremely legible, each letter had a stance to it, an attitude.

I felt uneasy. Something was wrong here, off kilter. "This letter," I said. "It's so…friendly. When Terry worked for me last fall he told me you two weren't even speaking. He said you hadn't talked to each other for *years*."

For a moment Fred was silent, then he said sadly, "This letter came out of the blue. When he married Heather he went off the radar, so to speak, like now he had a wife he didn't need anyone else."

Heather had come between them? Was that why he seemed out to get her? No will. If it turned out Heather was responsible for Terry's death, who would get his money? Fred was next of kin. What if Fred had written the letter himself, faked the signature? But you'd need more than that to even charge her, and besides, Fred had a chain of sporting-goods stores that covered the whole Midwest region. It didn't sound like he would be that desperate.

"I don't know why Terry says he didn't trust Heather," I said, frustrated. "It doesn't sound like he knew why himself. This letter means nothing—there's no specifics here, nothing that you can put your finger on."

Who could you trust? I certainly didn't trust Fred, but sometimes you just had to go ahead and take a chance and see where it led you. "One thing I do know," I went on, "Heather said Terry was worried about something, not sleeping. And last fall?" I took a deep breath. "He was worried then too."

"Worried? About what?"

"I don't know, he started to tell me, then—anyway, whatever it was, he said it all started with a woman you both knew. Her name was April. April Matasky."

"April Matasky?" He looked truly dumbfounded. "You've got to be kidding. She was years and years ago."

"Twenty years, Terry said. He said you and he came out West to Tucson, chasing after her. He called her a phantom."

"Jeez. A phantom." Fred rolled his eyes. "'Vampire' is more like it."

"You didn't like her?"

"I didn't like her at all."

"Then why'd you come to Tucson with Terry, looking for her, if you didn't like her at all?"

Fred looked edgy. "Let's just drop it, okay?"

"But it might be important."

"It isn't," he said firmly. "It was too long ago; just Terry reminiscing. Let's focus on Heather. Terry loved her. I don't want to go to the cops with this letter till I look into things on my own first. Come work for me. I'll *pay* you." He paused.

"Two hundred a day, plus expenses. Off the books. We'll go out to Terry's house tomorrow. You can tell Heather we talked on the phone and got to know each other. Hey, Chloe, I'm begging for your help."

I wasn't sure about Fred, but at least if I went with him, someone would be there who was on Heather's side. My headache was gone. What was I waiting for? "Okay, I'll do it."

"I'll pick you up here in my rental. No calling ahead. I don't want her preparing a grieving-widow act if that's not what she is."

Sam appeared, lugging Big Foot, back paws dangling. "This is a really *cool* cat," he said. "We're going to the house?"

"Not we," said Fred. "*You're* staying at the hotel and doing homework. You promised. Your mom will have a fit if you fall behind."

THIRTEEN

THE DESERT STRETCHED OUT on either side of Highway 92, pale gold grasses growing from red dirt. In the distance over on the right was the San Pedro River, the huge bare cottonwoods that bordered it a pale blur. It was a fine warmish day, sunny.

Behind the wheel of the rented white Toyota Fred was dressed just as last night, except the polo shirt was dark green. "Listen, when we see Heather?" he said. "Don't mention Sam."

"Why not?" I asked, mystified. "She must know Terry had a nephew."

"He's my kid, you know? I only brought him because we don't get to spend that much time together, his mother keeps him on a tight rein. But I don't want any involvement between them till I'm okay about her."

"You'll be okay about her," I said, tired of his paranoia, "once you meet her. Listen, I've been thinking about April Matasky."

"*Why?*" Fred turned to look at me. The car veered.

"Maybe whatever was bothering Terry wasn't about April, per se; maybe she was a metaphor for something else. Something that was going on in Terry's life then, back in November."

"Except we don't know what was going on in his life. That's why we're here in this car right now, going to see Heather. Just forget about April."

"A free spirit, that's what Terry called her. He said that made her dangerous."

"She was dangerous." His tone was reluctant. "Uncontrollable."

"So you and Terry come to Tucson, chasing her because she was *dangerous?*"

"We were callow youths."

"And how did you even know her if she lived in Tucson?" I persisted. "I mean, was she from Ohio originally?"

"No. Jeez. Look, I took a trip out West, okay, I stopped for a while in Tucson and that's where I met her. She came back with me to Ohio, but then she left so Terry and I came down here looking for her."

"Then she was *your* girlfriend, not Terry's?"

"She wasn't anybody's girlfriend. I don't think she had it in her to be a girlfriend," Fred said irritably. "I don't want to talk about this anymore, okay? I've got too much else on my mind. It was *twenty years ago,* Chloe."

I dropped it for the present, focused on our upcoming meeting with Heather. What if Peter French had changed his mind and told Heather about seeing me with Terry? Had Flynn told him my name? What if Heather took offense the moment she saw me? If only I could take her aside, explain.

"What's this bridge?" Fred's voice was tense. "Where are we anyway?"

"Almost to the turn," I said. "We're crossing the San Pedro River."

"A *river?* That's not a river, it's a *creek,* a tiny pathetic creek."

"I think this is the turn," I said nervously.

WE PASSED a small store, a wooden structure with a porch and a sign that said MEEKS'S MERCANTILE. I remembered its red and green neon lights shining out from the blackness the night Terry was murdered. Howard Meeks, the Pentecostal guy.

In the daylight, I could see that Prophecy wasn't really a town, more like a place the residents had given a name to. Houses, set widely apart, were scattered along both sides of the dirt road: adobe, straw bale, wood. Many had large garden plots somewhere near, mulched down for the winter. Behind, not far away, was the river.

We bumped along.

"It's right after this curve, I think," I said. "It was dark the last time." Dark, till I saw the rotating lights of the deputies' cars. I swallowed, some of the tension from that night coming back. "I hope I recognize the house—" I stopped as we rounded the curve.

The car swerved. *"Aw, jeez,"* said Fred.

Only partially obscured by the house was Terry's workshop. I hadn't seen it before, in the dark. It was the size of a small barn, painted a dark red that was even darker where the boards along one side were charred and smudged by smoke. In the sun, glass from a broken window glittered in the dry grass. I felt a little sick. Heather saw that every day. How could she bear it?

Terry had been shot in there. Was he already dead when the fire started or had it finished him off?

We reached the house and Fred parked the car, crookedly, behind an old blue Volvo. The same car Terry had been driving when I'd seen him last when we'd hugged, *a little longer than friends do.* What if we'd been somewhere more private? For a second Flynn leaned across the table at me in the interview room. *"Chloe, just tell me this—were you having an affair with Terry Barnett?"*

I came back, looked over at Fred. He was gripping the steering wheel, staring at the burned workshop.

"Fred?" My voice sounded oddly whispery. "You okay?"

"Kind of." He turned off the ignition. "Let's just do this."

As WE GOT OUT I caught the same scent of moisture I had the night of the fire. The gate in the low cedar fence that enclosed the yard had been open that night but today it was closed. Fred fiddled with the latch, nervously.

"You just raise it," I said. "Here, like this."

We entered the yard, dried-up blond grass bordered with flower beds, empty now but mulched with bark, in the middle the neat path of flagstones leading to the glassed-in porch. The house had gray cedar siding, probably was a small house in the beginning with rooms added on, so now it was large, really, sprawling. Some of the windows were stained glass. A pretty house, with a lot of shabby charm.

Fred knocked on the porch door, then tried the knob. It turned. "Not locked," he said. "So she must be here."

On the porch was a white wicker chair; bright red geraniums scented the air with a spicy sweetness. The big orange cat Heather had held in her arms that night in the living room sidled round my ankles. Pi-Pi, poor old Pi-Pi.

Fred knocked on the inside door. "Heather?" He tried the knob. "This one's locked. *Heather?*" he shouted. "Anybody there?"

"'Scuse me, folks?"

We turned. A tall man, seventy or so, gray hair in a brush cut, beaky nose, bushy white eyebrows, stood just outside. He wore a brown plaid shirt, long khaki shorts, wool socks, and big hiking boots like an ancient Boy Scout. "How can I help you, folks?"

"You can tell us where Heather is," said Fred. "I'm Fred Barnett, Terry's brother, and I came all the way from Ohio to talk to her."

The man looked stunned. "Terry's *brother?* For goodness' sake." His eyebrows fluttered like fat white moths. "She's in Tucson at her parents'. She probably won't be back for a while."

"For a while?" I said. "What about her class? The elder hostel?"

"She had to turn it over to someone else. Poor little thing. I don't think she's slept more than a couple of hours, since it happened. Lights are on all night, sad music playing." He looked bemused. "I'm Brandon Blofeld, by the way. I live next door."

He pointed at a simple cinderblock down the road. An ancient green VW van, spotted with rust, was parked in front, a big motorcycle behind it. A woman was just coming out of the front door. Blofeld. The couple who'd been in Heather's kitchen that night. The woman looked over toward us and waved.

Fred sighed as if giving up. "Listen, I want to take a closer look at Terry's workshop. Pay my respects. Maybe you can give Chloe here the address and phone number of Heather's parents."

"Hugh and Lucia Stephens." Brandon patted his shirt pocket. "Got it here somewhere. *Ah*." He pulled out a folded piece of paper. "Don't get too close," he warned as Fred walked away. "Structure's not that stable. Heather's got to get herself a crew, prop things up. But it's all too much for her right now."

I took out my notebook and wrote down the address and phone number Brandon gave me while Fred headed round the house.

"Brandon!" The woman was coming toward us, walking briskly down the road. She seemed his exact replica in female form, graying hair pulled back, same khaki shorts and hiking boots. A beautiful young man in black trailed along reluctantly a few feet behind her, the same young man who'd read "Fern Hill" at the memorial; the young Elvis look-alike.

"Is everything all right?" the woman called out.

"Fine, dear!" shouted Brandon. "My wife, Helen," he said to me, "and that's Damien, my grandson."

Now I remembered; Heather had had me call the Blofelds that night, to ask that Damien come over and be with her.

"Well, ciao," said Brandon Blofeld, backing away. "Maybe we'll meet again."

I watched him go. The trailing grandson had caught up with the woman; even in broad daylight in a faded black T-shirt, he still looked so luscious. I couldn't take my eyes off him. How could he be these people's grandson? He looked like he came from a different planet. *He* was the one Heather had asked to come stay with her the night of Terry's murder?

Well, so what.

But a whiff, just a whiff of doubt, entered my mind like one mutant cell; I staved it off and headed toward the back to look for Fred.

STANDING IN THE dried-out grass at the burned side of the shop, among the glass that glittered in the sun, his arms dangling at his sides, his face naked, Fred was crying in big shuddering sobs. He stopped abruptly when he saw me come round the house, took a large blue handkerchief out of his pocket and wiped his eyes. His nose was red and his eyes were tinged pink. Despite his good haircut and his clothes from the Gap he looked blurred, scruffy.

"I didn't even come to visit," he said. "Like Terry asked me to." He gulped. "It was a plea for help and I betrayed him."

Maybe I'd been wrong, completely wrong, not trusting Fred.

Instinctively, I held out my arms. The hug was brief, therapeutic. Even Flynn would have approved. I smelled sweat, tasted salt from tears.

He stepped back, smiling weakly. "I've been keeping it all inside, you know? 'Cause of Sam. He kind of stabilizes me. I—" He took a breath. "I was thinking again about Terry and me and Mike O'Reilly." His voice was gruff with emotion. "You remember Mike, don't you?"

"Terry's best friend," I said soothingly.

"They met in kindergarten. Best friends ever since. Mike's mother used to make this stuff she called Irish lasagna. With potatoes." He shook his head. "It was awful. I couldn't eat it, but Terry wolfed it down. He was just so—so *indestructible*."

There was an eerie silence. In the distance I could see the bare blurred trees that lined the river; smelled ashes, the ghosts of the fire. Pi-Pi appeared at the side of the shop, walking daintily through the rubble, sniffing at things. A big forbidding-looking padlock hung on the shop door, a remnant of yellow crime-scene tape nearby.

"I need to spend some time with Sam away from all this," said Fred. "I want you to go to Heather's parents' house this afternoon and use your powers of persuasion to get her to come home and meet with me, tomorrow. That's all the time I have left. I want to see her *here* in this house."

I nodded, a little dubiously.

"It has to be here," he repeated. "Maybe I'm wrong and she really loved Terry. But if she didn't, it won't be as easy for her to lie about things here, with Terry all around, listening."

FOURTEEN

ALL THE WAY TO TUCSON, I consulted my powers of persuasion. It wasn't like I was trained in sales. Was the letter Fred had shown me a fake? And if not, why hadn't Terry trusted Heather? What about Damien who Heather had had come over the night Terry died? I hadn't mentioned him to Fred. For all I knew, in his emotional state, Fred might have throttled him. Besides, Damien looked to be somewhere in his twenties, nearly half Heather's age.

But so what? Look at all those Colette novels. He looked like he could easily be someone's Chéri. But Heather in her baggy jeans, her unruly bangs, was certainly no one's idea of a French courtesan.

Hugh and Lucia Stephens, Heather's parents, lived on the northwest side, in the Foothills. I took the Ina Road exit, congested as always, passed a Super Kmart, a Target, the Foothills Mall. Crossed Oracle. Checked the address on my Tucson map. Saguaro Lane. Number 112.

Once I got off into the residential area, I was in the eternal spring of a Tucson winter. Borders of pansies and snapdragons edged some yards, but most were hidden behind tall adobe walls. When I turned onto Saguaro the walls got higher; the palms, paloverde, and oleander trees more luxuriant. Heather's parents weren't poor.

I pulled over in front of 112, shed the sweater I'd needed back in Dudley, almost three thousand feet higher altitude, and got out. There weren't any sidewalks, just a gravel path littered with the yellow paloverde flowers already blooming in February. In the high adobe wall was a wrought-iron gate, open an inch or so. A gray Ford Explorer was parked in the driveway next to a big bushy tree full of oranges.

I pushed the gate open. Small skittish birds yakked at each other and I could smell oranges rotting pungently. The sand-colored adobe house was low and so shrouded in greenery that the front door was almost invisible. I crunched across the gravel and came to a massive carved dark wood affair, framed by a scarlet bird-of-paradise. I pressed the doorbell.

Inside chimes played a tinkly melody.

After a while a woman opened the door. Somewhere in her late sixties, she had a wide, soft face, carefully made up, with graying hair pulled back, bits of it escaping in little curls around her forehead. She wore a long loose dress, probably to conceal some extra pounds. At the hem, Sienna-red lions and giraffes danced on a black background.

"Well, hello." She looked pleased to see me, as if she'd been sitting around just dying to talk to someone.

"Hi," I said. "Are you Lucia Stephens?"

"Yes?"

"My name's Chloe Newcombe. I'm sorry to bother you, I should have called but I was right here in the neighborhood. I'm looking for Heather."

Her face softened a little more with disappointment. "Oh, dear. I'm afraid you missed her. She went back home a couple of days ago."

"Excuse me?" I stared at her. "She went home a couple of *days* ago? Her neighbor told me just yesterday she was with you."

"Well, she's hiding out, you might say. She didn't tell me where." She eyed me curiously. "You're one of her friends?"

"I'm a victim advocate. I met Heather the night Terry was killed."

"A victim advocate?" Her voice rose hopefully. "Are you with the police? Have they arrested someone?"

"No." I shook my head. "I'm sorry. And I just work with victims, more like counseling, not law enforcement. But

Terry's brother, Fred, is in Dudley. He came all the way from Ohio to see her."

"Terry's *brother*." Lucia put her hand over her heart dramatically. "We've never met him. Oh, my goodness. Of course we'll have to get them together. But you helped Heather that night? Did she tell you— I'm so worried for her, she's—" She stopped, fluttery, breathless. "Look, why don't you come in."

So worried? I followed as she swished down a narrow tiled hall, one wall hung with a Navajo rug, past a door open to a living room with more Indian rugs on the floor and dark leather furniture. We reached a small sunny room, at the end of the hall, full of windows, with Mexican leather chairs and a farmer's table. The stuccoed walls were hung with more ceremonial masks than I could count.

"This is my cozy little nook," said Lucia too brightly. "Please, sit down."

I sat. The masks were painted in blacks and whites, reds and beiges. They seemed to watch me, not with benevolence. On the table were a coffee cup and a crossword magazine open to a puzzle, half done.

"Heather looked *awful*," Lucia said in despair. "I don't know what she did to her hair, it looks like she cut it with the kitchen scissors. So unbecoming." She hovered, babbling nervously. "And no makeup. Just a touch can make such a difference. But you can't tell her that. She's too proud, she's always been that way, ever since she was little." She stopped abruptly. "*What* am I talking about?"

"You're worried about Heather," I said.

She sat down across from me. "Terrified is more like it. You're a victim advocate, a professional. You— I thought—" She floundered. "*I don't know what to do.*"

"Maybe nothing," I said soothingly. "Just wait, be there if she needs you."

Lucia stared at me. "She didn't tell you, did she? About *Ivan*."

"Ivan," I said.

"Her ex. I'm sorry. What did you say your name was?"

"Chloe."

"Yes. Well, from the very beginning I tried to get her to talk to my therapist, but she refused completely. Of course, she hates therapists. Please, I beg you, don't mention this conversation to anyone." Her hands fluttered at her hair, smoothing it back. "Heather would be so angry with me."

"I'm bound by confidentiality," I said. "Anything you say to me stays with me. Ivan was her husband before Terry?"

"Yes. Ivan Fowler. They were divorced seven years ago. It was a terrible, terrible marriage. Heather doesn't like me to tell people, but he *abused* her."

My hands felt cold. I stared at Lucia, but I saw Evangeline, her red hair, her green blouse; like neon, in the cloudy light. "Abused her?" I said. "Physical violence, what?"

Lucia shuddered delicately. "I don't know the whole story. She hid things from me, from everyone, but I could tell something was wrong. The things he used to say right in front of people, so *cruel*. That she was ugly, not even his *type*. My therapist said he had to cut her down so she'd be small enough to keep. After a while Heather changed, she got so quiet, almost shy. It broke my heart."

I nodded, seeing Heather's stalwartness in a new way; defenses, built up over years.

"When she finally got up her courage and left," Lucinda went on, "Ivan took it very badly. He maxed out their credit cards, froze their bank account so she had no money to live on. She got a job, teaching art to little children, but it wasn't enough, she had to move back in with us. Then he'd drive by where she worked, follow her home; she was a nervous wreck."

I sighed. As a victim advocate, I'd heard it all before; so familiar, so dreadful. "What about restraining orders, orders of protection?" I said dutifully, though, God knows, I knew how useless they are.

"She got one once, and it—everything got *worse*. Calls

every hour all night, from different pay phones, hang-ups. She'd go out in the morning to go to work and the tires on her car would be flat. The police, they said they couldn't do anything unless they caught him in the act. It was almost like they didn't even believe her. In the act of what? I said to them"— Lucia's voice shuddered—"*killing* her?"

The masks on the wall stared down at me, representing God knows what dark pagan ceremonies. I saw Evangeline's face again, pleading, anxious. *"Chip will have a shit fit if he finds out the cops were here."* I felt my breathing getting shallow. Wonderful. Just what I needed, a panic attack in Heather's mother's cozy nook.

I took a deep breath and got myself under control.

"I understand what you're saying," I said, "but that was a while ago. I mean, he's not still doing it, is he? Harassing her?"

"He stopped for a while. We thought it was over at last. But then six months after Heather remarried, he started up again. That's what frightens me." Her voice rose anxiously. "He'd call, always when Terry wasn't there. And Terry didn't have a regular job, he worked at home. It was as if Ivan were watching the house, or had it *bugged*. Then the calls would stop for a while, start up again."

Creepily, as if on cue, somewhere in the house a phone rang. Lucia ignored it. It rang three more times, then stopped.

"But what about Terry," I asked. "Couldn't he do something?"

"She hid it from him." Lucia looked flustered. "I told you she was proud. I don't think she ever even told Terry how badly Ivan had treated her before she left him."

Was that why Terry didn't trust Heather, knew she was getting calls when he was gone and not telling him, thought it was a lover? I felt my breathing getting shallow again. "Lucia, what if Terry found out? What if he confronted Ivan? Ivan sounds really dangerous. Has Heather told the police about him?"

Lucia wrung her hands. "No."

"But if there's a chance that—that he came out there and murdered Terry," I said, "should he just be allowed to get away with it? That's how someone like him controls people, with fear."

"But don't you see, Chloe? It never did any good before. It always made it *worse*." Her hands went to her hair, twisting little bits. "You have to understand, Ivan's very credible, highly educated, brilliant, and so—*persuasive*. He's trained to be that way. He's—well, he's a therapist."

"A what?"

"A therapist." Lucia shrugged helplessly. "That's why she hates therapists. That's why she wouldn't go see mine."

"I'd rather be dead," she'd said, but I never, for a second, thought she'd meant it literally. I saw myself standing at the classroom door with my counselor list. "Oh," I said.

"Fowler Counseling and Consulting." She paused. "What's really ironic, if it weren't for Ivan, Heather would never have met Terry."

"What do you mean?"

"Right after Terry moved to Tucson from Ohio, about six years ago, he was in Ivan's office and he saw Heather's collages. Ivan had a series hanging up with the name of her gallery. When they got divorced he refused to give them back. Anyway when Terry saw them, he really liked them and wanted to buy one, so he went to the gallery, she happened to be there—"

"Wait a minute," I interrupted. "You said, not long after Terry moved here from Ohio? What was Terry doing in Ivan's office?"

"He was considering therapy. He'd recently lost his mother, Heather said, and Ivan is a very good bereave—"

"Lucia!" someone interrupted.

A thin, elegant white-haired man came into the room, deeply tanned, almost surreally immaculate in white walking shorts and a white polo shirt.

Lucia flushed. "My husband," she said to me. "Hugh, this is Chloe."

He nodded impatiently then looked importantly at his watch. There was more than a touch of the narcissist in the gesture, in the perfect white clothes, his tan. "Have you forgotten, Lucia? *The doctor's appointment.*"

"The what?" She looked confused. "Oh. Yes. Of course." She breathed out a sigh and said to me, "Why don't you give me your number. When Heather gets in touch, I'll have her call you."

I gave her the number and she scribbled it on the front of her puzzle book.

"We have to leave *now*," said Hugh. "And I can't find the car keys. What have you done with them? Nice to meet you, Carrie." His voice was dismissive.

"Nice to meet *you*," I lied back.

"We have to run," he added.

"It's okay, I understand." I stood up. "Please don't bother, Lucia, I can find my way out."

"Well, it was very nice to talk to you, Chloe," said Lucia, more sincerely.

God, I thought as I left the room, what a horrible man. What the hell is her therapist doing for her that she puts up with him? I walked down the hall, past the living room with its Indian rugs and leather furniture. It struck me now as a cold room, remote and overly planned, something to look at, but not to sit in, live in.

At my back, I could feel dead silence coming from the room I'd just left, the not so cozy little nook, as if they were waiting for me to be gone before they spoke. I reached the door, opened it, stepped out and closed it behind me. On an impulse, I tried the knob; it hadn't locked. I turned it quietly and pushed the door open again.

"Perfect stranger—" Hugh was saying loudly. "You think Heather wants you blabbing about her private life to every Tom, Dick, and Harry who comes along? I can't believe you told that woman about Ivan. You must be out of your mind. But what am I saying? Of course, you're out of your mind. I already knew that."

"She was nice," Lucia protested. "She's a victim advocate."

"You don't know who she is," Hugh cut in. "And the damn car keys, why aren't they hanging on the hook? I've told you a million times if you would only—"

I didn't need to hear this. I pulled the big door closed again carefully and crunched across the gravel. If what Lucia had told me was true, Heather was right, I knew that from my own experience: right not to tell, unless there was enough evidence against her ex to lock him up securely, with no bail, or chance of release. No wonder she was hiding out.

Evangeline, dead in her new green stretch blouse from Target and *it was all my fault. Oh, God, not Heather, too.*

I passed the scarlet bird-of-paradise, the orange tree with its sour inedible Tucson oranges, and went out the wrought-iron gate. The smell of the rotting fruit was overwhelming.

FIFTEEN

"A THERAPIST, abusing his wife." Fred bit into a shrimp taco. "I'm not surprised. They're all a bunch of sickos."

Fred, Sam, and I were having lunch at Chuey's Tacos. It didn't look like much, vinyl-and-chrome tables and chairs, linoleum floor, but it was the best Mexican restaurant in Dudley.

"But it doesn't make any sense for Terry to be in the guy's office right after he moved down here," Fred went on. "How would he even know anyone like that?"

"Looked him up in the phone book, probably," I said. "Lots of people see therapists after the death of a parent."

Fred shook his head skeptically. "He didn't go in for that kind of thing. Never did, never would."

"There're no atheists in foxholes," I pointed out. "Anyway, what difference does it make now? It's Heather I'm worried about. Ivan sounds seriously scary."

"According to her mom—but moms are always superparanoid. And if it's true, why doesn't Heather tell the cops?"

"She doesn't want him stirred up, I imagine. And she's right from my experience."

"Chloe." Fred pointed at me with a shrimp taco. "She tells the cops and then this Ivan guy murders her? That's bullshit. He'd be the first person they'd come looking for. You're still freaked about that client getting killed on your watch. But think, how'd she get killed? *The cops weren't there.*"

I set down my taco, half eaten, and pushed my plate away. "I don't want to talk about that."

"How 'bout this then? Heather hasn't told the cops because she's still hooked on this guy, maybe she even enjoys his phone calls, makes her feel special and that's why she never told Terry." Fred picked up tiny shrimp from his plate. "Don't look at me that way. Most people are weirder than anyone ever imagines."

"That's right and Ivan is a good example. How do you know what he'll do if she tells the cops? He probably thinks he's invincible. Fred," I said urgently. "You really need to rethink how you feel about Heather."

"You're always her champion."

"She needs one here," I said. "It's like you've already made up your mind, because from what you've told me, Heather kind of came between you and Terry."

"That's ridiculous," said Fred, a little too vehemently. "I just want the truth. You're forgetting about the *letter,* Chloe. And a substantial amount of money."

"The *letter?* Terry didn't trust her because he sensed she had a secret, is what I think." I said. "And money, it wouldn't matter much to Heather." My voice rose. "Ivan is our best suspect so far and you're making light of the whole thing. There's no real protection for domestic-violence victims. Anyone who's ever been one or worked in the field knows that."

"This pink stuff is *beans!*" said Sam suddenly. "I hate beans."

"You get beans every time you go to Taco Bell," said Fred.

"That's different. They're covered up with other stuff."

Fred looked patient. "You're in a Mexican restaurant. You always get beans in a Mexican restaurant. It's part of their culture."

He turned back to me, his voice placating. "We'll talk to Heather, see what she says, okay? Now we know she's around, we just have to find her."

I nodded, swallowing my anger. "Maybe she's back home. Barricaded in. If not, we could ask those Blofelds. She might have let them know by now where she's staying. Or the grandson."

"First we drop Sam. Your place this time? He's sick of that hotel room."

"Sure," I said.

WE TOOK SAM BACK to my house then drove out to Heather's. A thin winter rain drizzled down. The sky was grayish white, silver around the hidden sun. It was two o'clock. The blue Volvo was still parked in front of the house, in a puddle of water, but there was no truck.

We got out anyway, into the rain. Neither of us had an umbrella. Fred grabbed a newspaper from the back seat, and we divided it up. The air smelled rich and fecund, the rain pinging into puddles, blurring our view of the burned workshop behind the house. In the flower beds in the front yard, weeds were already sprouting.

We went through the porch to the inner door and Fred knocked, knocked again, louder. No one came. He shrugged. "On to the Blofelds."

Skirting puddles and holding newspaper over our heads, we walked to the simple cinderblock painted white. The old VW van and the motorcycle were still parked in front. Whoever did the gardening had opted for a yard full of no-upkeep irises, with a dirt path down the middle. A large wood sign hung by the door, with a roadrunner and THE BLOFELDS burned into it.

Fred knocked and after a while Helen Blofeld opened the door. Her nose was red and she wore a matching red turtleneck and red wool Fair Isle sweater buttoned clear up, though it wasn't really cold.

"Why, hello!" She seemed nervous, but not surprised; probably had watched our approach from a window.

"Mrs. Blofeld!" said Fred, in a hearty voice. "I'm Fred Barnett, Terry's brother. We met your husband the other day."

She nodded, unmoving, blocking the door.

"We really need to find Heather," I said. "Her mother told

me she's back in Cochise County. We thought you might know where she's staying."

"Well, I don't."

"Mrs. Blofeld—" Fred began.

"I'm sorry. I can't help you," she cut in and closed the door hard.

For a moment, we stared at its blank face, stunned.

"What the hell is going on?" said Fred. He raised his fist as if to knock.

"Forget it." I took his arm, pulling him away. "Let's go."

"Jesus Christ, what's wrong with those people?" Fred flung his sodden newspaper onto the ground, his face flushed bright pink with anger. "Total *assholes*." He kicked viciously at an iris. "Goddamnit! I need to find Heather!"

I picked up the newspaper and stuffed it into a garbage can near the gate. I made my face impassive, neutral, as we walked out to the road. I hate tantrums. I wasn't going to react and encourage him.

Fred stood in the road, clutching at his head as if it might explode.

"Goddamnit to hell," he said. "My whole life's flashing before my eyes here. I need some space. I need to think. I have to take a walk, clear my head."

He stalked off, heading for Heather's. God, I thought, Craig, just like Craig on his failed medication days. Fred needed more than a walk, he probably needed Prozac, Zoloft, Paxil, Effexor, Saint-John's-Wort; the litany of drugs Craig had tried and rejected spun through my mind. I knew it wasn't Craig's fault, but for a moment I burned with anger at him. *Chloe with her basically okay soul.* Then suddenly it was gone, leaving me alone standing in the road, in the rain that was ebbing, oddly refreshed.

A door slammed at the Blofelds' house. I turned.

Looking like a hologram of a rock star, Damien, in a black leather motorcycle jacket and black leather pants, walked down the path toward me carrying a helmet. Aha. Maybe something could be salvaged after all.

"Hi," I said.

He nodded and walked past me to the motorcycle. The pants had a line of silver studs all down the side to the ankle.

"Damien," I said. *"Wait."*

He was putting on his helmet. The rain had slowed now to a fine mist, beading on his beautiful face and leathers.

He beamed sapphire eyes at me. "What?"

"I'm Chloe," I said, crumpling my sodden newspaper, aware of my rain-matted hair, my general damp dishevelment. "I'm here with Terry's brother."

He rolled his eyes. "So I heard."

"I was there when you read 'Fern Hill' at the memorial," I said, trying another tack. "You were really good. Could we talk for a minute?"

"I don't think so." He looked at me impatiently. "I'm supposed to meet someone in Dudley."

"Heather?"

"No, not Heather. Leave her alone."

"Damien, what's going on?" I said in frustration. "I can understand you and your grandparents being protective of her, but this is Terry's *brother* we're talking about here."

"So what if it is?" he said scornfully. "It's not like he ever came to visit. Terry didn't even *like* him."

"Damien, they were family." My voice rose. "Things happen in families. People say things they regret and they're too proud to make up and then it's too late. Come on, Damien, help me out here. You're tight with Heather. Where is she?"

"I don't have a clue."

"Well, I have a feeling you do and you're not telling," I said, losing patience. *"Why?"*

"Why what? She's supposed to wait around in case Terry's shitty brother from Ohio shows up sometime? She's got a life. What is it with you and this guy anyway?"

Suddenly he grinned. It was a wide grin, that showed a chipped eyetooth. It took away from his beauty but made him ten times more likable. "Maybe you've been hoodwinked."

"Hoodwinked?" It was such an old-fashioned term, it made me smile too.

He got on his bike. "How do you know his brother isn't just acting nice so you'll help him? Everything I've ever heard about him, he isn't nice at all." He kicked to start the motorcycle. It roared, then sputtered and died. "Shit." He looked at me. "Anyway, maybe Heather's just sick of Barnetts in general."

"She was sick of Terry?"

"Naw. I didn't say that." He looked disgusted. "Maybe she should have been though."

"Why?"

"Saint Terry? Is that what you think? Hah!" He kicked again, the engine caught. He raised his hand in a salute, and roared off.

I watched him disappear down the muddy road. What was he doing living out here in the sticks with his paranoid grandparents? Was he in love with Heather, one of those crushes young men get on older women, like Chéri? Was that why he stayed? Did she love him back?

"Saint Terry? Is that what you think? Hah."

I looked around but didn't see Fred anywhere; he must have gone to the back to commune with Terry's workshop. I headed for the car, walking slowly.

In the distance, the mountains were invisible, shrouded in clouds, the river and its trees hidden too. There is something universal about rain; its smell and mist transport you to other times and places. Landmarks erased, I could have been anywhere, and for a few moments, I was back in New York City, in the Village, with James, so long dead now, running through the rain, ducking into a basement restaurant near Cooper Union. We ate lamb stew. I could still remember what we ate, after all these years. "The best city," said James. "The best city in the whole world."

"Sorry I was such a jerk." Fred was beside me.

"How do you know his brother isn't just acting nice so you'll help him? Everything I've ever heard about him, he isn't nice at all." I looked at Fred, bedraggled and sad, and I couldn't accept what Damien had said. I'd hardly known Terry, was beginning to forget him completely, but Fred was his *brother:* as long as he was alive, Terry would be alive too, just like James was for me. Then we would die as well and the world would close over us all.

"I understand," I said. "It's okay."

WE DROVE BACK toward Dudley in silence, the thin rain streaking the windshield, the heater on high to dry us out.

"I don't get it. I just don't get it at all," Fred said. "They know where she is, those Blofelds, I'm betting on it."

"My impression," I said carefully, "is that Heather doesn't want to see you because you and Terry didn't get along very well."

"Goddamnit!" Fred banged on the steering wheel. "She could at least give me a chance. And now it's too late, Sam's mom's due home. He's got this test coming up at school. I have to go back. I blew everything."

"Don't be so hard on yourself. I'll still be here investigating for you," I said. "The very first thing I want to do is check out Ivan. Right away, tomorrow."

Fred glanced at me. "Check him out, like how?"

I shrugged. "Go to his office. Talk to his staff. At least see what he looks like."

"Be careful."

The car was so hot, I felt faint. Suddenly, insubstantial as a wisp of smoke, I heard Evangeline's voice: *"No! Don't!"* And something else. I'd given her a list of therapists to choose from and she'd told me she'd made an appointment. But she hadn't.

So I should have known she might lie about calling the deputy, because she knew that was what I wanted to hear, just like she'd lied about calling the therapist. My stomach lurched. *I should have known.*

BACK IN DUDLEY, Sam stood waiting in the carport, holding Big Foot, unresisting in his arms. Fred pulled in behind my Geo and I got out.

"You like that cat?" I said to Sam. "Keep him."

"Wow!" said Sam.

"She's kidding," Fred said. "Get in the car."

Sam got in.

"Mailing address," said Fred. "So I can pay you."

I gave it to him.

"Look," he said to me. "Find Heather and talk to her. Tell her I really loved Terry, no matter what she seems to think. Set up a meeting at the house and I'll fly back for it. I'm not proud." He paused. "If worse comes to worse, and she won't see me, tell her I can draw on my rights as Terry's brother."

"Which are?"

"Well, I don't know. It sounds good though; it might persuade her. You've got my cell phone number if you need to get in touch. I'm a little hard to reach so keep trying, okay? But I'll call *you*."

"Right."

"Another thing." Fred looked abashed. "I want to apologize in advance, for anything untoward that might arise."

"Like what? Being murdered by Ivan Fowler?"

"Wow!" said Sam.

Fred looked worried.

"It's okay, I'll be careful," I said.

"Dad!" said Sam. "Why don't you just tell her?"

"Tell me what?" I asked.

Fred turned on the ignition. "Got to go," he said.

SIXTEEN

I GOT TO TUCSON and Fowler Counseling and Consulting at a quarter to twelve. It was in one of those ubiquitous stucco buildings with red tiled roofs, on a side street off Broadway near the El Con Mall on the east side of town. Parked in front was one of those not cheap but darling Volkswagens in lime green. I drove on past and parked a little ways down the street near a Circle K convenience store. I was nervous and I didn't have a plan.

It had been chilly back in Dudley but it was warm here—no, *hot*. I sat in my car, baking, while I composed a story and consoled myself with the fact that Ivan would have no idea who I was and, unlike Chip, would probably not have a weapon on the ready in his office. Then I got out and walked back to his office.

Gauzy white curtains, the kind you can see out of but not see in, covered a floor-to-ceiling plate-glass window by a blue-painted door. I pushed it open. A cactus, so large it resembled a green and thorny client, dominated the waiting area. There was a Persian-looking carpet, a leather couch, two matching leather chairs, and a coffee table with the usual array of wilted magazines. Beyond all that was a counter with a glass partition.

I went over, peered in, and saw a dark Hispanic woman sitting at a desk, working a calculator. Off to one side, a blonde sat at another desk, under a big white clock. When she saw me, the blonde got up, and teetered toward me in high black mules. Thin but curvy, she had hair that was a tousle of curls, and she was dressed in a red stretch blouse and a black skirt that ended three inches below her crotch—the kind of blonde that blonde jokes were made for.

As she came close I saw that her eyes were elaborately made up, her skin paled by makeup she probably didn't need. She slid open the glass and smiled. It was a warm smile, so friendly I regretted my thoughts about blonde jokes. "Hi! I'm Sally. Did you have an appointment?"

"We don't have anyone down till one-thirty," called the dark-haired woman in a tired voice.

Sally's brow crinkled and she tucked a curl behind her ear with her left hand. Her eyes were baby-doll blue and, under the pale makeup, her skin was like fine porcelain. "How can I help you?"

"Actually, I'm just making inquiries," I said. "For a friend. She's had a really rough time and she needs to see a therapist."

"Ah." Sally gave me a sympathetic look. "If only we could help our friends as much as we'd like."

"It's not like that," I said, getting her meaning. "She *wants* to see a therapist, but she just can't get it together to find one. I said I'd get her some names. I've heard of Dr. Fowler." I paused. "My friend's been terribly traumatized. Is he good with abuse, that kind of thing?"

"Oh!" In a triumph of reality over artifice, Sally's pale cheeks pinked with enthusiasm. "He's *fabulous* with abuse." She turned to the Hispanic woman. "Isn't he, Rosa?"

Rosa hit a key on the calculator and it clanked and whirred busily. Despite the modern office, Ivan Fowler seemed to be in the Iron Age as far as office machines went. She looked over at me. "What kind of insurance does your friend have?"

"Good insurance," I said.

"Dr. Fowler's really creative. He's not afraid to try new things," said Sally eagerly. "And trauma, he's excellent with trauma. He's one of the few therapists in Tucson trained in post-traumatic-stress rapid-eye-movement therapy."

"HMO?" said Rosa darkly. "Or preferred?"

"I'm not sure," I said.

Rosa looked frustrated. "Well, does she need a *referral?*"

Sally moved so she was blocking out Rosa. "She's our *business* manager," she said meaningfully. "Ivan—I mean Dr. Fowler is pretty full up but he occasionally takes cases he finds really challenging, no matter what the income. I mean I can't promise anything, of course, but have your friend give us a call. He—"

"Ladies," said a man's deep voice, soothing. "Done for the morning."

Sally turned. Her cheeks got even pinker. "Dr. Fowler."

I hadn't seen a patient leave, they must go out a back door. The man who'd tormented Heather for years, frightening her so much she was afraid to call the police, stood at the back, late-forties-looking, with stylish round glasses. His hair was dark brown touched with gray, and a wing of it fell exuberantly onto his forehead.

His eyes lit on me. "Unless—" He turned to Rosa. "Who's this?"

"Making inquiries," she said. "For a friend."

"Oh?" Ivan Fowler strode to the front. His stride was vigorous; it only took a second. On the short side and muscular, he was wearing well-pressed khakis, a green and blue madras plaid shirt with a tie that matched the green. Chip, what had Chip looked like, the one time I'd seen him in justice court? Boyish with a blond crew cut.

"Dr. Fowler?" said Rosa.

He ignored her. When he reached the partition he rested his hand on Sally's shoulder, but his eyes probed mine.

I tried to look neutral, innocent, and slightly distressed all at the same time. He gave me the willies, but I couldn't really pin down why except for what I already knew about him.

"Friends." He smiled knowingly. "Our greatest joy and our greatest sorrow."

"That's what I told her," said Sally eagerly. She paused. "Kind of."

"Sweet, sweet Sally." Ivan squeezed her shoulder, hard enough that his knuckles whitened, then released it. "Am I all booked up for eternity? I always have to ask the ladies, I don't know my own schedule. I never do, do I, sweet Sally?"

"Never," breathed Sally. She rubbed her shoulder.

"Uh, *Dr. Fowler*," said Rosa again, louder.

"Maybe I have space," Ivan Fowler said to me, "and maybe I don't, but—" He raised his hand. "Your *friend* has to call us. No matter how good your intentions, unless the actual prospective client has made the commitment, taken that step, your intentions mean nothing. Do you understand what I'm saying?"

"Of course," I said earnestly, taking on some of Sally's eagerness to please. "I *do* understand."

"Good." He looked at me intently for a moment, as if assessing my own needs as well. Then he looked away dismissively. "Sally. Let's go to lunch."

"Dr. Fowler," Rosa said. "If you could listen just a minute—"

But he was out the door.

I WATCHED OUT the floor-to-ceiling front window, through the gauzy curtains you could see out of but not in, as Ivan opened the passenger door of the cute lime-green Volkswagen. Sally pranced on the sidewalk in her high black mules. She seemed to float, smiling at Ivan dreamily. I thought about how hard his hand had squeezed her shoulder.

"Did you see *that?*" said Rosa, angrily.

I turned. She sat in front of the calculator, two bright pink spots on her cheeks. "What?" I said.

"How he ignored me. Sometimes I feel like walking out of here and never coming back." She hit a button hard on the calculator and it clicked and clanked furiously. Then it stopped. She ripped off a long narrow length of paper. "How am I supposed to run this office if I can never get his attention."

"I see what you mean," I said.

"Nice someone does. *She* certainly doesn't."

"Who?"

"Sally. We just hired her a few weeks ago." She looked at me meaningfully. "She doesn't notice anything but the doctor."

"She *does* seem to like him," I said cautiously.

"Worship is more like it. Bad move, the doctor likes a challenge." Rosa leaned back in her chair, still smoldering, opened a drawer in her desk and took out a brown paper bag. "Right now we're in the honeymoon period. But pretty soon she's going to realize she's getting nowhere, then there'll be the tears and the big scene."

"Oh, for heaven's sake," I said. "Then maybe my friend shouldn't—"

"Don't worry," Rosa cut in. "He's very good with the *patients.*" She took a sandwich out of the bag and unwrapped it. "It's just that he hires these bimbos who never work out. He doesn't seem to realize that every time they quit it doubles my workload."

I tsk-tsked sympathetically. "But he seemed so *nice,*" I lied.

Rosa's mouth turned down. "So's God, if you're on his side."

"Some men just can't commit." I leaned across the counter and said in a low voice, "Maybe it has something to do with his ex. I've heard he's still hung up on her."

For a second Rosa was motionless as if riveted to her chair. "His ex? You *know* his ex?"

I nodded. "You've never met her?"

"Before my time." She moistened her finger and picked up little crumbs from her sandwich, looking at me with avid curiosity. "He never talks about his ex. What happened to her?"

"She remarried," I said.

"Happily?"

"I think so, only her husband was murdered not that long ago."

"*Murdered.*" Rosa's eyes got very round. "You're *kidding.*"

"Actually you might have met him," I said, my voice light

as a feather. "I know he was in here at least once. His name was Terry, Terry Barnett."

"Barnett," said Rosa. "Oh, my God, *Mr. Barnett.* I *have* met him—it was just after New Year's. I didn't know he was—" She paused. "So *that's* what that was all about."

"What what was all about?" I murmured softly.

"We'd just closed for the day and he showed up hammering on the door. When I went to answer it, he acted really pissed off, *rude.* He said to tell Dr. Fowler that Mr. Barnett needs to see him right away. Then Dr. Fowler came out to the front and Mr. Barnett started shouting at him."

"He was shouting?" I said. "Shouting what?"

"Dr. Fowler hustled me out the back, so I didn't hear much, just a name. I thought she must be a patient. I had no idea she was his ex."

"Heather?" I said. "He was shouting about Heather?"

"*Heather.* That's his ex's name?"

"Yes."

She shook her head, looking disappointed. "Not Heather. April. He was shouting about someone named April."

April. In a split second, everything changed. I stared at Rosa through the opening in the glass partition, registering but not really seeing her, or the litter of paper on her desk or the big white clock behind her.

Terry, always so light and pleasant, driven to rudeness, *shouting* at Ivan Fowler. Shouting about *April,* and not twenty years ago either but just after New Year's, a matter of weeks before his death. So she and Terry had stayed in touch.

And Fred had pooh-poohed her being relevant—but then he was grieving too much to think clearly. I had to think for him and what I thought now was that April might be the key after all. A key that Terry had tried to give me, maybe even then fearing for his life, back on the bench in Agua Prieta, Mexico.

SEVENTEEN

APRIL, A FREE SPIRIT, dangerous. I stood beside my car outside the Circle K convenience store in the bright hot sun thinking about how I could find her. Obviously she had some connection with Ivan as well; it was even possible he'd been harassing her too. It could explain Terry's anger. If so, maybe she and Heather could both be persuaded to file complaints, it might get Ivan some real jail time. Buy time for some real investigating, time to build a solid case, because let's face it, the guy *was* a creep; harassing his ex, seducing his receptionists then dumping them.

After twenty years, there was a good chance April was married and had a different last name, but maybe she had relatives here. I didn't have anything else to go on. I walked over to the phone book dangling at the outside booth near my car. At least it was an unusual name. Matasky—not with an *i*. Wasn't that what Terry had said?

There were two listings, one for Charles W. and one for Charles M., and none for April. I jotted down the numbers, then just in case, I checked all the alternate spellings I could think of but didn't find anything else.

I went back to the car for my cell phone and punched in the first of the numbers. It rang for a while and I was about to hang up when someone answered.

"Hello?" a woman said. She sounded elderly.

"Hello," I said. "I'm sorry to bother you but—"

"Can't hear you!"

"I don't know if this is the right number!" I shouted. "I'm looking for an old friend of mine! April Matasky!"

"I don't want any more magazines. You talk to my son Chuck about that. I'm a widow and I'm not well."

"Could you put him on!"

"Chuck says for me to hang up on you people!!"

And she did.

Chuck. She must be the mother of Charles M. I went back to the phone booth and looked up the address. 505 S. Cholla Lane. I'd do it person to person this time. My map showed it over on the west side.

I took Speedway to Oracle. Traffic was heavy, but I was better at getting around Tucson than I used to be thanks to Craig—we came here all the time, to the multiplexes, where we'd seen so many movies, to Bookman's where we hung out browsing used books, to Ross's for cheap clothes. Now these places seemed like tombstones marking the various stages of our relationship.

Past the Tucson Mall, farther up Oracle than I would go today, was the Westward Look Resort, where Craig and I stayed when they had low summer rates, and even farther up Oracle was the Mountain View Rehab Center.

The sun glared off the windshields of six lanes of cars and trucks. I rolled up my window to escape their exhaust, feeling a headache coming on as I thought of Mountain View Rehab. Craig had gone in last year, battling an addiction to Percodan. A few weeks of therapy and then there was family week.

Family week. I gunned the engine and almost ran a red light. At the end of family week we'd all had to stand up and say we were codependent. Well, I wasn't, goddamnit. Maneuvered, shamed, into saying it, now I wished I'd stood up and said to all those smug counselors, the downtrodden relatives and exhausted loved ones, "Hi, I'm Chloe. Craig's pretty messed up and I don't know about you guys but I'm just fine."

A car honked and I blinked. Where was I? Not at family

week but stopped at a green light. What was I doing here? Looking for April Matasky, to save Heather from a sadomasochistic therapist.

NUMBER 505 WAS a pale yellow stucco house, landscaped with white gravel and dark green cactus. The neighborhood was slightly seedy in a pleasantly decaying kind of way. I parked near a stand of pink oleanders and sat in the car for a moment, cleansing my mind of family week, focusing on saving Heather. A lone male jogger ran past, panting and kicking up bits of gravel.

I couldn't sit here forever. I got out of the car. Sparrows chattered but other than that it was very quiet as I walked down a concrete path formed to look like flagstones.

I knocked on the door. A dog barked. Then from inside someone called, "Hey, dude, that you?"

Since I wasn't a dude, I knocked again.

The door opened. A boy, maybe sixteen with a shaved head and a gold earring, stood in the opening. "Aw, *sh—poop,*" he said. "I thought you were Turk."

"Guess not. Sorry. This is the Matasky residence, isn't it?"

His look was cagey. "Are you from school?"

"No. Why? Are you cutting?"

"I'm sick." He put his hand on his abdomen and winced theatrically. "I got a stomachache."

"Hey," I said. "I used to get them, too, when I was in school. Do you have an aunt April by any chance?"

"Skip," someone called. "You tell Turk you were sick today. That means you stay home."

"It's not Turk," Skip shouted. "It's some lady."

A woman appeared behind him and pushed him aside. She wore jeans and a man's striped shirt and her face was pale and tired looking, her hair partly bright blond and partly brown where the blond was growing out.

"Yes?" she said to me.

"She wants to know if I have an aunt April," Skip said.

"An aunt *April?*" she said.

"My name's Chloe Newcombe," I explained. "I'm trying to find someone called April Matasky. I looked in the phone book and thought she might be a relative of yours."

"Oh, my God." The woman patted her chest as if to ease palpitations. "It's déjà vu all over again. Just like *Ginger.*"

Ginger? I started to ask but the woman held up a hand. "Wait." She turned. "Skip, go to your room."

"Ma! I feel okay now."

"You stay home from school, you stay in your room. That's the rules. And no video games." She raised her arm threateningly. "Git."

"I might as well be *dead*," complained Skip.

When he was gone she turned back to me. "April isn't a relative," she said, "but I know about her—Ginger— Look, why don't you come in." Her voice was eager. "I'm Janet, by the way."

I came in. The door led directly into a living room dominated by a big TV. It was hard to tell much about the furnishings because every bit of available space was covered with jeans, T-shirts, socks, and underwear.

"It's kind of a mess," Janet said chattily. "Laundry. I've got four boys, Skip's the oldest, and a part-time job evenings." She moved a stack of T-shirts from a chair for me, and plopped onto the couch right on top of a stack of jeans. "I keep trying to catch up, but I never do."

"You said, 'déjà vu, like Ginger'? What did you mean?" I asked, hoping she hadn't asked me in just to escape the laundry for a while.

"She was trying to find April too." Janet picked up a couple of socks. "Ginger Crowlie. She came and knocked on the door, just like you, that's what I meant by 'déjà vu.'"

"Really?" I looked at her with interest. "When was this?"

"I probably wouldn't even have *remembered* but Chuck and

I had just bought the house, and I was lonely so I invited her in." She rolled a pair of socks into a ball and threw them at a pink plastic laundry basket across the room. They hit the side and fell onto the floor. "It was a long time ago. Before Skip was born."

And Skip was sixteen. Great. And now she'd asked me in too. Obviously still a little lonely. I edged forward on my chair. "What happened next?"

"Well, she kind of lost interest when she found out April and me weren't related but then it came up we both went to Amphi—we were three years apart but *we both had Mr. Dietz for science and Miss Schaefer for English*." She stopped, looking at me expectantly.

"Amazing," I said.

"I *know*. Anyway, we just started yakking away. We traded phone numbers and stuff, but then Chuck came home. I could tell he didn't approve of her, he's always been kind of straight. One time he—"

I couldn't take it anymore. "Janet," I cut in, "*Ginger*. What was her connection to April?"

She looked a little hurt. "They used to be roommates. They both bartended at Ace's, this punk bar—it had a terrible reputation. Torn clothes, tattoos, safety-pins-in-the-nose stuff— not Ginger, she was just darling. But I guess she and April had lost touch with each other. You know how it is."

"Ace's," I said. "Where's that?"

She picked up a couple more socks and rolled them absently. "It's gone, it burned down a few years ago."

God, so near and yet so far. "You and Ginger traded phone numbers?" I said. "You don't by any chance still have hers?"

"No." She made a face. "Chuck kind of put a damper on me and her getting together."

"So that's it? You have no idea how I can find Ginger?"

"Wait." Her brow furrowed. "I did run into her by accident, oh, five years ago. At the Tucson Mall. She told me then she was going to Devoe's Beauty College, studying cosmetology, and she was getting married, then one of the kids started to cry and all hell broke loose."

"Do you have any idea how I could reach her?"

"Just the phone book, but Crowlie wouldn't be her name anymore. I don't know what it would be…" She touched her hair. "You could try Devoe's," she said, "they might keep track of old students. Other than that, gee, I don't know. If you find her, say hi, okay?"

"Sure," I said.

I SAT IN MY CAR for a while in the quiet neighborhood, staring at the oleanders with their pink poisonous flowers. Hopefully, Ginger had found April and could tell me where she was now. I just had to find Ginger.

Ginger Crowlie, such a slender link but all I had and not even Crowlie anymore. And I was tired. I would go home, call Fred immediately, and get all the information I could about April. I would insist this time, and not let him put me off. Then I'd try and track down Ginger.

I sped down the I-10, turned off at Benson, drove through, and headed down the two-lane blacktop toward Dudley. It was nearly dark, the sky a deep purple, fading fast. At St. David, the whole town was quiet, the few stores closed down for the night, TVs going. After that there was no one out on the highway but me. The dark overwhelmed me, stealing my sense of purpose, of certainty.

How did I know I hadn't just wasted a day chasing after April? Maybe she would be no help at all and meanwhile I was in danger of losing a good job that I loved or had already lost it. I owed—what?—over a thousand dollars on my Visa bill. *I should have known that Evangeline might lie about the deputy.* And Fred. Let's face it, there was something a little off about Fred. Suddenly sadness closed in on me. I was isolated, a woman spinning her wheels.

When I reached Dudley I drove down Tombstone Canyon past the courthouse, my old office just behind it, on down where it turned into Main Street. I hadn't checked my mail for two or three days. I parked in front of the post office and got out. It was chilly again and the old guys that hung out on the wrought-iron benches in their ancient corduroy jackets and faded windbreakers were gone for the evening.

Inside, the counter was closed down, the trash cans stuffed with junk mail and unwanted catalogs, a few on the floor. The shallow fluorescent lighting belonged in a spacecraft. I opened my box, hauled out a stack of catalogs, my electric bill, and a bulky manila envelope with no return address postmarked Dudley.

Nothing from Craig. There never was. Except that one postcard. Yet somehow in his own inimitable way, by giving me Terry Barnett's phone number, Craig had managed to set me on a course that had totally screwed up my life. I saw him now in the airport parking lot, searching for the number of a guy who was a good carpenter, who could build a bookcase for me. *Here, Chloe, with your okay soul, take this.*

When I got home I threw the mail on the counter. My message light was blinking. Fred? I played it back. *"Chloe, remember me? Larry? Haven't heard from you in eons. Call me."*

Jeez. Larry, from another life, mine. I used to talk to him at least once a week. I was isolating myself, I knew it, but I couldn't call him, didn't have the heart, not now.

I punched in Fred's cell phone. It rang until a robotic recording kicked in. He hadn't even hooked up his voice mail so I couldn't leave a message. Damn.

I hung up, went and sat on the couch and stared at Terry's bookcase, the satiny wood, corners dovetailed so perfectly. I'd never suspected he'd be murdered less than two months later; no angel of death had hovered over his shoulder, any more than one had hovered over Evangeline's. But at least her death wasn't entirely surprising. She'd lived her life in chaos. Well, maybe underneath, Terry had too.

Fred, call me.

Ginger Crowlie. Devoe's Beauty College. I got up and called Tucson information, got the number and dialed it. It was after five but maybe they had night classes. It rang and rang until a machine told me their hours were eight to five.

At the kitchen counter, I sorted through the mail: I couldn't bear to open my electric bill, but I glanced briefly at catalogs selling things I couldn't afford before I threw them away. Then I ripped open the bulky manila envelope.

A bunch of hundred-dollar bills fell onto the counter.

What?

Amid the money I found an unsealed envelope addressed only to "Chloe." I tore it open. "Off the books," it said, "Fred." I counted the money. Twenty hundred-dollar bills. At two hundred a day, ten days' work paid for by Fred Barnett, who vehemently and adamantly didn't think April was relevant. I should be looking for *Heather*. Persuading her to talk to Fred, maybe even getting her to trust me enough to tell me about Ivan.

But she was hiding and how could I find out where? No one would say, at least not the Blofeld family. What about Diana and Peter French? I wasn't keen on talking to Peter after he'd ratted on me to Flynn but I'd have to deal with it. Tomorrow, in fact.

Right now, Fred and I had to talk. *"I might be a little hard to reach."* I called him again. The ring sounded somehow lonely. I imagined a couple thousand miles of fiber optics on Planet Telex, going nowhere, as it rang and rang, until the recording kicked in.

EIGHTEEN

I CALLED FRED AGAIN the next morning but only got the robot. Hard to reach. No kidding. Mourning probably, while his cell lay somewhere, completely uncharged. Why hadn't I gotten his home phone? Next I called Heather's just in case but no one answered there either. Then I called the beauty school. It was a business, someone had to answer.

"Devoe's School of Beauty!" The voice sounded awfully young. "This is Maria!"

"Hi," I said. "Maybe you can help me. I'm looking for an old friend who went to your school. Ginger Crowlie."

"I've never heard of her. Are you sure she goes here?"

"Not now, actually. Five years ago."

"Five years? Gee. I was in high school five years ago. Why don't you talk to my supervisor."

I waited. Five years ago, I was a grown-up. I was even a grown-up twenty years ago.

"This is Beverly, how can I help you?"

"I'm looking for a Ginger Crowlie. She went to your school—"

"*Ginger.* Of course. One of our best students. But Crowlie's not her name anymore, she got married."

"Well, do you have her last name, or a phone number?"

"I don't think I should be telling you that, honey. I mean it's a privacy thing."

"It's pretty important. I need to talk to her."

"I'll tell you what. She works over at Park Mall at the Robinsons-May Company. In cosmetics. Pretty Woman."

I called Robinsons-May.

"Pretty Woman, this is Nancy. How can I help you?"

"I'm looking for Ginger," I said.

"She won't be in till tomorrow afternoon, one to nine. Maybe I—"

"That's okay, thanks a lot."

I hung up. Big Foot watched me. "Cat," I said. "I am so smart. I found Ginger."

I'd have to drive back to Tucson tomorrow—I couldn't see myself asking Ginger about April on the phone while she was working. As for today, I had Diana and Peter French, hopefully in the phone book.

I found them in a shot: 32C Zacatacas Hill. It would be better to see them in person too. For all I knew Heather could be there with them at this very moment. I got in my car, drove down my hill, then down Main Street, and took a left up Brewery Gulch.

The chill had lifted and the air was back to halcyon. I rolled down the window. It was late morning on a working day, for those who worked real jobs with benefits. The tourists were gone and the unemployed of Dudley were out in their thrift store clothes, faded T-shirts, Birkenstocks, and expensive educations.

The bars all had their doors open, and I caught a whiff of stale beer and had a glimpse of the dark interior of the St. Elmo; shadowy regulars lined up on the stools at the bar, lit at the back by the neon glow of the jukebox.

Farther on was the Burnt Hyena, a local art gallery. Unlike like the ones on Main Street, full of Western paintings for the tourists, the Burnt Hyena was a collective; short-lived, probably, and full of local artists' work—brash, colorful, and rude.

After that, the street wound round past shabby wood houses, bereft in winter of their concealing greenery, front porches sagging, interspersed with fancy remodels painted in earthy San Francisco colors. Number 32 was way at the end; the C made it pretty high up on Zacatacas Hill. I parked next to a large pile of bricks near a flight of steps and got out.

The steps, cement with an iron railing, meandered up the stony hill and half disappeared from time to time behind big boulders, rabbitbrush, pyracantha, and winter-gray spiky ocotillo. Somewhere up there, someone practiced on a guitar, the same chords over and over.

I climbed, head down since some of the steps were crumbly and of unequal height. Finally they ended abruptly at a hedge of pyracantha, sporting bright red berries. I stopped and took a breath. All of Old Dudley lay below me, sun winking off the windows and the tin roofs of the wooden houses scattered randomly along the winding narrow streets. It seemed so out of time and too fragile; a bulldozer could come and level it to the ground in a matter of days or maybe hours.

In the middle of the hedge was a gate made of free-form geometric designs in a rust-colored metal. I pulled it open and encountered a tall birdlike figure of the same rust-colored metal. I heard a kind of hiss, saw bright orange sparks. Down at the end of the yard was Peter French, I assumed, in a mask, welding.

And there, so still that I didn't notice her at first was Diana French, queen of artistic Old Dudley. Botticellian pretty, she was wearing a black T-shirt, sitting on an ancient couch in front of the long adobe house, holding a blue pottery mug. The expression on her face was utterly quiet and dreamy, as if there were no other place she wished to be and nothing at all that she longed for.

A hint of marijuana smell tickled my nose. The air was balmy: springtime had stopped in early for a little visit. Guitar chords drifted across the hill. Sparks hissed. I felt vaguely disoriented as if I had stepped into a dream or a parallel universe.

"Diana?" I said.

She looked over at me, and smiled. "Hi."

The long house was built railroad style and had several doors. Diana stood up and started for one of them. She wore loose dark flowered pants and blue flip-flops with orange socks. "Come on in," she said.

Come in, just like that? We'd met so briefly at the memorial, I hadn't known she'd even recognize me.

I followed her inside to a kitchen. Except for the white porcelain sink, full of pots, the room was all aged wood; floor, walls, ceiling. Drying herbs hung from hooks near a scarred wooden table. Somewhere a phone rang.

Diana looked a little put out, the way people get when their phone rings constantly. "Hold on!" she said.

I held on, looking around. A brown jug on the table was full of pyracantha branches, dropping red berries. The refrigerator was nearly covered with photos, newspaper clippings, lists, announcements held on with an eclectic collection of refrigerator magnets; things stuck on top of other things as if nothing were ever taken down. I went over for a closer look.

Front right was a poster for an opening this Friday. Superimposed over a blurry snapshot of the artists was black lettering of their names, including Peter French and Heather. COME ONE! COME ALL! GROUP SHOW AT THE BURNT HYENA! ALL LOCAL ARTISTS!

Diana came back, and I stepped aside as she opened the refrigerator and took out a plastic bag. "Here you are," she said. "It's totally fresh, I made it less than an hour ago."

I took it. Inside was water and a block of something white. I had no idea what it was but nothing else was making sense either, as if it were all part of some art happening like they used to have in the sixties, organized by Diana.

"Puffy wanted the recipe," Diana said chattily. "It's totally simple. You boil the beans, grind them up with some water, strain that, throw nigari into the liquid, white clouds form, you strain that, put the curds in a press and *voilà!*"

It didn't sound exactly voilà to me. "But what is it?" I asked.

"Tofu, what did you think?" Diana's pale blue eyes widened. "Um, you are Puffy's sister, aren't you?"

"No, my name's Chloe."

"Oh. Oh, my goodness." She rolled her eyes and sat abruptly on a cane chair at the table. "You didn't come to buy tofu?" She looked puzzled. "Haven't we met before?"

I nodded. "Outside Terry's memorial service. I'm looking for Heather. I thought she might be here."

"Heather." Her voice was despairing.

"What about Heather?" A man's voice, loud, just on the verge of menacing.

Peter French stood in the doorway. Up close, he was so rawboned you could have made an anatomical drawing of his skeletal parts. He had a short black beard, a large nose, and a tangled mass of black and gray curls. His faded blue T-shirt and jeans were dotted with burn holes where sparks must have hit them.

The man I'd seen across the square in Agua Prieta and later at the memorial. Who had seen me too, with his cop's eyes, and pointed me out to Flynn, started a chain reaction that had maybe lost me my job. I kept my face expressionless.

He looked at Diana. "What's *she* doing here?"

"Peter," said Diana reprovingly. "This is Chloe, and she's looking for Heather."

"Chloe? That's your name?" He snorted. "Flynn didn't say."

"Flynn?" Diane gave a little shriek. "Peter! What are you talking about?"

He jerked his head toward me. "Ask her."

I might as well play it straight. Well, I had no choice. "Last November," I said to Diana, "I had dinner with Terry one night, over in Agua Prieta. Peter saw us there. After Terry was killed, he thought the police should know about it."

"You?" Diana looked at me hard. "That was *you* Terry was seeing when Heather and I were down in Mexico?"

"I don't have anything to hide," I said, feeling pretty sure Flynn, closemouthed with my name, wouldn't have mentioned the other sightings to Peter. Which surely meant Heather, thank God, wouldn't know either. At least not yet. "Terry asked me to dinner. I thought he was a nice person. I didn't know he was married. Then he told me and that was that."

There was a little silence.

Peter still looked hostile, unconvinced, but Diana said sadly, "Terry always did hate to be alone."

"I need to find Heather," I said. "For Fred—Terry's brother. He was down here from Ohio, trying to find her."

Peter looked annoyed. "We know *that*."

"You said 'was.'" Diana's eyes widened. "Is he gone then?"

I nodded. "Back to Ohio. But he'll fly down again if she'll agree to talk to him."

"I don't think so," said Diana dubiously. "She says he's *awful*."

"But she doesn't even know him," I protested.

"That's because he and Terry never saw each other," Diana said fiercely. "Their connection was irretrievably broken. That was the word Terry used, 'irretrievably.'" Her voice rose. "Heather didn't even want to talk to Fred when Terry died, to let him know. I had to make the call for her."

"He's not anywhere near as bad as you make him sound," I said in exasperation, but I felt uneasy.

Peter smoothed his beard. His face was stolid, still hostile. "He came a little late, don't you think?" he said accusingly. "Years go by and nothing, then the minute Terry's dead this guy shows up. What's his motive? Thinks he can claim some of the money Terry left Heather, is my guess."

"Well, I think you're wrong." Suddenly I was sick of all this group hysteria about Fred. No one had actually met him but me. "Motive?" My voice rose. "You want *motive?* His brother was murdered. Maybe he was shocked into awareness. How's that for a motive? Or you could try guilt, pain, a need for redemption. Will they do? What else do you need? His own brother, in spite of whatever it was that came between them."

Peter and Diana looked stunned.

"Oh, my God," breathed Diana in awe. "It sounds so *right*.

When you say it like that, I feel just awful." She looked at Peter guiltily. "Maybe we should have encouraged Heather to see him."

"If I could talk to her," I said, "maybe I could make her see that."

"We don't know you, lady," Peter said wearily. "We don't know if you're honest, or have Heather's best interests in mind. And I feel responsible for her, now that Terry's gone."

"Just let me give you my number," I said. "Ask her to call me."

"When she gets in touch," said Peter stoically, "I'll convey that message."

ALMOST AFTERNOON and the sun shone straight down. Diana hurried out after me, her flip-flops slapping on the cement behind as I was about to close the gate.

"Here, have some tofu anyway." She smiled and handed me a plastic bag. "A peace offering. I'm really sorry we were so rude. Have you ever actually met Heather?"

"Yes," I said. "I was at the house the night Terry was killed. As a victim advocate for the county attorney's office."

Diana looked surprised. "A victim advocate. What's that?"

"We do all kinds of things for victims. Crisis intervention, courtroom accompaniment for hearings and trials, whatever we can do to help."

"Then maybe you can understand what Heather's going through." She brushed back her hair self-consciously and looked like she might cry. "She's a really strong person, in a way, but really vulnerable too."

"Diana," I said, "she's hiding out. Why?"

Diana looked flustered. "She's—oh, you know, sick of *people*. Feeling sorry for her. *Staring*."

"Just that?" I said. "Nothing specific?" I wanted to mention Ivan, but if Heather hadn't told anyone, it would get back to her, and she would never trust me then.

Diana shrugged. "Isn't that enough? I know how she feels. All Peter and I want is peace. We're retired from the world up here. I work at the food co-op most mornings, keep busy the rest of the day. Peter just wants to do his art."

"He doesn't like me much," I said.

"It's not that." She lowered her voice. "He's suspicious because he used to be a cop. He still acts like one sometimes. I mean, he hangs around that Flynn like—oh, I don't know." She bit her lip. "He can be moody, but he's a good person, really. It was his goodness that made him be a cop. He thought there was such a thing as justice. But there wasn't, so he quit. I'll put in a word for you with Heather."

"Diana," I said, "did Terry or Heather ever mention someone named April? April Matasky?"

The bright sun shone on her blond hair, picking out bright gold wires. She squinted in its glare. "I don't think so," she said. "Why? Who is she?"

"Just someone Terry used to know."

"Oh." Diana backed away a little.

"Listen," I said. "I want to help Heather. If I thought Fred was like you say, I wouldn't be here. Basically, I'm just trying to get at the truth."

"There's all kinds of truth," she said. "Sometimes it's best not to know everything."

"Like what?"

She hesitated. "I've already said too much."

SHE'D NEVER HEARD OF April. Did she know about Ivan? And what had she meant, there's all kinds of truth and sometimes it's best not to know everything? I had a feeling under different circumstances, without her surly husband so close, she might have talked more freely. Maybe I should stop by the co-op one of these mornings and try again. When I got home I stuck the tofu in the fridge and called Fred. No answer.

Okay, he'd said he might be hard to reach so keep trying. He'd said hard, not impossible. He had my number. Sooner or later, he'd call me, wouldn't he?

I remembered his tears, standing out by Terry's workshop. Was he okay? I felt uneasy again, not just for Fred, but about him. The things people said, they didn't jibe at all with what I knew of him.

I fed Big Foot and opened the refrigerator. I hadn't even had lunch. What the hell was that? Oh, tofu. I've never been much of a fan. Then again, this was homemade. I dumped the block into a bowl, got a knife and cut off a cube.

My God, it was good, the flavor kind of like bean sprouts, but the curd so delicate it was like tasting a spring breeze. You were supposed to fry it, weren't you? Throw it in when you stir-fried vegetables. I didn't have any vegetables except frozen peas. I ate about half the block then I called Fred again. No answer.

NINETEEN

I GOT TO PARK MALL a little after two and headed for Robinsons-May. I hadn't been to a department store in ages. Inside it was oh so cool, yet glittery. Cosmetics were just inside the door and the air was heavy with fragrances. There were so many counters, and the flattering lighting turned the women who staffed them into goddesses. More goddesses stared haughtily down from large banners, in the act of sailing, playing tennis, tending children, yet their hair and faces remained immaculate, not like me, a makeup peon.

Pretty Woman was between Estee Lauder and Elizabeth Arden and only one woman was behind the counter, a gorgeous redhead in a lavender smock. She looked bored. Except for the staff, the store was nearly empty.

I came up to her. "Ginger?"

Her eyes were bright green, enormous. "Yes?" She smiled. Up close I could see little laugh wrinkles around her eyes but they did not detract from her looks.

"My name's Chloe," I said. "I got your name from Janet Matasky."

"No kidding," she said with no undue enthusiasm. "How's she doing? Still making babies?"

"Four boys now." I paused. "I'm looking for April Matasky."

Ginger looked stunned. *"Really."* Her eyelashes fluttered, like tiny butterflies. "My God."

"I have to talk to her," I said. "It's important. Janet said you and April used to be roommates and you'd lost touch and were looking for her. I was hoping you'd hooked up again."

Ginger picked up a brochure, and fanned herself with it. "Honey, I haven't seen April for probably twenty years."

"No." My shoulders sagged with disappointment. A long trip to Tucson and for nothing.

Ginger tsk-tsked. "I would have told Janet the whole story and she could have told you but she was such a yakker, I couldn't get a word in edgewise. April vanished, just up and disappeared from one day to the next."

"I don't understand," I said. Vanished, twenty years ago? But Terry had gone to see Ivan, shouting April's name, in early January. "How can that be? What—I mean—"

"I even filed a missing persons report," said Ginger. "For all the good *that* did."

"Wait," I said. "Tell me the whole story, from the beginning." I looked around, suddenly aware of bright lights, salespeople. "Is it okay to talk here?"

"Sure. It's dead right now, as you can see." She tossed her head. "Tell you what, I'll give you a consultation. That way we can talk without anyone getting on their high horse about it." She pointed authoritatively at a high chair next to the counter. "Sit."

I obeyed.

"April and I worked at the same place, this crummy bar, Ace's, way back when." Ginger sighed. "I kind of took care of her. I mean, someone had to." She tilted back my chin and studied my face with a cool and expert eye. "You know, I like that little line you draw under the eye, but you might try a softer color. Gray instead of black. And your blush is too pink."

"It is?"

"Yes. You want a yellower undertone." She tsk-tsked again. "You don't use foundation? How come?"

"I don't know," I said helplessly.

"Well, it's never too late. We'll go with Basic Beige and then the Burnt Rose blusher." She wiped at my face with a damp-ish sponge and began to apply foundation.

"How come someone had to take care of April?" I asked.

"She had, you know, *complications,* underneath. Like she didn't have any—" Ginger paused with her sponge. "I want to say sense, but it's more like *brakes.* She was such a flirt and she never knew when to stop. A blonde is a blonde is a blonde, but let me tell you, when she flirted, she was, like, *dazzling.* Guys were always getting the hots for her, then she'd move on and they didn't know what hit them. Broken hearts and busted egos."

"Wow," I said. "Sounds like a recipe for disaster."

Ginger shot me a look. "Maybe, but there wasn't anyone current when she disappeared. She'd settled down a little after we became roommates."

"How long was that?"

"A couple of months. She'd had her own place, but she went off for a while and when she came back, she still had her job but she'd lost her apartment. She paid me rent and all, it was a big help." She sighed. "Then, like I said, from one day to the next, she was gone."

She paused to draw a line under my left eye, then my right. She dabbed some shadow on the lids. "I'm going with mauve, it'll really perk you up."

"So you filed a missing persons report?" I prompted.

"After a couple of days. I wasn't concerned at first. I got back to the apartment from a date, and she wasn't there but I just figured she'd met some guy. But then she didn't show up for work that next afternoon—we both had the four-to-midnight shift and she *always* called in if she wasn't going to show up. That's how she was able to keep the job. That's when I started to worry."

"And?"

"I waited another day and she still didn't show or call in, so at that point I knew something was wrong. I went to the police and filed the report. I talked to a detective but he never really did anything." She shrugged. "He said she was an adult, that she'd probably just taken off with a guy."

"Well, I mean, had she ever done that—taken off with a guy?"

"Yes—" Ginger leaned over the counter. "But not without telling me. Not only that, *all her clothes were still there.* And April was a woman who liked her clothes. Who goes off and leaves all their clothes anyway?"

"Not me."

"I kept them for months, hoping she'd show up. Then it got, you know, *creepy,* and it felt too weird to wear them myself, so I gave them all to Value Village." She raised her eyebrows. "Somebody scored. She had some cool stuff."

This was getting me nowhere. April had vanished one night simple as that. "Terry Barnett," I said. "He's from Ohio and he has a brother, Fred. Do those names ring a bell?"

She brightened. "Not Terry, but yeah, there *was* a Fred from Ohio. I waited on him a few times but I never knew his last name."

"No kidding."

"Fred the dead." Ginger smiled. "That's what April called him. She could be dead-on accurate, really wicked that way. He was so stiff, like he had a poker you know where." She laughed.

Poor Fred, barmaids mocking him behind his back. But he was hardly stiff now, slackened by time, or sorrow.

"Back then," Ginger went on, "we both liked guys with, you know, *attitude.*" She rolled her eyes. "Stupid us. I've got me the sweetest husband now with no attitude at all. Those attitude guys are losers, as far as I'm concerned. You know what I mean."

Alas, I did.

"Fred the dead was just passing through town," she went on. "He came in the bar a few times. Away from home and slumming, that's the impression I had. He got the hots for April like half the guys in the bar. Anyway, she needed a break so she took off for Ohio with him. Then she came back a week or so later. That's how she lost her apartment and had to move in with me."

"Wait." I stared at Ginger. I was getting a timeline. She and April had been roommates a couple of months, she'd said, a couple of months after April came back from Ohio and went missing. "She went off to Ohio, then came back, right? So Fred must have come back too, later, with his brother, looking for her."

Ginger looked surprised. "No. Fred never came back."

"Are you positive?"

She nodded. "I'd have remembered. I worked at Ace's for a year at least after that." She laughed. "Ohio was pretty boring, from what April said. We laughed about it. If Fred had shown up again, she would have given him the heave-ho, believe me."

Maybe that was just what April had done, given them both the heave-ho. But then why wouldn't her roommate, and presumably her confidante, know about it?

Ginger lined my mouth with a little pencil. "I'm going with Chocolate for the liner then I'll use Chocolate Rose for the lip color."

"Chocolate Rose," I said.

"I still have it in the back of my mind, she'll come bopping in one day and say 'Hi, Ginger, let's go to the mall.'" She smiled sadly. "She loved to shop." She applied lipstick to my mouth, then stood back. "Not bad."

The lipstick felt dense and heavy. I took a tissue from a box nearby and dabbed at my lips.

"The worst of it is, no one else seemed to care," said Ginger. "Not like if she'd been a schoolteacher on her way to Sunday school instead of a barmaid at Ace's."

"What about relatives, Ginger? Didn't they care?"

"She was from San Diego. Her parents were divorced and

her mom remarried, had a different last name, which, stupid me, I'd forgotten if I ever knew it. God knows about her dad, she never mentioned him. But she said to me once, I'll never go back to San Diego, no matter what."

"What about other people that worked in the bar, didn't they care either?"

"The owner sure didn't, and she'd already gone off once. The only other person that really knew her was Tod. He and April were pretty tight, but he was a real asshole, I never understood why she couldn't see that. And he got really pissed at me for filing the report."

"But why, if he and April were tight? Why wasn't he worried too?"

"He didn't like cops." She shot me a look. "Some of the regulars at Ace's did a little dealing, he didn't want any cops around. I said they were tight, but in the end, Tod only ever cared about himself."

"What happened to him? What's his last name? Do you remember?"

"Hines. Tod Hines. Last I heard, he was managing a health food store at the Tucson Mall, if you can believe that." She made a face. "Power Nutrition."

She whirled the chair around so I could see the mirror. "At least you got a nice makeup out of all this. Pretty Woman costs an arm and a leg. You can try for similar colors, in a cheaper brand."

I couldn't look. "Wonderful," I said hurriedly. "Maybe I'll get that Chocolate Rose lipstick."

"Good choice," said Ginger.

She found a lipstick and bagged it. "That's twenty-six forty-eight."

Christ, for a lipstick. I usually paid seven or eight dollars. I handed her a twenty and a ten and watched her ring it up. "Let me give you another name," I said, "see if it will ring a bell. Ivan Fowler."

"That does, for sure." Ginger handed me my change. "He was April's shrink."

"No kidding."

"Remember? I said *complications* underneath. April didn't talk to me about them, I guess she told everything to Mr. Fowler. Ivan, she called him." Ginger smiled sadly. "Or Ivanski, sometimes."

And there it was. The link that tied April to Ivan. I stared at her. Mister, not doctor. He would have been just starting out, twenty years ago.

"She thought he was the greatest," Ginger went on. "I mean like, better than Freud or something. She talked about him all the time, Ivan said this, Ivan said that."

Talked about him all the time. Then Terry would have known about him twenty years ago. That must be why he'd gone to see Ivan when he first moved to Arizona six years ago. Not for therapy, but to ask about April. Gone to see him because he didn't know April had vanished. But why had he gone to see him again this January?

"Ginger," I said, "did anyone ever question Dr. Fowler about April?"

"I tried two or three times, but his office always gave me the runaround."

"Did you tell the detective about him?"

"Yeah, but I told you he didn't really work it. He just put on a show for me." Ginger stared past me at the other glittering, gleaming counters, all staffed with women pretty as they could be. "I kept on hoping but in my heart I *knew*."

"Knew what?"

"That April was dead. Someone murdered her way back then, some sex pervert is my guess. Probably dumped her body in the desert like so much trash. And they got away with it. Because no one thought she counted. Who knows—maybe they killed some other women too and they're out there now, laughing about it."

"*SOME SEX PERVERT. Out there now laughing about it.*" Chilled, I stood in the mall, used my cell phone to get the number for Power Nutrition, dialed it and asked for Tod Hines.

"Tod's in Phoenix till next week," said a woman with a chirpy voice. "Maybe I can help you."

"No, thanks anyway," I said.

I went and bought an Orange Julius. I always buy Orange Juliuses in Tucson because my first Orange Julius was at little place on Eighth Street in the Village, years ago when I lived in New York. I will probably never live there again and sometimes it makes me sad, so I always buy Orange Juliuses, when I'm at a place that has them.

I sat on one of the big couches at Park Mall, a single woman in slightly faded black clothes and exquisite makeup, and thought about it all.

Okay. So Ivan Fowler had been April's counselor. What if, when Ivan was counseling April, he'd fallen in love with her? And he'd started to try to control her, change her wild ways, and she'd resisted. Uncontrollable, Fred had said; not like Sally and maybe even Heather, and Ivan was clearly a total control freak. Not only that, he was a man with status in the community, free, apparently, to harass Heather. So why not also free to murder an unimportant barmaid in a punk bar and get away with it?

Just a scenario, but it made sense in a lot of ways.

In the end, April had been a throwaway person. Blond, flirtatious April Matasky now probably dead, her body dumped out in the desert somewhere like Ginger said. Bones now; buried deep so the coyotes wouldn't dig her up. Her family in San Diego had never come looking for her, maybe didn't even know she was in Arizona, maybe didn't care. She'd had troubles with her family, God knows what kind, and run away and the family had given up on her.

All those guys with broken hearts and busted egos but the only person who'd cared that she was missing was Ginger. Ginger had probably been a lot like April back then but Ginger had survived, come through into, I hoped, a reasonably normal life: teaching women how to look like someone men couldn't live without.

Why hadn't Fred and Terry shown up at Ace's? Could they have gone to see Ivan first instead and he'd told them April didn't want to see them? But no, Fred had never heard of Ivan. But Terry had. Years later, when Terry returned to Arizona he'd gone to see Ivan. It had to be about April. Ivan could have given Terry some convincing story, and that was that.

My bet was that Terry had finally found out that Ivan was harassing Heather, learned what he was really like, and he'd started wondering again about April, done some digging. What if he'd discovered something that linked April's disappearance to Ivan and had gone to confront him? Oh, Terry, you idiot, didn't you realize how dangerous he was?

Terry was an idiot? What about me? In a snit, Rosa had told me about Terry coming to the office. What if she repeated that to Ivan when she cooled down?

And Heather. If Ivan had murdered April and gotten away with it so easily, why not others, too, over the years and why not Heather next?

BACK IN DUDLEY I stopped at the Circle K and bought the *Review*. It was just after five, light fading, cold setting in. "Police Baffled by Barnett Slaying," said the headline in the lower right corner. At home, I turned on the heater and fed Big Foot. Then I nuked a shrimp and vegetables bowl with some of Diana's tofu, and scanned the article as I ate. Flynn's name jumped out at me, but he said nothing I didn't already know.

Fred had met April first, in the bar. Why had he never heard of Ivan, when Ginger said April talked about Ivan all the time? Fred the dead. No one liked him. I did. What was wrong with me? I couldn't trust my own instincts anymore. I had two thousand dollars of his money, and though I liked him, something was not right about Fred.

I rinsed out my bowl, thinking, here I am, charging along: blatantly showing up at Ivan's, talking to Rosa behind his back. The thought of Ivan lay in my mind like a heavy weight. Heather was at least hiding out, but I wasn't. I needed to be a little more careful. A lot more careful. Well, at least I had a gun.

I dried my hands, went into the bedroom and turned on the lights. I walked over to the chest where I kept it, opened the top drawer and rummaged gingerly under my slips and bras. Didn't feel anything but underwear.

What?

I rummaged more thoroughly, then took the drawer and dumped everything onto the bed. The gun was gone.

TWENTY

FRANTICALLY I WENT THROUGH the rest of the drawers even though in all the years I'd owned the gun, I'd always kept it in the same place. No gun. I dumped all the drawers out onto the bed. Still no gun. It had been there the night Flynn had interrogated me. I'd taken it out and sniffed the barrel. Put it back.

Flynn.

I'd told him I hadn't taken it out of the chest of drawers in my bedroom for at least a year. He would know exactly where it was. *"At least you got some guy on fire investigating,"* Stuart had said, *"willing to do anything, no matter how sleazy, to get his man or woman."*

Goddamnit. *"If you think of anything else call me day or night,"* said Flynn as he handed me his card. I got my purse, unzipped the inner pouch and found it. I punched in the home number.

"Flynn here. Leave a message."

"This is Chloe," I said, between my teeth to the machine. "You think you can come into someone's house when they aren't there and take anything you want? Supercop, doesn't need a search warrant? Who do you think you are anyway, *God?* Well, you may think so—"

There was a click. "Flynn here."

"You dirty rat, you took my gun," I said.

"I'll be right over."

HANDS ON HIS HIPS, Flynn in his ubiquitous dark brown leather jacket, jeans, and running shoes stood at the door to the bedroom, looking at the piles of sweaters, T-shirts, and, oh no, *bras and panties,* scattered on the bed. He rubbed his chin. I imagined the stubble rasping over his fingertips. "Chloe, Chloe, Chloe." His voice was sad.

He turned to me. "Now why the hell would you think I'd come and take your gun?"

I stepped back. "You knew where it was. I told you. And the last time I saw it was right after you interrogated me." I stared at him accusingly. "It was a thirty-eight, like my gun, wasn't it? The gun that killed Terry."

Flynn's eyes turned to lumps of black coal. "This is an ongoing investigation. I don't share that kind of information with civilians."

Civilians. "Well, I think it was a thirty-eight," I said, "and you took it for evidence."

Flynn snorted. "Right. And instead of getting a search warrant, doing everything legal so it would hold up in court, like an asshole I came here and stole it."

I felt my face flushing with embarrassment as I had the sudden realization that I was an idiot. "I panicked," I said defensively. "I was *scared.* You were the first person I thought of."

Flynn nodded. His eyes scanned the bedroom again, but he didn't go in. "Anything else missing?"

"Not that I can tell offhand."

"Who else knew about the gun?"

"I don't know." I paused. "Craig."

Flynn raised his eyebrows. "Craig?"

"He's my, um, boyfriend. *Was.*" I dithered. "But he's in South America. He went there—" I paused. In November, after which I immediately took up with Terry. "Oh, a few months ago."

"You lock your doors?"

"Only when I'm home."

"Not when you're gone? *Smart.*"

Flynn backed away from the bedroom in disgust. Big Foot

sidled past me and sniffed at his running shoes, black with red and white stripes. Then he rubbed against them, purring loudly.

Flynn sighed wearily, disengaging his foot from the cat. Probably a dog man or hated animals. "Okay, Chloe, let me give you the speech. Keep your doors locked whether you're home or not. That's just good sense. Most crimes are crimes of opportunity. Why offer up temptation? Second of all, guns are the first thing a thief looks for. And where do people keep guns? In the bedroom. First choice, bedside table; second, *chest of drawers.*"

He squared his shoulders authoritatively. "Okay. Let's take a look at your locks. The one on the kitchen door is shit."

"Oh," I said.

Flynn glanced around the dining room area, then strode across it to the front door. "Dead bolt. That's marginally better." He peered into the darkened living room. "What's this? *French doors?*"

I shuddered.

Flynn strode into the living room and tripped on the edge of the coffee table Craig had made. I stifled a burst of hysterical laughter. Undaunted, he went to the French doors. They were secondhand to begin with, ancient, put in by Hal, my brother's lover who had left me the house. "Locked?" he asked.

"Yes."

He barked scornfully, gave a tug on the knobs and the doors burst open.

"Hey!" I said.

"Not even properly installed." His voice was triumphant.

"Flynn!" I said. *"Someone stole my gun."*

He strode back. "Crime of opportunity, is my guess," he said. "Like I said. Someone took a stroll through your unlocked house and hit the jackpot. But this isn't my jurisdiction. I'm here as a courtesy. Keep your hands off the drawers until you file a report with the Dudley PD."

I'd already touched the damn drawers, all of them, probably smudging everything there, but what did it matter? Two years ago my neighbor Lourdes had had a DVD player and some jewelry stolen and, understaffed and underfunded, the Dudley PD hadn't even dusted for prints.

I could be in danger, but Flynn wasn't concerned. Oh, no, not at all. I should tell him everything—Terry's letter to Fred, Ivan, April, my fears for Heather—but it was mostly a jumble of hearsay. And God knows how he would handle Heather. He would take over and never tell me a thing. No. I would figure this out on my own, like I was getting paid in hundred-dollar bills to do, get some concrete evidence that Flynn would accept. Then he would see, he would just see.

He made me so mad, I wasn't even afraid anymore. I wanted to hit him, beat on his chest with my fists till he keeled over.

"Thanks for all your support," I said icily as I walked him to the door.

"No problem."

AFTER FLYNN LEFT I took all the dining room chairs and wedged them under the doorknobs of the kitchen door to the carport, and the front door, and under each knob of the French doors. I arranged silverware under the bedroom window that had a broken lock, so it would clatter and wake me if anyone tried to open it. Then I went to bed.

Big Foot leaped up beside me and I stroked his fur, thinking of him rubbing against Flynn's running shoes. "You dumb cat," I said. "You don't know who your friends are."

It was hard to fall asleep with one part of me trying to stay alert, listening, but finally I did and dreamed of Flynn, holding hands with a beautiful young girl, blond, wearing a diamond engagement ring around her wrist. You're the one who's unfaithful, I said to Flynn, then the young girl turned wild, clawing at Flynn with fingernails like talons. April; I saw her as clearly as a glossy photo in a magazine, half beautiful young girl, half banshee. Then, as I watched, the bright fresh skin slid slowly off her face, till there was nothing left but a skull. I felt an almost unbearable sadness.

She's gone, said Flynn.

TWENTY-ONE

"Looks like a crime of opportunity," said the uniformed young policewoman, echoing Flynn as she filled out the report. She was built like a little tank and her chubby pink face was set in what appeared to be a perpetual smile. "You need to get in the habit of—"

"Locking my doors," I cut in. "I know."

She clicked her pen shut. "That's about it," she said, still smiling as she backed toward the open kitchen door. "You have *a real nice day.*"

"You *too.*"

I watched her go. She had dusted for prints, but that was probably a token acknowledgment of my probably former position at the county attorney's. They would go in some file somewhere never to be looked at again.

Last night's dream was still with me, April's face as clear and lovely in my mind as if we'd actually met, filling me with sorrow and free-floating anxiety. I still hadn't reached Fred though I'd tried several times earlier that morning. My God. What if Fred and Sam never made it home? What if they never made it out of Arizona? Lots of people knew he was looking for Heather. Maybe he was getting to be a threat. But to whom? Not to Ivan Fowler, why would he be? And I had no address for Fred, not even a town. Just Ohio. Stupid, stupid.

I called my lawyer. I didn't plan to mention the gun being stolen. Stuart would kill me if he knew I'd called Flynn.

Stuart laughed when he heard my voice. "You still at large?"

"Do me a favor, okay? Run a Google search for me."

"Sure, but you know, you should get yourself a computer, Chloe. You really should."

"Yeah, right, I'm so rich right now. The name's Fred Barnett, in Ohio. He's in sporting goods, has a chain of stores, to narrow it down."

"Barnett? Isn't that the last name of the guy—"

"Just a coincidence," I interrupted. "What I need is a home phone number, if possible, or at least an address. Write down what you come up with and I'll get back to you. Take your time. This afternoon would be fine."

"This afternoon." He chortled. "Chloe, you're so good to me."

"I know," I said, as I hung up.

Crime of opportunity. Maybe so. Maybe not. The theft of my gun made everything more urgent. It was time to do something more useful than obsessing about April and anyway all I had left was Tod Hines, the bartender at Ace's, and he was out of town. Besides, if you got hung up on one theory, you missed everything else. I dialed Heather's number just in case she'd finally come home.

It rang a few times, then someone picked up.

"Hi! This is Terry Barnett."

"Terry!" I almost shouted.

"Leave a message at the tone."

A machine. Of course. Heather hadn't put on a new message. Shaky, I hung up.

The Frenches weren't the only friends Heather had. There was Damien. If I could get him to trust me. Get him when he was away from his grandparents' house. What about that bookstore, the Cranny? Right here in Dudley. Heather had been at a poetry reading there, the night Terry was killed. I could check it out.

THE CRANNY IS IN a small shabby wooden house on the Gulch, up from the bars near the Burnt Hyena Gallery. There is no such thing as zoning in this part of town. A bulletin board hung by the red front door, covered with index cards hoping to sell eight-track tapes CHEAP, used CD players and VCRs, plane tickets, water filters, and offers to house-sit.

There was also a big poster advertising the opening at the Burnt Hyena Gallery, a larger version of the flyer I'd seen on Diana and Peter's refrigerator.

The hand-lettered sign on the door said OPEN, and I went in. A bell tinkled. Someone had torn down a few walls to create one fairly large room. The place had the ineffable moldy smell of old books; they lined all four walls in shelves reaching to the ceiling. On the pale sanded wood floor was a big thread-bare Afghani rug, and on that were a couple of worn leather armchairs. A young woman, all in black, sat in one of them, head bent over a book. Her short hair was henna red and three silver hoops pierced one dark eyebrow. She didn't look up.

"Good morning," I said.

She glanced at me for a second and sighed. Then she got up from the chair and, still holding the book, walked past me out the door. The bell tinkled.

Well. There seemed to be no one else there. To one side was a coffeepot and some Styrofoam cups at the end of a long table, half covered with books that turned out to be poetry. I browsed them. Mostly from small presses: thin, elegant books, beautifully done, and read mostly, I figured, by competitive graduate students. I selected something called *Tuning,* sat in the chair across from the one the young woman had vacated, and opened it at random.

It wasn't exactly in a poem format, more like prose with spaces instead of punctuation. The room was very quiet. Next to me a fern on a plant stand audibly shed crinkly brown leaves. For a few minutes I stepped into the world of the book. It seemed to be about a country where people had to rent the air and could only make love in private compartments on buses.

Then I heard a kind of rustling sigh, and someone said, "Still here?"

I looked up. A large man, in denim pants and shirt and a tan buckskin vest, walked out from a door in back. He had a white beard, neatly trimmed, white hair pulled back in a ponytail, and resembled Santa Claus on his day off, if Santa were an aging hippie.

"Oh," he said. "I thought you were Miranda."

"I said good morning to her, and she left."

The man chuckled. "She likes to be alone." He sat heavily in the other chair and looked over at the book I was reading. "David Antin," he said.

"It's pretty interesting."

He harrumphed and nodded. "He writes some fine essays, no matter what he calls them. I'm Stan Wakowski. Retired from teaching English. My wife died, I thought, what are you going to do with yourself now? Didn't need to make money, so I opened a bookstore, new and used, and all these smart dropout kids showed up. Fine with me, I like kids."

"It's a nice place." I paused. "Speaking of kids, I was hoping to run into Damien here."

"That Damien." He shook his head. "Too much time on his hands."

"I guess he's pretty bored living with his grandparents out in the middle of nowhere," I said. And, judging from his ready conversation Stan was kind of bored too.

"Sure he is. But it was his grandparents or jail. The judge wanted him out of Tucson, somewhere he couldn't get into trouble. It's a condition of his probation."

His *what?* But I nodded wisely. "Kids and drugs," I said, hazarding a guess.

Stan looked amused. "He told you that? It was for drugs?"

"Not exactly." I was dying to learn more, but I had to tread softly. "I guess I just assumed, I never really asked."

"Damien's not a druggie." He tugged at his beard. "Poor Damien. His name came up when I talked to that hotshot detective, ah, *Flynn*."

"Oh, really?" Hotshot detective. For no good reason I felt my cheeks getting pink. "How come his name came up?"

Stan glanced at me. "You must know about Terry Barnett?"

"Yes."

"Detective Flynn wanted to know if Heather had been at the poetry reading here the night Terry was murdered."

"She was, wasn't she?" I asked.

"Sure she was. I saw her come in."

"Did you see her leave?"

He shot me a look. "No, but Damien did. He got here late and spoke to her as she was leaving. Ten-fifteen or so. I guess other people must have seen her too. Damien came to mind because he called me the next morning to fill me in about Terry and that's when he mentioned seeing Heather leave. I told Detective Flynn that."

I nodded, imagining Fred and maybe Flynn too, thinking: nice, convenient. Damien not only comes over to sit with Heather the night of Terry's murder, but he also calls Stan the next day with an alibi for her.

"Anyway," Stan was saying, "that's how Damien's name came up. He was close to the Barnetts."

"Damien and Heather are very close, I understand," I said dutifully.

"Heather can sense an underdog from a mile away," said Stan. "She saw through that pretty-boy façade to the lonely guy underneath. She took him in, brought him here one day, introduced him to people in Dudley. Gave him a life. Damien worships her for that, to the dismay of all the twenty-something single women in town."

"Ah," I said.

He frowned. "Don't get me wrong. She was true blue as far as her marriage went." He put his hand over his heart. "I could swear to it. Tight little community like this, total fishbowl. Anyway this Flynn, saturnine kind of guy, but he sure perked up when I mentioned Damien. Wanted to know all about him, his connection with Heather, what he does with himself, that kind of thing, probably knew already about Damien being on probation."

"What is he on probation for?" I finally asked.

"It's no secret. Assault."

I stared at him. *"Assault?"*

"It wasn't his fault," said Stan forgivingly. "It was his clothes. All that black leather and velvet." He smiled, shaking his head. "He was in a bar in Tucson, dressed that way, and some redneck cowboys took offense. One of them followed him out to the parking lot, called him a pussy, that sort of thing. Damien was a little drunk and he threw a lucky punch. Probably couldn't do it again in a million years." Stan chuckled. "Broke the man's nose."

"Substantial but temporary disfigurement," I said, unable to resist showing off. "A class six felony, probably pled down to a misdemeanor, and taken off his record when he successfully completes probation."

"Don't tell me," said Stan. "You're a cop too?"

"No. I'm a victim advocate," I said defensively. "I help victims through the criminal justice system."

"Sounds interesting," Stan said, his voice warming up twenty degrees or so.

I realized what a fool I was, so used to sneaking around, I'd forgotten the effect honesty has on people.

"And you like David Antin's writing," Stan said. "You know, I enjoy having young people around, but I'm starved for grown-up conversation. That's what I miss most about losing Anna, my wife. She loved to crochet and she loved to talk. Talk and crochet, crochet and talk." He stood up. "Can I get you a cup of coffee?"

TWENTY-TWO

I HAD TWO CUPS of strong black coffee and learned a whole lot more about Stan's wife, but nothing further about the Barnetts or who might have killed Terry. After I left, I focused on what he *had* told me. Damien was the one who'd supplied the alibi for Heather. Damien who worshipped Heather and had *come* late, as she was leaving. So where was Damien during the poetry reading? Well, Mad Dog Flynn knew as much as I did. Let him investigate Damien.

Finding Heather was number one on my list. If Heather confided in anybody, if anyone knew where she was, surely it would be her best friend, Diana French, who worked at the Natural Foods Co-op mornings, only a couple of minutes away. Diana alone without her watchful hostile husband to shut her up.

Once the co-op had been small and cozy and right on Main Street. But as tourism grew the businesses that served the locals got pushed out, replaced by antiques stores, a title company, art galleries, and jewelers of the two-pair-of-earrings-for-ten dollars variety. Now the co-op was just outside town, in an unscenic area near the huge mining pit, in a big building that used to sell furniture. I pushed open the door.

Inside it was nearly empty. The place smelled of freshly ground coffee. The sun came in strong through the big plateglass windows and glinted off jars of herbs, natural jams and jellies, bottles of organic juices, and row after row of nutritional supplements.

Behind the register, a young woman with spiky platinum blond hair was reading a book. Another woman in an ancient

Peruvian sweater, long brown skirt, and Birkenstocks, two blond toddlers in tow, drifted among the aisles. I didn't see Diana.

I went over to the register, interrupting the young woman in a yawn.

"Excuse *me*," she said. She had a tiny gold earring through one nostril, which looked painful. "Slow morning."

"I'm looking for Diana French?" I said.

She nodded. "In back, bagging."

I walked past the frozen organic dinners, tofu burgers, and the slightly wilted organic vegetables, to a vast back room, but saw no one in it.

"Diana?" I called.

"Hello? Back here."

Then I saw her, standing at a table to one side, a tin cup in her hand. I walked toward her.

Her blond hair was pulled back tight, revealing more of her face, bare of makeup, and as sweet as ever. She wore a long olive-green velvet jumper, over a black T-shirt. The velvet's nap was worn off in places. Peter was like a big barking dog. Without him around she seemed much more accessible.

"Have a seat." She gestured to a spindly chair pulled up to the table.

"I'm still looking for Heather," I said, sitting gingerly on the chair.

For a moment she didn't say anything. She opened a plastic bag, dipped the tin cup into a large cardboard drum, and filled the bag with rolled oats. She fastened the plastic with a wire twist and stuck a label on it. "She *knows* you're looking for her."

"Then you've talked to her?"

She nodded. "She feels like it would be too painful to talk to Fred, till she's more grounded. He can wait a bit, out of respect for Heather's feelings. You see what I mean?"

"Fred's suffering too," I said. "I've spent time with him. He's very, very sad about Terry. Especially since they didn't always get along. You know how it is, Diana, people get into arguments, take positions, then they can't back down."

"I do know. I really do. It's not me, it's Heather." She sighed. "I hate being in this position. I'm trying to be fair, but it's hard. Heather is my best friend, but you know, I've had to do so much for her since Terry was killed; man the phones, call everyone, set up the memorial. Some things she needs to do for herself." She sighed again, looking exhausted. "But I can't force her."

"It must be really hard on you," I said sympathetically.

She plopped down on a folding chair. "Not as hard as it is for her. I keep telling myself that. But how can she heal unless she faces up to things? She doesn't face up very well. She hides behind her art, ignoring everything around her."

"She's probably still in denial," I said. "It takes time, sometimes a very long time."

"That's right. You said you were a victim advocate, you must see this kind of thing every day. But Heather…well, Heather's always been kind of in denial. Especially where Terry was concerned."

"Where Terry was concerned?"

She gave me a look. "Think about it. Remember how you said you met him? He came over to build you a bookcase, and asked you out to dinner? Didn't happen to mention he was married?"

"Umm," I said.

"Don't you see how he tricked you? Terry was so nice, so charming. He kind of cast a spell. You didn't realize you were being charmed, because of the nice part."

I stared past Diana out the back window, smudged with dust and dirty spiderwebs. It was as embarrassingly apt a description of my encounters with Terry as any I could have come up with.

"What are you saying?" I asked her. "Terry was in the *habit* of cheating on Heather?"

"Not exactly." Her skin reddened. "At least, not lately."

"Not lately?"

"Well, not for maybe a year. We thought he'd finally reformed. Peter was so disappointed when he saw Terry with you, and in *Mexico*. Terry always took his little flirtations to Mexico, where no one knew him. We used to joke about it— uh—oh, Terry's gone to Mexico again."

There was a little silence, during which I felt nothing. Nothing at all. Then I said doggedly, "So he *did* cheat on her, regularly."

She bit her lip. "I don't really know what went on. I mean, he'd pick women no one knew, women just passing through or visiting. Women who didn't talk, would keep a secret."

Keep a secret. I felt my face flush, clear down to my neck. I bent over as if to look in my purse to hide it.

"Oh, maybe he never actually physically cheated," Diana went on. "Maybe it was just little flirtations, like I said."

She stood, picked up another bag and began to fill it. She was so carelessly pretty in her green velvet jumper with the nap worn off, standing on a cement floor, filling a plastic bag with rolled oats. Even though she was essentially performing a menial task in a chilly back room, somehow she reminded me of Marie Antoinette, in her shepherdess days in the hamlet at Trianon.

"Heather's not exactly a girly girl," she said, "but Terry loved her. He just couldn't help himself, seduction was so easy for him. I think that's why he was always so mistrustful of her, even though she never gave him any reason to be."

"Doesn't that strike you as weird," I said, "when *he* was the one who couldn't be trusted?"

"It's not so strange. If you can't be trusted yourself, then how can you trust other people? I mean, you assume other people are like you, you know?"

She paused. "Please don't get the wrong idea," she added, backtracking. "Terry was very honest in most ways. I thought since Terry tried to fool you, you'd understand."

In spite of myself I could feel anger rising, partly at Terry, but partly at Diana, as if we'd waged some subtle battle and she'd won. "It wasn't—" I began.

"Diana?" The platinum blonde was at the door.

I stopped, swallowing my words.

Diana blinked. "What?"

"We're out of tabbouleh mix up here," said the blonde, "and I've got an antsy customer who wants some. Is there some back there you can bag for her?"

Diana dropped the bag she'd been holding and some of the oats spilled out. "Shit." She looked around. "Tabbouleh mix, tabbouleh mix." She walked over to a pile of boxes. "I saw some. But where? Oh, I'm so *behind*."

"I'm sorry," I said. "I'd better go."

Diana turned. "Please," she said pleadingly. "Don't—"

I interrupted. "Say anything about this conversation. Don't worry. I won't."

I walked back through the front of the co-op and out the door, still trying to fully digest what Diana had told me. She probably wouldn't have, if she hadn't been so frustrated about Heather, with no good way to talk about it with the people she knew, people who also knew Heather and had known Terry.

Saint Terry. Hah.

Outside it had gotten breezy. I stood by the door and took a few deep breaths. My anger at Diana slowly evaporated. It wasn't her fault and I couldn't say one hundred percent that my meeting with Terry had been so innocent, not even on my part. What if I'd been home when he brought over the bookcase and we'd hugged then, instead of outdoors in public in front of the junk store?

April had seemed so important. Now I wasn't so sure that she meant anything at all. Had all the things he'd said to me on the bench, in the square in Mexico, been lies? Lies about screwing up, obsessing about April, lies about how sorry he was for not telling me he was married; all part of some well-rehearsed script to get my attention and my sympathy. A *line*.

I walked slowly over to my car. Down on my left was the

old mining pit, deep as a mountain was high, and bare; terraced sides crumbling, nothing grew on them or ever would; a murky pool of acid poison at the bottom. At the far end of the parking lot, a tumbleweed rolled slowly, over and over. As I opened the car door, the wind gusted, billowing an old empty plastic bag, scattering the leaves left over from fall.

TWENTY-THREE

"'GONE WITH THE TUMBLIN' tumble-weed,'" I sang, driving out to Prophecy. I'd called Stuart about the Google search, but he wasn't home. Fred still wasn't answering and I wanted to talk to him more than ever, tell him the letter from Terry, *his whole case* against Heather, was less convincing than ever. It was like Diana said, if you couldn't be trusted, then you couldn't trust.

Except, as I drove down the highway, I had some second thoughts. Fred's whole case against Heather might be unconvincing but the scenery had changed: now she had the most classic of motives to kill Terry, jealousy.

Another thing, even if most of what Terry had told me was lies, I still had no explanation as to why he had gone to see Ivan about April, not very long before he was murdered. Angry, shouting. Terry wasn't like that.

I turned onto the dirt road, went past Meeks's Mercantile on the corner, past the hodgepodge of houses and gardens. Except for the night of the murder, I'd been coming out here in Fred's rental so I figured the nosy Blofelds wouldn't recognize my car.

It appeared no one was home at the Blofelds' anyway—no Volkswagen out front and Damien's motorcycle wasn't there either. The old blue Volvo was in the same spot in front of Heather's; the truck nowhere to be seen. I drove round to the side so the Blofelds couldn't see my car if they should return.

I raised the latch on the gate and Pi-Pi, the orange cat, scuttled under the house, as if sensing I was now the enemy. But I wasn't, I wasn't; I just needed to know. More weeds were beginning to poke up through the bark mulch of the empty flower beds, the result of the recent rain. No one had been back, then, to pull them up.

I went down the flagstone path to the glassed-in porch. A card was wedged in the space where the door met the frame. I took it out.

Howard Meeks
Ministry of Christ

Poor Howard, come to offer Heather help from the Lord and she wasn't home. I knocked, just in case. I knocked twice, but no one came. Through the glass I saw the wicker chair, the geraniums. They seemed as healthy and profuse as before. Someone must be watering them. Feeding the cat, too, for that matter. Damien?

The door to the porch hadn't been locked when Fred and I were last here. I tried it and it still wasn't.

As I walked into the porch, the phone began to ring from inside the house. I stood and listened till it stopped and the machine kicked in, heard the blur of Terry's voice, smooth and tranquil.

A cat, and plants. I had those too. When I go away, my neighbor Lourdes takes care of them. I hide a key for her, over the door. I raised my arms and felt along the ledge of the inside door. Nothing. What about a rock? But there weren't any. The doormat, dummy. I pulled up a corner and there was a key. I picked it up and looked down the road. No one. I could go inside, look around. If I got caught, that would be it, no one would ever trust me again.

Again? Who trusted me now?

I unlocked the door, put the key back under the mat, and walked inside, pulling the door behind me so it caught. I went down the hall to a rectangular living room, the room where the night of the murder I had sat on the couch with Heather, the mouse-brown person; doing my victim advocate routine and failing utterly to connect.

Now sparkly motes, some colored by stained glass, danced

in the sun that shone through long windows framed in a richly burnished wood. Faded rag rugs were on the satiny wood floor, potted ferns everywhere. Two more of Heather's collages hung on the wall, transcending the odds and ends of magazine clippings, newspaper print, bits of wood, sparkly things, and other people's trash they were made of. Beautiful but dimmed, as if ever so slightly out of focus, with a faint layer of dust, of loss, in the house where two people had once lived.

And now one.

I tiptoed, needlessly, into the kitchen. The counter had been wiped down. There were no dishes in the sink or drainer. The tiled floor was smudgy looking. On the wall was the beautiful collage I remembered from the night of the death notification. Beer-bottle caps and labels transformed into an ancient Russian icon. I went closer for a good look and noticed a caption pasted underneath: "Drunk."

I didn't want to think Heather might have killed her husband in a fit of jealous rage.

I opened the door at the far end of the kitchen and found a room full of sunlight and chaos. A wooden stool lay on its side by a drawing table. Uncapped squeezed tubes of paint, beads, gold and silver paste-on stars, bright stickies used as rewards for first-graders, and clippings from fashion magazines littered the floor. A jar streaked with paint residue, which must have once held water, lay among crumpled wads of paper.

Heather's studio.

A fly buzzed urgently, beating itself against a sunlit window. Then, standing there, it hit me. Diana said Terry had been faithful for a year. What if Peter had told Heather about seeing Terry in Mexico with a strange woman and it was the last straw; she just couldn't take it anymore? What if Heather had killed Terry in a jealous rage over *me?*

Guiltily, I closed the door. I walked through the kitchen, out the back door and closed it behind me.

Even after all this time, there was still a faint odor of burning in the air. Across the field, down by the river, the trees had that smoky look they get before they start to bud out. In front of me was Terry's workshop. A few days ago Fred had stood, just there, in the dried-out grass at the burned side of the shop, among the glass that glittered in the sun, crying.

I walked over to the door, padlock dangling from the hasp now, but it seemed too risky to unhook it and go inside. A beam could fall, hit me on the head and knock me out. I'm not especially brave. Next to the door was a big oil drum, overflowing with burned bits of wood and crushed newspapers. I pulled out a newspaper. The *Sierra Vista Review,* dated a week or so after Terry's death.

Under the newspapers was something else: black, shiny plastic. I pulled it out. A videotape. Not a rental; plain label with something faded and unreadable scrawled on it. Thrown away, so why would anyone mind if I took it? I shoved it into my purse. Then without warning, rage overtook me. I kicked viciously at a charred bit of wood on the ground. I had two thousand dollars in cash but, let's face it, my job was in jeopardy and I was broke, broke, broke; heading for financial disaster all because Terry Barnett had felt like playing around.

"Goddamn you, Terry!" I shouted. "You stupid *shit!*"

Too much. I backed away, skirted the house, headed for the front as fast as I could without actually running. My knees were shaking.

I got in the car, made a fast U-turn, and drove back down the road, past the hodgepodge of houses, spooked by my own anger. Why was it, someone so pleasant when alive, could be so threatening dead? Because I thought I'd known him and I hadn't?

My throat was dry. At the turn to the highway, I stopped at Meeks's Mercantile, to get something to drink.

A bell tinkled as I opened the door. The place was packed with boxes of slightly aging lettuce, tomatoes, potatoes and onions, canned goods, bread, even a video rental section. A deli case was near the back and Howard Meeks, in a white apron, stood behind it. The light shone off his pink-rimmed plastic glasses and his pale red hair.

"Good afternoon," he sang out. His voice was surprisingly melodious. "What can I do you for?"

"Good afternoon," I said, my voice unusually melodious in response. "My goodness, you've got a little bit of everything here."

"Sure do. Even got lottery tickets. Gambling's against my religion but people will drive clear to Dudley or Sierra Vista just for one of them tickets and we lose business that way."

"I see what you mean."

"Do you now?" He leaned over the counter toward me. His pale blue eyes behind the plastic-framed glasses were twinkly and utterly benign. "It seems like I seen you around, but I can't think where."

"Actually, I think we met the night Terry Barnett was killed."

Howard blinked. "Oh."

"I'm looking for Heather."

He sighed. "I haven't seen her lately, she's been out of town. What I think is she couldn't stand being around the memories. She'd still come in the store after it happened, but every day it seemed like she was paler and skinnier." He looked woeful. "A terrible tragedy."

"Yes."

"And they haven't even arrested anybody. Me and the wife, we lock our doors at night. Always have. Got those illegals coming through this area all the time. They'll steal all right, but they're not murderers, just come to the U.S. to make money to feed the wife and little ones. Doris'll give 'em water and food even, sometimes. It's the Christian thing to do." He sighed again.

"I just don't understand it," I said. "Terry got along with everyone."

"That's why I put my money on an outsider. Excuse me, I

mean if I was a bettor, I would. And partly 'cause of the white car too."

"The white car?"

"We're open till nine, see, but after I close there's still the cleanup. I heard it make the turn and I looked out. It was a stranger's car, so I paid attention. I'm used to the regulars, they go in and out, I don't even notice. Couple people here own white cars, but the engine sound was different from those. I told that Detective Flynn about it. He checked with everyone on the street to see if anybody had a visitor that night."

"And did they?"

Howard shrugged. "One of the Lamberts came in the store, said they did, but they never told me if their visitor was driving a white car."

"You could ask them," I said.

He shook his head. "Don't like to. They're strangers. Used to be I knew everybody round here. Prophecy was a religious center once, know that? Pentecostal. Had our own little church, but it's gone now, burned down. They said it was arson."

"Really?"

Howard's eyes gleamed. "Never found out who did it either. But that was a long time ago, before all these new people moved in." He leaned across the counter. "Some folks, they go to church every Sunday, kind of for sanitary reasons, like brushing their teeth. I like to be with the Lord every day. I tried to talk to Heather after Terry was killed but that Flynn wouldn't let me near her."

"I guess he felt he was just doing his job," I said.

"Well, and I was trying to do mine. What I was put here on this earth to do. It's all in the readiness because sometimes salvation comes when you least expect it. When all the worldly things have failed you." His pale eyes met mine. "Have you been saved?"

"No," I said.

"It's never too late!" His voice was hopeful. "You ever hear of Brother Louis?"

"No," I said hurriedly, foreseeing what was coming. "Umm, I was looking for your drinks cooler."

"Sure. Right over there. Brother Louis's dead now, but his message lives on. Which is: it's all in the Bible, every word, you don't need to go anyplace else. Brother Louis was a healer, he healed a whole lot of people. You name it, heart trouble, liver disease, blindness, diabetes, *cancer.*"

"Wow. Really." I opened the cooler door, grabbed a bottle of spring water and brought it back to the counter.

"That's a dollar seventy-nine."

I gave him a couple of dollars and he handed me the water in a brown paper bag, then the change. "Included a little gift." He winked. "Free of charge."

BACK IN MY CAR, I snuck a peek at the free gift. A pamphlet of some sort, *The Life of Brother Louis.* There was a drawing on the front, of a strong-jawed man, smiling, wearing a hat. I opened it up and found a blurry black-and-white photograph of Brother Louis with a light shining round his head. On the facing page was a facsimile of a letter from the FBI dated 1938, certifying that the light was, in fact, a halo.

Well.

I drove back to Dudley down Highway 92, thinking about Heather, then for the first time in a while, I thought directly about Evangeline, and about her husband, Chip. Of Chip working on the house for her, fixing up the prison, a way to shame Evangeline into putting up with him, but instead she goddamn broke his heart. He had to have been thinking of Evangeline day and night, to have been so ready with his gun, not even knowing she was going to show up.

When someone has us in their thoughts we cannot escape them.

All at once I had a weird feeling of sudden danger. My

throat tightened up. The empty two-lane blacktop ahead seemed precarious, yet there was absolutely nothing there, not in front or behind or on either side. I forced myself to slow down, pulled over to the side, stopped. I took a few long deep yoga breaths, filling my lungs, letting them out slowly.

Outside the car the dried blond grasses grew in clumps, innocent mountains rimmed the horizon. The winter sun was already low behind them, casting an eerie golden light. There was not a soul in sight, no cars, no houses, just the big empty gilded desert and my unreasoning fear.

BACK HOME, inside my house, things were topsy-turvy, with all the dining room chairs gone from the table, wedged under the doors. I went back outside and tested them. Not bad. I went back in and added some more silverware in columns to a couple of other insecure windows in the living room, then I called Stuart. This time he was home.

"You did the search?"

"Yeah. What's your connection with this guy, anyway?" he said. "If it's the right Fred Barnett, he owns this company Barnett Enterprises."

"Sporting goods," I said.

"Right. Sporting goods." Stuart laughed. "Started that way, but he's got his finger in a lot of pies now, real estate being the most concrete. The rest is obscure, dummy corporation stuff, if you ask me. He must be loaded. How do you know him, anyway?"

I was surprised. Fred had said the stores covered the whole Midwest region, but somehow I didn't think of him as really rich. "I know all sorts of people," I said, to keep my edge with Stuart. "What else did you find out?"

"Made a bunch of speeches to business organizations. Oh, and Barnett Enterprises was investigated a couple of times—some kind of complicated tax fraud."

"Oh?"

"Didn't go anywhere, either time. Oh, and he got divorced—finalized this January."

"Really." Sam's mother. I didn't know she and Fred had gotten divorced so recently. Maybe that accounted for some of the pain he was in. "That's it?"

"That's it."

"So, do you have a number for me?"

"Not a home number. I got the one for the main office, in Cincinnati."

I wrote it down. An office. Damn. I would have to wait till tomorrow.

"You feel like hot dogs?" Stuart said.

"Listen, when I get out of this mess I'm in, I'll invite you to dinner at my house," I said. "I promise."

I hung up, called Fred just in case and got the usual. Loaded? It didn't jibe with the Fred I knew, but then nothing I'd heard about Fred did. But maybe his being rich explained why I hadn't been able to reach him. Really rich people are different, aloof, isolated: owned by their money. Maybe he'd thrown some at me, to free himself from the burden of investigating. Or was he using me in some other way I didn't understand?

Investigated for tax fraud twice. Fred, Fred. What if more investigations were looming, not so easy to get out of, bankruptcy threatening? Wouldn't he get Terry's money if Heather didn't? That would fuel his animus against her. I should use some of that money he'd thrown at me to check him out more thoroughly than just a Google search. But how? When he was so far away, up in Ohio.

I nuked a diet dinner and threw some salad together from a bag. I sat in the living room in front of the blank TV and tried to eat but

I wasn't hungry, stewing about Fred. Then I remembered the video I'd found in the oil drum outside Terry's workshop. I got it from my purse, popped it in the VCR, turned on the TV and pressed play.

It started somewhere in the middle, as if whoever had been watching had stopped there and hadn't bothered to rewind the tape. I saw a blurred black-and-white image like an ancient snapshot of a man in a white suit.

"And this lady," he was saying, "this poor unfortunate soul, she come to me, had a big old tumor right on top of her head. Oh, it was an ugly thing. And I says to her, 'Sister, God loves you. Do you believe?' 'I do, I do,' she says.

"And the Holy Spirit come upon her and that big ugly tumor, it was a cancer is what it was, well, it fell right off her head. And she's here tonight! She's got that big ugly tumor with her! In a jar full of alcohol! It don't look like nothing now, it's all shriveled up. That's what happens to the Devil when the Spirit of the Lord comes up on him!"

A man behind him rose. "Amen, Brother Louis!"

Brother Louis, Howard Meeks. Ever hopeful of salvation for others, he must have lent it to Terry. Howard standing behind the deli counter in his ordinary little shop and this, *this,* was going on in his head. Another world, eerie and fantastical as a fairy tale. Who knew? Who ever knew who anyone was?

Spooked, I stopped the tape. Outside, in the quiet, I heard a car coming up my hill, stopping close to my driveway. I went into the kitchen, peered out nervously through the carport window, but the car had started up again, taillights heading away down the dark street. I went to bed.

TWENTY-FOUR

"Barnett Enterprises. This is Stephanie speaking."

"Hi! Could I speak to Fred Barnett?"

"Mr. Barnett isn't available right now," said the voice on automatic pilot. "Maybe I can help you?"

"This is personal," I said. "I'm a friend. Could you give him a message, please. Have him call me as soon as he gets a chance. Tell him it's Chloe."

"Chloe?" Her voice was dubious.

"He'll know who that is. Tell him it's important. I'm at 520-555-1803."

I hung up and paced the floor nervously. I really needed to see Heather more than anything else right now. What about that art opening at the Burnt Hyena? The flyers were all over town. It was tonight and Heather might go to something like that. I could check it out, see if she showed.

Meanwhile, what the hell was going on with my job? Lucinda there all alone, fielding calls from victims who irritated her. Was she working on Melvin, to persuade him to let me come back to work? Or was she beginning to look for a replacement?

Lee Thomas.

Lee is the widow of a judge who was murdered. She has power in Cochise County, and we were friends. I used to lunch with her from time to time, back when I was a normal person with a job. I punched in her number and got Sandy, one of a series of Cochise College students she has working for her.

"Oh, Chloe, Mrs. Thomas went to Santa Fe. Corney has a big show there." Corney is Lee's daughter, a photographer.

"Could you have her call me when she gets back, as soon as she has time?"

"Sure."

Stalled, I spent the rest of the day cleaning out the refrigerator and all the kitchen cabinets, calling Fred's cell phone and getting no answer.

IT WASN'T HARD to figure out what to wear to an opening at a gallery like the Burnt Hyena. Black. I had plenty of that. Black silk sweater, black stretch pants, black boots with two-inch heels. Damien, Peter, and Diana would probably be there. If Heather showed, I didn't want them spotting me, hustling her away before we had a chance to talk. Maybe I could do something about that.

I rummaged through the medicine cabinet and found a metal tube of colored gel called Street Punk hair highlights in Rita Red that I'd picked up one day at Target. I don't know why except it had seemed irresistible. I brushed it through about half of the front of my hair. The color was cakey and unreal, but actually it looked good. I put on the twenty-six-dollars-and-forty-eight-cents Chocolate Rose lipstick and a ton of eyeliner and mascara.

I stared at my image in the mirror. I looked super. I really did. Goth. Me, Chloe, the defiant Goth rebel. Free to be whoever I wanted. I should look like this more often, no longer actively working for the county attorney and all.

I found some Scotch tape, a spool of thread, went outside, closed the carport door behind me, and locked it. Then I bit off a piece of thread and taped it across the crack at the top of the door so it wouldn't be noticeable, memorizing exactly where, then put the tape and spool in my purse.

I decided to walk, it would be hard to find parking and it wasn't that far. In my fancy boots I swaggered down the street, tripping from time to time on the potholes. Even my walk felt different, when I was a defiant Goth rebel.

The Gulch was brightly lit and smelled of booze around the bars, marijuana in the alleys. Near the St. Elmo, a man in a black cowboy hat, blue and red striped cowboy shirt, probably as much a cowboy as I was a Goth, came up alongside me. "Honey bun! It Halloween already?"

His eyes were blurred and pink with alcohol. Asshole. I stepped off the curb to let him get ahead. He ambled away in the direction of the Burnt Hyena, swerving a little.

Radiohead mourned from the gallery. The drunk began to sing tunelessly, "'I'm proud to be an Okie from Muskokee,'" as he headed for the small crowd standing outside, drinking wine from paper cups. On the fringe I saw Diana French. She had a long blue and gold Indian scarf round her neck and was the only one not wearing black, which for some reason, pleased me.

The drunk waved his arms like a windmill at the crowd. He came up directly to Diana. "Pretty lady!" he shouted, swerved and kissed her on the cheek.

Diana looked stunned. Someone laughed.

Out of nowhere, Peter French appeared, elegantly tall, spectrally thin. He grabbed the drunk by his shirt collar and pulled him away. Someone shouted something and the drunk backtracked. I slipped, unnoticed, through the crowd and into the gallery.

Inside were lots more people, blocking the art. The room was brightly lit. *"Wish it was the sixties,"* whispered Radiohead anxiously. The wood floors had been stripped, somewhat inadequately, the walls painted white. In the center was maybe one of Peter's pieces, a full-sized Medusa-like bust, metal zigzag pieces for hair.

I headed for a long table in back, close to where a band was setting up. The table was covered with white paper and represented the bar. Behind the table, pouring red wine from a bottle into Dixie cups, was a good-looking man in a black suit that was too ancient to be serious. Larry.

My old friend Larry who'd been too sick to go to the mall with me that day in November. What a relief. Someone I knew, someone to give me credibility. He smiled with recognition, seeing right through my defiant Goth-rebel look.

"Look at *you*," he said, "Chloe transformed. I love that stuff on your hair." He looked at me with concern. "You never called me back. What is going on in your *life?* We haven't talked since that desolate phone call *months* ago. I hope you ditched whoever he was."

"Not a problem," I said lightly. "Is the wine free?"

He gestured at a coffee can. "Donation. We'll have to get together, do the mall."

"Sure." I rummaged through my purse for a dollar bill, and dropped it into the can. I picked up a cup of wine and took a few sips; vinegary as if it were left over from some long-ago previous opening. "How's Nelson?" Nelson was Larry's partner, a counselor of all things.

"Suffering."

"You broke up?"

"No." Larry's eyes twinkled wickedly. "That doesn't mean he isn't suffering. What, you're making the art scene now?"

"Actually"—I lowered my voice—"I'm looking for Heather Stephens."

He raised his eyebrows. "*Heather.* Really. I don't know her, but I've watched her at these openings. She'll probably be here. She's—"

He stopped as the lights dimmed.

"What?" I asked. "She's what?"

Larry put his finger to his lips. "Later. The open reading's about to start. Damien's on first, I think. Killer looks."

Damien. Great. People were sitting down on the floor. I sat too. Now that everyone was sitting I could see a spotlight had been rigged up, aimed at the front wall. Damien, in full leather-

and-velvet regalia, stepped through the crowd and sat down on a chair under the spot.

"Don't I get an introduction?" he said. "Let's not and say we did. You can all clap now."

Several people beat their hands together as I sipped my puckery wine. Someone whistled.

"Thank you," said Damien. The spotlight made shadows on his face, lengthened his eyelashes. "I'm just going to read one. It's new and it's called 'Heartbreak Ridge.'" He paused. "Kind of a Western poem."

"That's not Western!" shouted a man with a gray beard, sitting near me. "Heartbreak Ridge is in Korea."

For a moment Damien looked disconcerted. "It is?"

"Read," someone shouted.

"Anyway," said Damien, recovering his composure. "It's still in progress. So I hope you'll forgive me if it's a little uneven and it rhymes. 'I went up to Heartbreak Ridge,'" he began hesitantly, and paused. "Maybe I'll call it 'Breakheart Ridge.' Yes." He took a breath.

I went up to Breakheart Ridge,
A lonely place, where I once lived.

I settled back on the uncomfortable floor, a little clumsy from the effect of wine. One cup. I was out of practice. I've been known to drink, but not lately. Around me the room seemed surreal. Damien went on.

A woman I knew was living there,
Making things beautiful out of thin air.
I smelled the smoke, I heard her cry.

Smelled the smoke? I suddenly came out of my torpor. The poem was about Heather.

I thought I could save her,
I don't know why.

He stopped suddenly, staring at something behind me. I turned to look. Heather was standing near the door, wearing her sunglasses and a black and silver turban. She took three steps back and out the door. Damien watched her go.

"You know," he said, "this poem's not done and I've already lost someone. I think I'll quit while I'm behind."

People began to clap.

"I see you all agree," he said. *"Hasta la vista."*

Damien got up, walked through the crowd and out of the door too. After a moment I followed.

WITH THE LIGHTS INSIDE still dimmed, it wasn't as bright outside as when I'd arrived. It was chillier now and goose bumps rose along my arms. The wine hadn't exactly numbed my senses, more like made me extra aware. Two men in jeans and black T-shirts, holding hands, passed me; "She doesn't know who she is, if she did—" A black pickup cruised slowly by. Down a ways, people were coming and going at the bars, and a teetering couple embraced in the parking lot.

Across the street, Damien and Heather were sitting on a bench. I dodged another pickup and went over, coming up from the side so they didn't see me right away.

"I didn't know Heartbreak Ridge was in Korea," Damien was saying disconsolately. "It *sounded* Western."

"Well, it isn't," said Heather. The turban was kind of Miami Beach retro, black jersey shot with silvery threads that were coming loose from the fabric in little prickles. "And the poem needs work." She touched his arm. "Why don't you just forget it?"

"Excuse me," I said.

They both looked up at me politely, taking in my Rita Red streaked hair and black mascara.

"I'm Chloe," I prompted. "Chloe Newcombe."

"Oh, *shit,*" said Damien in disgust. "You again." He turned to Heather. "She's the one that came over with Terry's brother, looking for you."

"Fred?" Heather flinched. "Oh, no. Is he here *now?*" she cried out in alarm.

"He's gone back to Ohio," I said. "Heather, please. Can't we talk? We met in your kitchen, remember?"

Heather looked at me curiously.

"Leave her alone, for Christ's sake," Damien said fiercely. "You don't have to talk to her," he said to Heather.

"Give me a break," I protested.

"Heather!" someone called.

A man detached himself from a group across the street by the gallery and strode over. Peter French. Maybe I should just give up.

"What's going on?" he asked. His mass of black and gray curls stood on end as if his tangle with the drunk had electrified him. But he looked at me without recognition, for which I was grateful.

"Peter," Heather said wearily, "it's all right. Everything's all right. And Damien. Why don't you back off, both of you? Go inside and listen to poetry. Okay? I'll be fine."

"I REMEMBER YOU NOW," said Heather. "You cleaned up the broken glass from the coffeepot."

That was what she remembered? Not the scene in the living room? So trusting. Damn Terry for violating that trust. But I looked at her with gratitude. "I came to your class too. With a counselor list. I'm sorry. I guess it was kind of pushy."

"No, it was thoughtful. Just—not my kind of thing. *Damn it!*" Impatiently she pulled off the black jersey turban and held it up. "I look like a *dork* in this and it gives me a headache. It's my friend Diana's. She keeps trying to glamorize me, but I'm hopeless."

Her bangs were mashed flat from the turban. She ran her fingers through them but it didn't help. "Fred's gone back to Ohio? Are you sure?"

"Yes, I'm sure."

"Littleton." She laughed, a little shakily.

"What?" I had a sudden impression of students being massacred in Colorado. "Columbine?"

She shook her head. "No, no. Littleton, *Ohio*. Near Cincinnati. That's where Terry grew up. Little Town, that's what he always called it, because it was." Her voice was teary suddenly and heavy with fatigue. "I never thought—that's—that's where he is now. Buried in Littleton."

She sagged back on the bench as if overcome and took off the sunglasses. Her eyes were red and almost swollen shut.

I wondered if she knew about April Matasky. Would Terry have talked about her? Would Ivan? I could pound her with questions, try to get her to tell me about Ivan, but she looked so fragile under the streetlights, I didn't want to blow it again. Just persuading her to see

Fred would be a major victory. But for whom? If they did get together, I would have to make sure I was there.

Uncertain if I was doing the right thing I took a breath. "Fred really wants to talk to you in person, Heather. He's willing to fly back here, if you'll agree to meet with him."

"Do I have to?" Heather picked at a silver thread in the turban, drawing it out, letting it drift to the ground. "One reason I didn't go to the funeral was so I wouldn't have to deal with him." She sighed. "But now I wish I had. Terry's so far away from me there."

"I know Fred and Terry didn't always get along," I said. "What happened between them?"

"Nothing had to *happen*." Head down, Heather pulled out more threads. She looked up at me. "Fred's a jerk. You want to know how Terry described him? When Fred comes into a room, all the life goes out of it."

For a moment there was silence. Fred the dead. But he had loved Terry, I was certain of that.

"Wow," I said finally. "Isn't that a little harsh?"

"Harsh? Everything I think is harsh. When I wake up in the morning, Terry being dead washes over me in these big waves, like I'm *drowning*. I can hardly get out of bed."

She stared down disconsolately at the turban, the silver strands loose and unraveling. "And now I've wrecked Diana's hat."

"Fred could have changed," I said. I hoped it was true. "Will you think about it?"

"All right!" Heather appeared to be hyperventilating. "All right. I'll think about it." She stood up and put the turban back on a little crookedly, then the sunglasses.

I'd done it again, blown it. "Wait," I said.

But she walked away.

"How can I contact you?" I called after her.

"At Diana and Peter's."

"Stay there," I said urgently. "Be careful. Don't—"

Suddenly cymbals clashed, drowning me out. Then drums and a guitar; the band was starting to play. The poetry reading must be taking a break, or had died from lack of participants. Couples emerged from the gallery and began to dance in the street. Her fatigue suddenly gone, all alone, Heather began to dance too, swaying confidently to the music; a good dancer, which somehow surprised me.

"Heather," someone said. "Poor little ugly duckling."

I looked up. It was Larry, like a handsome god in his black suit, taking a break from tending the bar.

He sat down beside me companionably. "She could probably use a shoulder to cry on right now. Little ugly duckling making first-class art. The dark star. Why is that?"

"Why is what?" I said, not really listening. "Could you do me a favor? Could you ask Nelson if he knows anything about a therapist who works in Tucson. His name's Ivan Fowler."

"Ivan Fowler. Okay. What's the—"

"Larry!" someone shouted. "We need you!"

"Damn." Larry stood up. "*Sorry.* I'll call you."

I'D HAD IT FOR the night anyway. I trudged back down the Gulch, in my uncomfortable boots. Home seemed miles away, and I would have to pass more drunks. Before the St. Elmo was a brick-paved alley, a shortcut. I turned onto it. Mangled beer cans and broken bottles littered the bricks; the smell of urine was strong, gagging.

I stepped round a used condom, gross, it was like walking through a toilet. Coming up on my left was an abandoned house. Then I heard a sound from the yard. *Oooph.* Alarm bells went off in my brain. It sounded weird, wrong. I peered over but bushes blocked my view. Heard it again, louder this time. *Oooph.* And again. *Oooph.*

Human, I was sure. I parted branches; the yard was a mass of weeds. I smelled the sickly sweet smell of vomit, saw four men, gray in the moonlight, two of them holding the arms of a third—striped shirt, black cowboy hat. The drunk who'd kissed Diana. I froze in fascination. The fourth man, back to me, raised his fist, hit the cowboy in the stomach. *Oooph.*

The cowboy's hat flew off and he lolled forward, vomit dribbling down his chin, but the man kept on hitting and hitting. Panic dried my mouth. His silent fury was palpable; deadly— radioactive. I felt sick.

God, he was going to kill him. I should do something, but I couldn't seem to move.

Then from somewhere a window flew open. "Break it up, you guys, I called the cops!!"

The fourth man turned toward the window. I could see him now. His face was set in a cold malevolent mask, hair wild, eyes glittering. He couldn't see me, thank God, obscured by the bushes. Peter French.

I fled for home.

TWENTY-FIVE

SHAKY, I PAUSED AT the carport door to check the thread and tape. Still in place. I unlocked the door, went inside. Had the cops come and arrested Peter French, a former cop himself? *"He thought there was such a thing as justice,"* Diana had told me. Dispensing his own now, apparently. I could still see his glittery eyes, feel his rage as he hit the cowboy again and again. And what had the poor guy done, after all, nothing so much, nothing to get—like that.

Jeez. Poor Diana. He must be tough to live with. I locked the door with the lock Flynn had said was shit and wedged a dining room chair back under the knob. My phone was blinking, and I hurried to check it, but it didn't register any new messages. Two calls, both unavailable on the caller ID. Fred? It was ten here, midnight in Ohio, but I didn't give a damn if I woke him up. I called his cell phone again but got the usual nothing.

Littleton, Ohio, Heather had said, near Cincinnati. I picked up the phone, dialed the operator and got the area code and got a number, an actual number for Fred in Ohio but when I punched it in, it just rang and rang like the cell phone. No answering machine. Still, at least now I knew where he lived.

Wearily, I tugged off the uncomfortable boots and went into the bathroom. The woman in the mirror had crossed the line from daring to tackily grotesque. Hopefully the change had happened on the way home and not at the gallery. "You cheap hussy," I said to the mirror.

The phone rang.

I tore out of the bathroom and got it on the second ring.
"Hello?"

"Hello," said a man's voice, unfamiliar. "Am I speaking to Chloe?"

"Yes, you are."

"Well, *good*."

"Who's this?"

"I've done a little research, Chloe, and I'm very concerned about you." The voice was soft, soft to the point where it would have been tender had there been any love in it. "I think we should talk."

I shivered involuntarily. "Who is this?"

"I believe you were in my office just the other day. This is Dr. Ivan Fowler."

Rosa. Rosa had betrayed me.

OR WAS IT ROSA? I'd parked down the street, but not that far. Had I been the only unfamiliar car around, and he wrote down my license number? I'd been an idiot, going around as if I were invisible, invincible. I took a few deep breaths to get the shiver out of my voice. "Talk? About what?"

"You had a pretty close call, not so long ago."

"I have no idea what you're talking about," I said.

"What was her name? Evangeline?"

"Evangeline," I said blankly.

"I get nervous about husbands myself. Especially these suicidal types, they have nothing to lose." His voice was like some sticky-sweet syrup. Was that what he'd done to trusting Heather over and over—called her and hypnotized her with his sticky voice?

"I prefer wives," he went on. "It's relatively rare that a woman will do what he did. Rare, although it does happen."

I sat down, clutching the phone hard, propping my arms on the counter for support. "Dr. Fowler," I said as evenly as I could, "what does any of this have to do with you calling me at ten o'clock at night?"

"Why, concern for you, of course. I'm a professional, I know the impact of something like that can be enormous. Have you thought about therapy?"

My knees were shaking. "Not really." I was furious at myself, that I could let myself be so intimidated. "Since you're a professional, *Doctor* Fowler," I said, "I'm sure you're not trying to sell me some therapy, so what is the purpose of this call?"

"I could ask you what was the purpose of your visit to my office," he said reasonably. "After all, I am a therapist. Unconsciously, maybe it was a cry for help. You've been through a lot. But consciously, you probably think it had to do with my ex-wife. Well, you have to understand: she won't let go."

"Really."

"The divorce was bitter. And afterward, she spread ugly rumors about me. That I was *stalking* her. She has some unresolved issues about men in general, her father—" He paused. "But of course I can't, in good faith, go into that. Do you like irony?"

"Do I like what?"

He chuckled. "Irony. Here's a piece of it for you. You know how Heather met Terry?"

"No," I said, wanting to hear what he would say.

"She met him through me. I introduced them, so to speak."

Introduced them. Because Terry had seen Heather's collages hanging in his office? The nerve. Just an example of the half-truth a manipulator like him would use.

"Hardly the behavior of a stalker, wouldn't you agree?" he went on. "I thought when she remarried these ugly rumors would stop, she would move on with her life. Then you showed up. The woman I'm seeing now, Sally, you met her, such a wonderful *clear* person. She has no character armor. Heather has so many defenses I'm surprised she can still breathe."

"What are you saying?" I said. "You think Heather sent me?

You're totally wrong. She had nothing to do with that visit. She doesn't even know about it."

"Would she have to? She's subtle."

"What does that mean?"

"All she had to do was win your sympathy, and she's an expert at that, believe me," he said. "You're the victim advocate, dedicated, already on her side. So you ask around, gather up rumors and hearsay and you go on a campaign: a crusade to wipe out that vision of poor Evangeline that's been haunting you."

I clutched the phone, feeling sick, almost faint. It was close enough to the truth, I felt as though he had peered into my soul.

"It must have been horribly traumatic," he went on. "It's skewed your judgment. How have you been sleeping?"

"Fine."

"I'm glad to hear that. But post-traumatic stress can mask itself as many things. I know Tucson's pretty far away from your little hill in Dudley, but if you'd like to come in and talk—I do some consulting, gratis, for the right person."

My little hill? "I'd have to think about it."

"You do that. Sleep well."

He hung up.

SLEEP WELL? Where was he calling from? I checked my caller ID. A pay phone in Tucson. At least it was Tucson but hadn't Lucia told me—Ivan had called Heather constantly, always from different pay phones. Was he going to start doing that to me now?

"Your little hill in Dudley." He actually knew where I lived. Could he have stolen my gun? Leaving me nothing to defend myself with but chairs and silverware? *Flynn.* Should I call Flynn? I picked up the phone. But what did I have on Ivan, really? Did it constitute harassment, calling someone and offering them free counseling? Besides, this wasn't even Flynn's jurisdiction. He would think—God knows what he would think.

I looked around the room, consoling myself with my mini-fortress armed with dining-room chairs and columns of silver-ware. I removed the chair from the front door, walked outside and stood on my porch in the cold, looking down at the town of Old Dudley warily, as if I might see the lights of Dr. Ivan Fowler's darling lime-green Volkswagen heading up my hill for our first therapy session.

How small Old Dudley seemed, constricted by hills. And all of New Dudley, glittering in the distance, fit into a little bowl between two mountains. Space. I needed space. I wished I could just fly away from it all, go someplace I could breathe more freely. With no job, I could, if I had the money.

I walked back inside to my bedroom, turned on the heater and the electric blanket, undressed and put on my pj's, but I wasn't tired at all. Big Foot jumped on the bed, kneading the covers, purring. A cat. Right now, I needed a big barking dog. Through the chinks in all the curtains I felt Ivan's eyes looking in.

Then the sound of a car coming up the hill made me jump. It slowed as if to stop, then kept going. Eleven-thirty. Cars went by my house day and night. Was I going to panic every time?

Why didn't Fred call? I thought mournfully. Not that I was sure I could trust him either. *"Hoodwinked."* That's what Damien had thought. The letter from Terry, possibly phony. And Terry's words, *"weirdly needy—nothing ever enough for him."* A big-time tax evader too.

I clicked on *City Confidential,* Bigfork, Montana, where nobody locked their doors until some guy in a wheelchair murdered someone. Safety was only an illusion. But ha ha, Ivan Fowler wasn't going to drive to Dudley and kill me, like he had possibly killed April, might in the future kill Heather. He was seeing a wonderful clear woman with no character armor.

Dammit, dammit to hell. Where was Fred? You didn't give someone two thousand dollars and then just vanish. It was nearly two a.m. in Littleton. Was he there, sleeping, dead to the world? What if he was just dead? *What about Sam?*

I lay there debating whether I should call the police in Littleton, tell them it was a dire emergency, have them run by the house to check, rouse him if necessary.

I had most of the two thousand dollars, and I'd certainly earned it between the trips to Tucson and browbeating Heather to meet with him. Besides, it was only money. *I would go to Littleton myself.* I could check out Fred on his own territory, talk to people who knew him now, not as Fred the dead, or Terry's horrible brother. And if he wasn't home, I could camp out on his doorstep till he returned.

People always come home eventually.

Ohio

TWENTY-SIX

I'VE NEVER UNDERSTOOD why people like aisle seats, sacrificing a view of the world from thirty-three thousand feet for easy access to the restroom. The sky was cloudless for a thousand miles, with a thousand miles of brown winter emptiness below. Then we flew into the clouds and out of the West and I began to consider where I was going. When I think of Ohio it has the same mystical resonance as New Jersey.

What actually was I doing? What if Fred never showed up at his house? But I would still be able to check him out, find people who knew him, and besides, he'd told me he was going home and there was a big and thriving business to run. If worse came to worse I could go to the main office. Unable to concentrate on the airline magazine in my lap, I dozed fitfully until we began to descend.

"Going back to see the folks in Cincinnati?" asked the man in the seat next to me.

"What?" I said, startled. I looked at him; a salesman type, brown eyes, beige hair, bland. "No. Not really. I'm going to Littleton."

"No kidding." The man chuckled. "I know it pretty well. But most people *leave* Littleton, grow up there and move somewhere else soon as they graduate high school. Not much of a town anymore." His tone sounded as though he were talking about the Village of the Damned.

I raised my eyebrows. "Oh?"

He looked apologetic. "No offense. I grew up in a small town myself. In fact, we played basketball against Littleton."

"Then maybe you know a good motel there?"

He laughed. "This must be your first visit."

"Yes. I'm not even sure how to get to Littleton."

"Well, you won't have a choice of motels, there's only one. Let's see, Littleton's about forty-five minutes from the airport. You'll be coming off the freeway onto Route 29 and then to—" He stopped. "Hope you got a map."

"Well—"

"Better get one. The motel is just before you hit Littleton proper, on the left. It's called the Wayside."

The plane broke through the clouds. Below was Cincinnati, everything covered in snow with the Ohio River a thick ribbon of pure silver winding through it. Ohio or not, it looked like an enchanted kingdom. We passed low over the silver ribbon, then the plane circled, glided down and hit the runway with one little bump.

"Welcome to Cincinnati, folks," said the pilot. "The temperature outside is a brisk fifteen degrees."

THE RENTAL CAR KEYS were like slivers of ice in my hand. My black boots with two-inch heels were awkward in the snow but they were the only boots I owned. Gloves. I had to get some gloves right away. Luckily my full-length black coat was warm, left over from when I lived in New York. It had a moth hole on one sleeve and too much shoulder padding but at least it was black. I opened the map I'd bought in the airport terminal, put it on the passenger seat and started the car.

It was close to five, and twilight dark. The freeway was jammed with rush-hour cars, their lights ghostly, but the traffic thinned after a while and then I turned onto Route 29. I stopped at a convenience store just off the freeway and bought some coffee and two hot dogs. There hadn't been any food on the plane except for some dry pretzels and I felt like I was starving.

"Cold tonight," said the big bald man at the counter cheerily. "S'posed to get down to *five*."

"How far is Littleton?" I asked.

"'Bout thirty miles. Take it easy out there in the snow. Don't you get lost."

Don't you get lost. Back outside the freezing cold found gaps in my coat and made my teeth chatter. I got back in the car. Already the hot dogs were cold, but I wolfed them down. The heater had warmed things up by now, but my arms and legs were cramped with tension. I decided I wouldn't try to locate Fred tonight. I'd bought a book at a fancy bookstore at the airport, in love with its title, *Motherless Brooklyn,* but all I wanted was to be warm in bed watching television. Ancient vestigial television memories rose in my mind. Something like *The Rockford Files*. Yes.

I headed down the road, which seemed to get narrower and narrower with every mile. Houses were scattered on the low snowy hills along the way, lights inside blurred by the twilight. I was the only one out driving. I drove through several tiny towns; so close to the road, I could see white plastic chairs frigid on the porches of the houses, see televisions on, through the windows.

It felt as though I'd entered another world entirely, one that had nothing to do with my life or my concerns. I was moving through a vacuum. Everything now was a silvery blue-gray, the snow, the sky, except for the sharp black outlines of trees, and a tinge of rose and gold in the west. The whole world around me was as beautiful as any world I'd ever seen, and twice as lonely.

Then it was dark.

I SAW THE BLUE neon sign first, WAYSIDE MOTEL. The place was small, red brick with white trim and just off the road on the left. Tiny lights glowed over some of the units. I counted two cars. Not the height of the tourist season, if there was a tourist season. I parked in front of the office and got out.

A sign on the door said OPEN. Ten steps and I was chilled to the bone. Inside, it was warm enough to make you weary, and smelled of burned chocolate. The walls were dark wood veneer, the carpeting a dull blue. On every surface were little china baskets of dusty artificial generic flowers on plastic lace doilies. There were two on the front desk, next to a bell. I pushed it and it screeched.

"Hello?" I called.

An old woman, with pure white hair in tiny curls, came out from a door behind the desk. "My goodness, I'm sorry. I didn't hear you come in," she said. "I must have dozed off. You look cold. There's coffee over there."

She gestured with her head at a Mr. Coffee at the end of the counter which accounted for the burned-chocolate smell. Ancient coffee.

"No, thanks," I said. "I'd just like a single room."

She pushed over a form for me to fill out. "Now where would you be coming from on a night like tonight?"

"The airport. I thought I'd look up a friend of mine, Fred Barnett," I said as I filled out the form. "He lives here in Littleton."

"You don't *say.*"

"I guess I'll wait till morning to find him though." I handed her my Visa card. "I'm not sure of his address. Maybe you know of him?"

"Why, that name does sound familiar. But I'm not from around here. I came down from Michigan to help out my daughter. My son-in-law owns the motel, *he* grew up here, but he's in Cincinnati at the hospital there." She paused and lowered her voice. "*Tests.* That's why my daughter called me, so she can be with him. It doesn't look good."

"Oh, dear," I said.

"The Lord does send us trials," said the old woman.

"Still, it's how we confront them that matters," I said, falling right in.

I pushed the form toward her, and as I did, she patted my hand. "You're a good girl," she said.

LIGHT SNOW was falling outside when I walked to room 11, which turned out to be almost as cold inside as out. I flipped on the light, found controls for the big box heater under the window, and turned it on full blast. The smell of singed dust filled the air. Most of the room was bed, covered with a faded blue quilted comforter. The walls were the same dark wood veneer as the front office, with a basket of the same kind of generic flowers on a blond wood chest of drawers. The TV was chained to the wall so I wouldn't carry it off with me when I left.

I threw my carry-on onto the bed, and still wearing my coat, went into the bathroom. A strip of paper wrapped round the toilet seat certified it had been sanitized thoroughly. Thirsty, I tore off the wrapping on a glass by the sink, filled it and drank. The fluorescent light over the mirror revealed a dozen lines in my face I hadn't even known I had.

Discouraged, I came back out, sat down on the bed and opened the drawer of the bedside table. Inside was a Bible and the phone book.

I looked up Fred and there he was, listed, at 120 Poplar Street.

I thought about calling but instead I took a hot shower, crawled into bed, pulled up the heavy covers and clicked on the TV. I fell asleep almost at once, and woke up at eleven p.m., nine Arizona time, to the light still on, Jay Leno yakking, and the room so hot I could hardly move. I threw off the comforter, staggered to the heater, turned it down, turned off the TV and the light.

I lay awake most of the rest of the night, wondering what I'd thought was so great about leaving my comfortable house, my cat, my life, to end up in an old motel in a cold climate. But at least here I didn't have to put chairs under the doorknobs or stack silverware in front of the windows. Maybe I wouldn't even dream about Flynn.

TWENTY-SEVEN

WHEN I WOKE, the sun had lit up the thin fiberglass curtains and shot a knife of light through a chink where they didn't quite meet. I looked at my watch. Eight o'clock. I sat up in bed, grabbed the phone and dialed Fred's number. No answer.

He could be gone by now, already at work. Sporting goods. A chain of sporting goods in a town like Littleton? He must commute to Cincinnati, to his main office. Unless he was home, of course, had been all along, shot dead in his living room, by his own hand. What about Sam? Shot dead as well, spared the pain of living? That seemed a little over the top. Cool it, I thought, seek out the sane.

Was Sam's mother back from her trip? I looked in the phone book to see if Fred's ex still had his last name and was listed, but didn't find any more Barnetts.

I got up, showered, dressed, and walked outside. The sun shining off the snow was so bright it hurt my eyes. Everything was blanketed in white, except, thank God, the roads and the parking lot. The snow crunched beneath my boots, crisp with the cold. I turned my ankle getting into the rental car.

Damn, damn, *damn*. I wanted: bacon, eggs, toast, orange juice, and lots of coffee, good coffee. I got a container of orange juice, a sweet roll, and bad coffee at the convenience store across from the motel. The woman at the register, in her forties, colorless, had a mean curl to her mouth as if angry about having to work a register, or maybe just about life itself in general.

"What do most people do for a living around here?" I asked her.

"Honey, they don't." Her voice was scornful. "They work somewhere else. Commute to Cincinnati, mostly."

"No sporting goods store?"

She stared at me.

"Never mind. Could you tell me how I get to Poplar Street?"

IT TOOK ONLY FIVE MINUTES to get through town: video store, bar, arts and crafts supplies, a coffee shop, a church. Then I turned onto Poplar. HERITAGE ESTATES said the sign at the entrance. A small development. Snow was piled on the edges of the street that wound round brick houses, red, white, and tan, set maybe a quarter acre apart. An older development from the size of the trees, in three basic styles, all variations on ranch.

Fred, rich, with an empire, chose to live here? Well, Terry had chosen to be buried in Littleton, it must have some mysterious charm I just couldn't see. Maybe in summer it would be different, people outside, big leafy trees, lawn mowers going, children skateboarding, but now in winter it seemed utterly abandoned, as if the houses were empty boxes, put on display.

Number 120 was several curves down, near the back edge of the development. Snowy farm fields stretched beyond it. It was a tan brick house with gray-green shutters, the driveway a pristine rectangle of snow. No one had been in or out of that driveway for a while. I parked at the curb and got out, shoving my freezing ungloved hands deep into my pockets as I trudged up the rectangle.

The door, gray-green as well, had a big brass knocker, but the frame had a doorbell. I pushed and heard no echoing chime. I lifted the knocker, so cold it sent daggers of pain through my hand, and rapped sharply three or four times. The sound reverberated loudly but no one came.

Most of the windows had curtains, drawn closed. I trudged around the house through the snow till I found one I could see in. I stood on tiptoe and saw a large room, brick fireplace, orange shag carpet, two matching brown leather recliners side by side facing a television. Christ. A room in the heart, the very heart, of Middle America.

And neat. Not just neat but empty, so empty. No newspapers or magazines lying around. Not even a *TV Guide,* at least from my vantage point.

I went back around the house to the big garage. The shuttered windows there matched the rest, but these were uncurtained. I peered through the closest and saw one car inside, a '56 Chevy. I mean I think it was a '56. Tail fins. Turquoise and white. Ah. It all made sense now. I'd fallen through a time warp and was back in the fifties. I'd entered the Twilight Zone.

But surely Fred, of Barnett Enterprises, didn't drive around in that Chevy. He must have another car. From the looks of the driveway he hadn't been home for a while. Which meant that probably his bullet-riddled body wasn't lying on the floor somewhere in this house.

"Hello?" said a woman's voice.

I jumped guiltily and turned in the direction of the voice.

A woman in dark glasses was standing at the corner of the house, wearing a brown knit floppy hat, a pink chenille bathrobe partly covered with a heavy brown coat, and big black boots. With most of her hidden it was hard to tell, but probably she was middle-aged. Her nose was red.

"Can I *help* you?" Her voice was accusing.

"I'm sorry," I said. "I was looking for Fred Barnett."

"Fred?"

"Yes. This is his house, isn't it?"

"And who are *you?*" She sniffed loudly. "Selling something?"

"I'm not selling anything," I said. "I'm a friend of his."

"You can't be much of a friend or you'd know he doesn't live here."

"But he's listed here in the phone book," I said.

"That's Fred Barnett *senior.* Neither of the Barnett boys have really lived in Littleton for years. The house—" She sneezed suddenly, pulled a tissue out of the coat pocket and blew her nose. "The house belonged to Mr. And Mrs. Barnett senior, they're both deceased."

I should have known. This was the house where Fred and Terry had grown up. The house where Terry had sat with his mother, dying, while the snow fell outside. Clearly he'd loved his mother very much. Was that it? Why Terry couldn't be faithful? Too afraid to take on responsibility and return to the pain of that world of loss?

And where had Fred of Barnett Enterprises been while his mother lay dying?

"Hello?" The woman was staring at me.

"So who lives here then?"

"No one. Fred keeps the utilities on." She jabbed at the air with the tissue. "Don't ask me why. He only comes here maybe every two or three months."

"I'm from out of state." I held my ice-cold hands out, palms up, in a gesture I hoped was placating. "We really are friends. All I have is his cell phone number and I haven't been able to reach him. I've been worried."

There was a long silence, while the woman looked up at the sky, then down at the ground. She shuffled her feet. "You should talk to Fanny Snyder," she said finally.

"Who's that?"

She sneezed again and wiped her nose. "I have this god-awful cold. I stayed home from work to rest and now I'm probably getting pneumonia. You go back into town, all right?"

I nodded.

"You can't miss her house, it's right on the main street, block and a half past the Methodist church on your left. Five-oh-five. A white frame two-story. Fanny's the one that looks after things here for Fred. It's just like her; she'd be running the whole town if there was anything left of it to run. Tell her Dee sent you." She sneezed again. "Excuse me, I'm going back to bed."

THE SNYDER HOUSE was on a small hill, the front yard terraced. I climbed the brick steps that led up to the porch, wide enough to accommodate one of those old-fashioned gliders. In summer you could sit out here and watch the street, feet propped up on the railing, but now the railing was iced with a thick layer of snow. The door was varnished oak with two little windows but they were curtained and I couldn't see in.

I rang the bell. After a moment the door opened and the air around me warmed up considerably. A large woman in wire-rimmed glasses and an untidy bun of gray hair looked out. She wore a red apron over a blouse printed with merry antique cars, neither of which concealed what used to be called a bosom.

"Fanny Snyder?" I said.

"Yes?" She peered at me over her wire rims. "What can I do for you, young woman?"

"Uh, my name's, oh, Chloe Newcombe." Something about her direct stare made me stammer slightly. "I was looking for Fred Barnett and a woman named Dee told me to come talk to you. I'm a friend of his."

Her face softened. "Goodness gracious. My, my, my. Don't just stand out there, come in, come in, out of the cold." She stepped back and I walked into a hall carpeted in deep rose.

She hovered around me solicitously. "Now take off your coat, hang it right there."

I hung it on a hook near the door.

"Look at you," she said sternly. "Those fancy boots won't keep your feet warm. And for heaven's sake, where are your *gloves?*"

"I flew in from Arizona," I said apologetically.

"Well, I got six or seven pair somewhere around here, don't

you leave without some. Come on back into the kitchen, warmest place in the house." She looked at her watch. "Nine o'clock. You had a good breakfast?"

"I hardly had anything." A voice rang in my ears, mournful as a child's. Was it really mine?

"That's not good. Come on back to the kitchen, I'll fix you something." It wasn't an invitation, more like a command.

I followed obediently past a living room, lace curtains at the windows and a lot of dark wood furniture, not veneer, past a flight of stairs, with a runner in the same deep rose carpeting, to the kitchen, all old white appliances and speckled linoleum on the floor. Bright crayoned drawings on yellowing construction paper hung on the walls.

"Grandkids did the artwork when they were little," said Fanny, with a touch of pride. "You sit down right there next to the window."

I sat at a round table, near a large drawing of a black and red fighter plane dropping a series of bombs like little turds. Above a row of neon-purple African violets, the window was all steamed up. I had an urge to write my name on it.

"Milk noodles," said Fanny triumphantly. She set a bowl in front of me.

And that's what they looked like, wide noodles in a rich broth of buttery milk. I dug in. I hadn't had a real meal since I left Arizona. The broth had an almost spicy edge to it. She watched me eat.

"Oh, my go—gosh, it's *heavenly*," I said.

"You've got to brown the butter. I make the noodles from scratch like my mother did, it's an old Mennonite recipe. My mother was Mennonite until she went to college. The preacher came to see my grandfather, just before she left, said to him"— she snorted—"'I'd rather see my daughter dead and buried than go to college.'"

She hovered till I was finished, then sat down and looked

at me sharply. "You said Arizona, so you must have been a friend of Terry's too."

"Yes, I was."

"The last I heard they hadn't arrested anyone for his murder. Is that true?"

I nodded.

Fanny sighed. "Terry's buried next to his folks, at the Presbyterian cemetery. Fred had me handle the arrangements; Mary Barnett and Terry had planned everything out when *she* was dying, so there wasn't too much for me to do, really." She paused and looked at me questioningly. "Terry's wife didn't come to the funeral. I wondered why not."

"Some people can't handle funerals," I said.

"No one can handle funerals," said Fanny sternly. "You just go anyway. Think how Fred must have felt, he and Terry at odds for so many years. And Fred freshly divorced too."

"Fanny," I said. "What were Fred and Terry at odds about?"

"Plain old-fashioned jealousy's the root of it." She looked sad. "Fred Barnett senior wasn't around much—school superintendent—and Terry was his mother's favorite. That always rankled Fred." She shrugged. "Maybe it drove him too. He was the one who turned out to be successful. Terry was a dabbler. I'm not surprised, sometimes favorites don't try as hard. At the funeral people were going on, you know the way they do, since no one had been charged with killing Terry."

"Going on about what?"

"Why, that Fred might have done it."

"*No.*"

Fanny tsk-tsked. "It's just nonsense."

"People—" I paused. "Well, people don't seem to like Fred very much."

"That's right." Fanny looked at me thoughtfully. "Fred has a lot of drive and he likes to win, his father was the same way. So people are hard on him; a small town like this, you don't want to stand out, act too special." She sighed. "His dad wasn't ever around, like I said, so it was Mary Barnett that kept everything going in the home. How those boys loved their mother, do anything to please her. Terry knew how to do that naturally, but Fred, he always tried too hard."

"I need to talk to him," I said. "Dee told me you handle his affairs here."

"Only since his divorce. His wife used to. His ex, I should say."

"I came all the way here and I'd really like to see him."

"He lives outside Cincinnati, about a half-hour trip. But—" She paused, her brow wrinkling.

"I don't have much time," I urged. "I have to go back to Arizona tomorrow."

"He's been out of town, some conference in Detroit, but I know he's due back this morning. He'll be home now most likely, because after these conferences, he likes to—what's that word he uses? Decompress?"

"Decompress," I said.

She stood up, took my bowl and spoon, carried them to the sink, turned on the water. Then she looked back at me. "Well," she said, "I'll tell you how to get there. Let me write it down. But you should wait a bit. Maybe till afternoon."

TWENTY-EIGHT

I LEFT FANNY'S feeling pleased with myself. Now it made sense. Fred had been out of town. At a conference in Detroit. He must have kept his cell phone off so he wouldn't be distracted. Since I had plenty of time before going to see him, I drove slowly down the main street till I got to the Presbyterian church, where Fanny had said Terry was buried. It was a substantial building of beige brick with a white spire. The graveyard was there beside it on the right, with a high black wrought-iron fence around it. Outside in front of the church, a man was shoveling snow off the sidewalk. I stopped and rolled down my window.

"Excuse me?" I called.

He bounded over. "Hi, there! What can I do for you?" Under a hat with ear flaps, his skin was rosy, his smile big and filled with improbably perfect dentures.

"I wonder if you could tell me where Terry Barnett is buried?"

The smile faded and his face turned solemn. "Of course. Ah, you wouldn't by any chance be"—his voice turned hopeful—"the *wife?*"

"No, I'm just a friend."

"Oh." He looked down at his feet sadly for a moment, then looked up and gestured with his head at the graveyard. "He's buried right alongside his mom and dad. Barnetts were here way back before the town incorporated. Cemetery's full of them along with Snyders, Haskells, O'Reillys—"

"O'Reillys?" I cut in. "I've heard of Mike O'Reilly. Wasn't he Terry's best friend?"

"That's right." He ruminated. "I guess Mike'll be buried here too. Not soon, I hope. It's kind of sad, the way people's kids go off to the cities, don't care anymore about being buried where their families have been for generations. This'll all just be a piece of history soon." Then he chuckled. "*Mike O'Reilly.* Real piece of work, that Mike." He paused. "But you can't help liking him."

"Does he still live here? In Littleton?"

"Sure does. At his grandparents' place, just outside town off Sycamore Road. Not too far from the highway as you go out headed southwest."

He shifted his weight on the shovel. "Seems like just the other day, Mary Barnett would come to the cemetery with Mike and her boys, they had picnics among the graves. Some folks thought that was morbid, but as Mary always said, the dead aren't half as scary as the living."

"Sorry." He looked abashed. "I didn't mean to go on and on. You asked me where Terry was buried. You go through the gate, straight down the center road, take the first left, Terry's down about four graves." He glanced at my car. "That's a rental, isn't it? You used to driving in snow?"

"No."

"Maybe park by the gate, walk it from the street then."

I turned to go.

"Miss?"

"Yes?"

"Church is open if you feel the need."

"Thank you," I said.

I drove down to the big wrought-iron gate in the middle of the fence, both sides open wide, and saw what he meant by walking it. Acres of seamless white, unplowed. Big skeleton trees, a lot of headstones. I got out and put on some gloves Fanny had given me before I left; green chunky wool with a design of black and white snowflakes and a big hole in the middle finger of the right hand.

The snow crackled under my fancy useless boots. I trudged

down the center road, and turned left. My feet were so numb by now I felt no pain.

Down four graves, three Snyders and a Haskell, I came to a small temporary-looking metal cross, next to two large granite headstones: Mary Elizabeth Barnett, Frederick George Barnett, the letters forming their names dark and permanent-looking against the gray granite.

In front of the metal cross, on top of a mound of frozen pale roses, lay a wreath of holly, the leaves still a deep shiny green, the berries bright red. Gingerly, I pushed the flowers and wreath back a little, cleared snow around the cross and uncovered a metal plaque.

TERENCE HAROLD BARNETT.

Really, really dead, laid to earth next to his mother. The permanence of it all softened the anger I'd been feeling. I stood still for a moment, thinking this, then something caught my eye, jutting out from the flowers. A wooden handle. I picked it up. It had a sharp beveled blade. For a moment it made no sense, then I understood. It was some kind of woodworking tool, for Terry the carpenter. Had Fred put it there? It seemed to be the kind of thing he might do. It made me sadder than the grave, the cross, the wreath, and all the flowers.

I looked around. Beyond the three Barnett gravestones were more Barnetts, a George, an Agnes, and a Henry, but there was no one alive except me in the entire graveyard, no one on foot passing by the wrought-iron fence, no car on the street.

"Terry," I said. "I want to help. For Fred and Heather. Give me a sign?"

The silence was so profound it rang in my ears. I waited, thinking of Heather, Fred, myself even. How hard it was to be sure of anyone's love. And April. How did she fit in? Or did she fit in at all? Behind me I heard a car go by on the street. Someone shouted something out the window. Then the silence returned. I waited some more until the cold got to me, then I walked numbly back through the snow to my car.

I RETURNED TO the Wayside Motel, changed into dry socks, and put my boots on the heater while I called my neighbor Lourdes, who was supposed to be feeding Big Foot.

"Everything is fine here," she said. "I don't understand why you went to *Ohio*, Chloe."

"I had to."

"A job?"

"Kind of."

"Well, your phone's been ringing its head off. If it rings next time I'm there, you want me to answer? It might be your *boss*." Her voice lilted up, hopeful for me. "Maybe she wants to give you back your job. I could give her the number of the motel."

Maybe it *was* Lucinda. Or Fred, back from his meeting and trying to reach me. On the other hand, maybe it was Ivan Fowler. "No," I said hurriedly. "Don't answer it."

My feet relatively warm again, I tugged the boots back on, relatively dry, and went out to the car, got in and headed west out of town toward where Fred lived.

I LOOKED AGAIN AT the house number Fanny had written down for me, looked again at the house in front of me. I'd done it twice and both times they matched. The house was a three-story white brick with columns, and I guessed six bedrooms at least, standing on several acres. Fred really was rolling in it, like Stuart had said. The two thousand dollars he'd mailed me was probably just spare change to him.

I parked behind a Jeep Cherokee, Fred's? But wouldn't he park in the four-car garage that dominated one end of the house? The long driveway and all the walks and sidewalks were clear of snow. As I got out, I noticed a woman sitting on an ornate wooden bench by the front door, half hidden by a column. She was smoking. I headed toward her. It took a while.

"Hi," I said. "Fred Barnett lives here, doesn't he?"

She took a long drag on her cigarette and looked me over for a moment before she answered. She wore a neon-pink ski parka and matching pants, fur gloves and fur-lined boots. Her hair was probably not naturally blond, but whoever had colored it had been an artist. She looked rich and pampered and the outdated shoulder pads on my black coat swelled to absurd proportions.

"Yes, he does," she said finally. She coughed, several times; patted her chest. "Excuse me," she said. "My iron lung. The creep won't let me smoke inside, so I'm out here freezing my butt off."

I blinked at the contrast between her words and her polished appearance. "Is he home?"

She nodded. "I came over to get him to sign something, but of course you can never talk to Fred until he's good and ready." She blew out a stream of smoke and looked me over some more.

I stepped back.

She smiled a little sardonically. "Don't worry. I don't give a shit who you are. He's round the back, on the court."

The court. I stared at her. He was playing tennis in the snow?

"Go on back, give it a try. Why not?" She laughed ominously and gestured at a stone walkway. "Just follow that round the house."

I trudged past privet trimmed into a thick hedge, till I came to an opening and walked through. I heard the sounds first— *boomity, boomity, boomity*—then, as the walk turned again, I saw the court; basketball, not tennis, surrounded with mounds of snow from where it had been cleared.

In the center, some friend of Fred's, a medium-sized man in his forties, wearing a navy blue band of fleece to protect his ears, navy blue sweatshirt, shorts, and big athletic shoes, was dribbling a basketball.

Shorts. In this weather. His legs were tautly muscled as if he worked out a lot. On his face was a look of such utter concentration his features were a blank mask. *Boomity, boomity,*

boomity, faster and faster, as if the ball were an enemy he was determined to subdue. He threw it then and it swished through the net.

"Excuse me?" I said loudly.

He retrieved the ball and started dribbling again, as if I weren't even there, but unless he were deaf, he had to have heard me. Rude. A guy on a power trip.

"Hey!" I shouted.

He stopped dribbling. "Goddamnit!" He threw the ball hard and it lodged deep in a mound of snow. He glared at me. "What the hell do you want?"

"I'm looking for Fred Barnett." I paused and added defensively, "It's important."

"Oh, yeah?" He put his hands on his hips. "You don't decide what's important, I do," he said arrogantly. "And I don't work out of my goddamn house. Sales reps are supposed to call my *office.*"

"I'm not a sales rep," I said.

"Well, *whoever* the hell you are, you got something to say to me, you call my office. That's how it's done. Make an appointment."

"I told you, I'm looking for Fred. And I don't even know who *you* are."

"Who the hell do you think I am?" he said. "Some guy who wandered onto the court from the street?"

"What do you— *What?*"

"*I'm* Fred Barnett, stupid. What were you expecting?" He laughed nastily.

"I—you—it's—" I stuttered.

For a moment he looked at me in disgust, then he turned and strode away to the ball in the snow, retrieved it and started to dribble again. *Boomity, boomity, boomity.*

A lot of things suddenly made sense. Through a glass darkly, then face-to-face. Embarrassed, I stood for a moment in shock as Fred Barnett pointedly ignored me. *"When Fred comes into a room, all the life goes out of it."*

I turned and trudged back round the house to my car, the sound of Fred Barnett's basketball reverberating in my ears. Fred the dead. On the snow by the ornate wooden bench where the woman had been sitting was a cigarette butt, imperfectly snuffed, sending a thin stream of smoke into the air, but the woman was gone.

TWENTY-NINE

"DAD, WHY DON'T YOU just tell her," Sam had said. Yeah, right.

It was three-thirty. I drove back the way I'd come, munching on an apple Fanny had given me, along with the gloves, on my way out of her house. Just before Littleton, I stopped at an Ameri-Stop Qwik Mart and went inside. The place was very hot, the windows blurred with steam, an ancient Ferlin Husky song playing softly from a radio. A dark-haired thirtyish woman in brand-new jeans and a bright red down vest was desultorily tidying up the shelves of Doritos, Fritos, potato chips, and bean dip.

"Hi!" I said. "Are you from around here, by any chance?"

"All my life," she said cheerily. "For what *that's* worth."

"I'm looking for Sycamore Road."

"It's just ahead, if you'd of kept going you'd of seen it. Who're you looking for on Sycamore?"

"The O'Reilly place?"

"That's off Sycamore, on Chestnut. You go—"

"Wait," I said. "Let me write it down."

THE LANDSCAPE WAS hilly here, dotted occasionally with big old farmhouses, all of them white. The matching snow lay in drifts on the hills and in the valleys. Overhead the clouds had begun to thicken, filtering the sunlight down to a silvery gray. I drove slowly, glancing from time to time at the directions I'd written in my notebook. Left at Sycamore. Two miles on right. Pass farm with white picket fence. Chestnut. House, green shutters.

I saw the farm, up ahead, passed it and turned onto Chestnut. It was a smaller road, though not much smaller, and still paved. Everything in the state of Ohio seemed have been paved, tamed, and fenced in long ago. As I turned, the clouds closed in and completely hid the sun. Close to four o'clock and already dusk. I felt far away from anything familiar, as if I could drive through this landscape forever and still get nowhere.

I focused again on the directions, looking for a house with dark green shutters. There it was, a big old Victorian farmhouse set back from the road, O'REILLY in red paint on the mailbox. The driveway, thank God, was cleared of snow.

I drove up slowly. An old gray Ford truck was parked just under the basketball hoop nailed above the double garage door. A far cry from the elaborate court at Fred's. I parked behind the truck, got out, crunched through the snow, and climbed the rickety wooden steps up to a wide porch.

The house was shabby, flakes of white paint littered the damp porch floor. By the door was an old-fashioned chrome-and-vinyl kitchen chair, the vinyl marbled yellow, with a big tear in the middle, stuffing leaking out. No doorbell, just a plain wood door. I knocked.

No one came.

"Hello?" I called loudly.

Then light snow began to fall.

Damn. I didn't want to get stuck out here. I went hurriedly back down the steps. I should give up but I only had the rest of this day. I'd have to leave for the airport in the morning. The snow fell faster. Futility overwhelmed me.

Then I heard something. Music. From behind the house. A song I knew, though I couldn't place it right away. A girl group. I walked gingerly through the snow and ice toward the back. Smelled, somewhere, wood burning. The light snow had already turned into big heavy flakes.

"'My one and only—'"

"'Baby,'" I finished. The Ronettes, singing "Be My Baby," transporting me out of this world of snow and ice to an ancient golden summer, the music drifting through a balmy evening. For some reason this cheered me up considerably.

I rounded the back and saw the source of the music; coming from a smaller building, about a hundred yards from the house. Partially obscured by the snow, the place looked relatively new, boards painted white with no trim, a minimalist style of construction. The music changed as I approached.

"Sugar Mountain." Ah. So sweet in the icy cold.

As I reached the door, Neil Young's voice yearned for the barkers and the colored balloons and I almost didn't want to knock. But I did, then knocked again, louder, because I didn't think anyone could hear me over the music. "Hello!" I shouted. *"Hello!!"*

I heard a shout, muffled by the music.

"What?" I called.

"Come in! It's not locked!"

I turned the knob and pushed open the door. Heat blasted out. Inside, the walls seemed to be made of silver. An enormous cast-iron wood-burning stove stood in the middle of the room. I didn't see anyone.

"Mike? Mike O'Reilly?" I shouted.

"Who's there?"

"I'm looking for Mike O'Reilly!"

I still didn't see anyone. I advanced into the room. The music stopped. A man in a red and green plaid flannel shirt came round the wood-burning stove. "What—" He stopped.

"Chloe," he said. "You like Neil Young? I always did. I kind of got out of music till I discovered Napster. Before they made you pay, I downloaded almost five hundred songs. Think of it! Not just the oldies that I used to like, but all the best rock groups ever, all in my library! I got R.E.M. *Automatic for the People,* Springsteen, of course, U2, and Nirvana. *Nevermind.*

It's great!! And then, my God, there's even newer ones too. Radiohead!!"

It was Fred. It was Mike O'Reilly. It was Fred.

"I *knew* it," I said.

THERE WAS A LONG silence while we stared at each other. I could almost hear the snow outside falling to the ground it was so quiet.

"Why?" I said finally.

"Credibility."

I stared at him. "*Fred* has credibility?"

He came a little closer, looking earnest. "He's Terry's only living relative. That carries a lot of weight."

"Not with Heather, it doesn't," I said. "She knows Fred and Terry haven't spoken for years."

"That's just it. Don't you see? Terry and I always kept in touch. The letter I showed you was to me, not Fred. If something screwy was going on in the marriage, Heather had to figure I'd know about it. Even if Terry told her Fred was a jerk, Heather wouldn't be on her guard with him like she would be with me."

It kind of made sense, but I felt hurt, left out of the loop. "You could have told me," I said.

He shrugged disconsolately. "I could tell you didn't trust me, the way you stood up for Heather. I didn't know if you'd go so far as to lie for me."

"So you went away and left me hanging. You never even answered your phone."

Fred, no, Mike looked contrite. "Don't be mad. I accidentally left my cell at Jill's house, my ex, when I dropped off Sam. I got it back this morning." He ran his fingers through his hair. It had grown out of the good-haircut category since I'd seen him last and he needed a shave. "It hasn't been that long and I called you all day today."

"Great," I said. "You want to hear what I've been doing today?" And I told him.

Mike began to laugh. "You tracked down Fred! That's amazing. A real charmer, huh? The fancy blonde's his ex. Nancy. I can't believe he makes her smoke outside in the middle of winter. Well, yes, I can. It's just like him. No wonder she hates him." He plopped down on an old leather couch, still laughing.

"I don't see what's so hilarious," I said huffily. "It was embarrassing."

It was boiling in the room. I took off my coat, walked over, and sat next to Mike.

He looked at me apologetically. "Look, I'm really sorry. I'll nuke some coffee, okay? We'll talk."

He got up, headed to the back, where there was a makeshift kitchen with a refrigerator and sink. I looked around. Through the windows the snow fell steadily outside, filling the room with a pale light that shone off the silver walls which had pink fluff showing at the edges. Insulation, I realized, shoved in between the wood studs; the walls hadn't been drywalled yet. Everything had a temporary feeling to it, the only thing that looked new and intact was a desk with a computer, and a couple of elaborate speakers.

"This place has saved my life," said Mike, returning with two cups of coffee. "Terry and I built it when he was looking after his mom. The big house gives me the creeps. I spent too much time there, watching my grandparents, well, basically, *dying*. When they finally did die, they left me everything 'cause I took care of them—a bunch of money and the house—so I quit working."

"You worked?" I took a sip of the coffee and looked at him doubtfully. "Doing what?"

"Jeez. Don't give me that look. Believe it or not, I was the A number one salesperson for Barnett's Sporting Goods."

"You worked for *Fred?*"

He nodded. "I was good too. Not just good, but fantastic, the best. I made a lot of money. Jill, my ex, got to go to grad school, we had a really nice house—then, I don't know, something happened. First I lost track of Jill and Sam. Then I lost track of myself. I'd be pitching some idea to a group and I'd go all clammy. Words would be coming out of my mouth and I didn't even know who was saying them. When I quit, I thought maybe I could become some kind of artist, like Terry." He sighed. "But I couldn't even get it together to finish putting sheetrock on these walls."

"But you got it together enough to come out to Arizona."

He nodded. "Terry getting murdered changed my life. Put me back on track, I could feel the old energy coming back."

He stood up, turned on lights, walked around the room, closing all the curtains. "There's a blizzard out there and I bet you don't know how to drive in the snow. You might as well sleep over."

"In the big house with your dead grandparents?"

"There's a room in back where Sam sleeps when he's here." He came back to the couch. "Look. Since I was pretending to be Fred, I couldn't tell you everything. I had two theories and I kind of focused on Heather but Fred is just as viable, really." He shrugged.

"Fred?"

"Want some chili? I was just about to heat some up. I make up big batches and I live off it for days. Gringo chili, not Southwestern. But it's pretty good."

"Sour cream? Shredded cheese?"

"Sure." The chili was spicy and sweet with a touch of cinnamon.

"Good, huh," said Mike. "I put in a little honey."

"It's great. Now, what about Fred?"

"At the visitation—" He sighed. "It was awful, people filing by this open coffin and inside it was *Terry*." His voice thickened. "But it wasn't. His spirit was gone." He shuddered. "I took Fred aside, and I said I know you and Terry had problems but we need to find out who did this. And Fred said, if Terry chose to lead the kind of life where he got himself murdered, then so be it. In other words, he deserved it."

I shivered. "Cold," I said.

"That's Fred, a bitter guy, and after Nancy told him she wanted a divorce he got even worse."

"Broken heart?" I said.

Mike snorted. "More like ego. And she got a chunk of his money too. I don't know what he expected, he treated her like shit. He treats everyone like shit once he thinks he has them."

"Well, you have to do better than tell me Fred's a jerk, if you're planning on him being a suspect. And he's got nothing financial to gain from Terry's death, Heather gets all the money."

"God knows what lurks in Fred's cold heart," said Mike darkly. "Vengeance, maybe."

"Vengeance for what?"

"God, I don't know. For Terry being Terry. Like Fred was deranged from his divorce and had to blame somebody. Let me finish. For the visitation, I had to borrow a blazer from Fred. My old jackets all had moth holes in them. I forgot to return it that day. It was just hanging in my closet and one day I took it out for some reason, and I went through the pockets. Guess what I found?"

"A gun."

"No. An airline ticket stub. Fred went to Tucson early in January, right after his divorce went through."

"You're kidding. *Early* January?"

"Yeah. Not late, he wasn't there when Terry was killed, I checked that out—he was at a two-day conference making speeches. Fred hops on a plane whenever he feels like it, but all his business ventures are in the Midwest. When I saw that stub I knew for sure I had to take matters in my own hands. What the hell was he doing going to Tucson?"

"'*Mr. Barnett*,'" I said. "Now I get it." The room was getting chilly. The stove needed more wood. I picked up shreds of cheese from my plate. "He told Rosa his name was Mr. Barnett."

"What are you talking about? Who's Rosa?"

"She works for Dr. Ivan Fowler, you know, Heather's ex. Rosa told me a man came to see Dr. Fowler just after New Year's, a Mr. Barnett, he was really rude, yelling at her. I just assumed it was Terry, but I bet it was Fred. It sounds a lot more like him than Terry."

"Fred went and saw Heather's ex? Fred doesn't even know Heather." He looked at me skeptically. "Boy, that makes no sense at all."

"That's because you've been hanging out here, and *I've* been investigating. Fred went to see Ivan in January for the same reason Terry did, six years ago when he moved down to Arizona. Mike, he went to see Ivan about *April Matasky*."

"April?" Mike flung out his hand, knocking over the pint of sour cream. "She's nothing, *nobody*."

"Everybody's somebody," I said irritably, righting the sour cream and jamming on the lid. "I had a talk with Ginger, who was April's best friend. I've been trying to reach you for days about this, and now you're going to sit still and listen."

AFTER I'D FINISHED telling Mike everything, he sat quietly for such a long time, I wondered if he'd gone to sleep.

"Jeez," he said finally. "You really think this Ivan guy might have killed April?"

"He's definitely creepy. Creepy enough to kill someone under the right circumstances. Now that I know you're not Fred, I think he and Terry looked up Ivan instead of going to the bar.

Who knows what he told them. What did they say when they got back to Ohio?"

He shrugged. "Not much. Shit, they were only gone about a week, like they got there, turned around, and came back. The feeling I got from Terry was, *don't ask*. Besides, I kind of didn't want to know. I'm basically a peaceful person and April was just trouble."

"It never once came up later?"

There was another long silence. The burning wood snapped and hissed in the stove. Mike looked tired. For a moment, he stared off into space, then he whooshed out a breath. "We both avoided April as a topic of conversation. She was—well, she was kind of a sore point between Terry and me. He knew I didn't like her after seeing the way she acted when she was here."

"How was that?"

"Like your basic slut. It was early summer when Fred brought her back, the last summer me and Terry and Fred all hung out together." Mike sighed. "Maybe the best summer of my life—except for April. She was too wild, too crazy. Like some whirling dervish. I remember, one time, we went to a bar over in Clifton, that's this little town not too far from here. They had a band. We all got pretty pissed. April danced with everyone in the place." He looked disgusted. "She had on some kind of thin blouse, you could see her nipples. And she wasn't even that good-looking when you saw past the clothes and all that makeup."

"Well, then," I said huffily. "She obviously deserved to be murdered."

"Come on, you know what I mean. Besides, that's not all. I—" Mike's face got red. "It's hard to explain. She was staying in the motel. She called me up, with some lame excuse, and asked me to come over there. So like a dope, I did. And she— I don't know how it happened. She started telling me what a drag Fred was, getting my sympathy. Anyway." He sighed. "She got me in the sack."

"No," I said. "You *slept* with April?"

"I told you, she was awful."

"Then so were you."

He looked hurt, but I wasn't buying. "Come on, it takes two." My voice rose in annoyance. "And who are you to judge her, anyway? You don't always get it right any more than the rest of us. Look at Terry, how unrealistic you are about him."

Mike looked surprised. "What do you mean?"

"He wasn't so perfect either. I mean, he asked me to dinner in Mexico without bothering to tell me he was married."

"So? He probably saw you as a friend."

"I don't think so. Mike, he went out on Heather *all the time,* cheated on her, everyone knew. He had *affairs.*"

"Affairs." Mike laughed loudly.

I went on, "That's why Terry was suspicious of Heather; he couldn't be trusted himself. Another thing, if April went for you, I bet she went for Terry too. Or vice versa."

"Vice versa? He went for her? I don't think so." Mike got up, went to the stove, opened the lid and jabbed inside with the poker. He did it several times. Jab. Jab. His back was rigid, like a stubborn kid who's been scolded. "Terry didn't go for women," he said over his shoulder. "They went for him."

"Okay, okay," I said in exasperation. "She went for him. What's the difference? There was something between them or Terry wouldn't have gone to see Dr. Fowler, *April's counselor,* when he first moved to Arizona."

"Jeez." Mike put his hands to his head. "You're making me crazy. So he went to see April's counselor. So what? That doesn't prove there was anything between them. Terry was off his rocker a little bit, his mother had just died. He watched her suffering for a *year.* He probably needed help and he remembered April mentioning this counselor."

"You told me Terry would never see a counselor."

"Maybe I was *wrong*. I'm not perfect either." He glared at me. "Terry's dead. What do you want to pick on him for?"

"I'm sorry, okay? Let's just drop it."

"Fine with me."

He came back to the couch, sat down. Neither of us said anything for a while. The fire in the woodstove ticked, ticked. A log shifted. Beyond, I could feel how the snow muffled the room, enclosed it in a profound silence.

Then Mike stood up again. "I have to get out of here. Think. I'm taking a walk."

"But it's snowing," I said.

"I've got good boots."

THIRTY

GONE OFF IN A HUFF, just like the last time, at the Blofelds'. Great way of dealing with things, Mike. Another spoiled brat, just like Craig, but instead of going off to South America to live life on the edge, this one was hibernating like a teenage boy in his playhouse, with his music and his computer. *Mike O'Reilly, whose mother used to make Irish lasagna.* Well, how long could he tramp through the snow? I glanced at my watch: seven forty-five. I'd give him fifteen minutes.

I sat on the couch for a while, listening to the fire tick, tick, and relenting a little. I shouldn't have laid into Terry the way I did; not to Mike, his best and oldest friend. Now he was mad at me, the messenger.

So many people were mad at me—Lucinda, Damien, the Blofelds, Peter French, probably even Heather—when all I wanted was to find out the truth and get my life back. Self-pity, cloying and saccharine, overwhelmed me. I should go home, lay it all out to Flynn, see what he made of it. Lulled by the silence of the snow, I fell into a repetitive series of fantasies of Flynn and me in some companionable space that existed nowhere in this world, hashing it out together, laughing over cups of coffee, while Flynn's chin hair grew black and prickly—

Something whooshed and thunked outside and I came to with a start. A chunk of snow falling off the roof. I looked at my watch: eight-thirty. I'd been sitting here for forty-five minutes. Where was Mike? Oh, Jesus, lying outside in the snow somewhere, freezing to death all for the love of his best friend Terry. I leaped up, put on my coat, Fanny's gloves, found a black wool scarf on a hook by the door, and underneath on the floor—hooray! galoshes; small enough for me, Sam's probably.

OUTSIDE THE SNOW had stopped, leaving a blank white world. Overhead, the sky was starry and profoundly black. Mike would stand out here, dark against the snow, but there was no sign of him.

"Mike!!!" I shouted, half tramping, half slipping through the snow in the clumsy galoshes. "Mike!"

Then down the driveway I saw footprints that doubled back to the house and up the porch of the big Victorian grandparents' house. The gray truck was still in the driveway, with my rental car. The house was dark. I went up the porch steps anyway, past the chrome and yellow vinyl chair with the stuffing leaking out, and tried the door. It wasn't locked so I went in.

I stood in a pitch-black hall. "Mike?"

Then my eyes adjusted and at the end of the hall, through a door, I saw a faint red glow and walked to it, floorboards creaking. Sitting on a stiff-looking couch covered with a dust-cloth, in front of an electric heater, was Mike.

Walking in the snow?

"Hi," I said. "Did you plan to sit there till I called the cops?"

"I had to think." He hunched forward on the couch, and cleared his throat where his voice had gone rusty. "Guess I was a jerk. Again. Sorry."

"It's okay." I walked over and sat beside him, raising a little puff of dust that tickled my nose. In the darkness around me, I saw the dim shapes of covered chairs, lamps beside them like sentinels, and a rose pattern on the threadbare rug where the heater glowed.

"So how did it go?" I asked. "The thinking?"

He took a couple of deep breaths. "Well, I have an idea why Fred would have gone to see this Fowler guy in January."

"Oh?"

"Because that's when his divorce became final. I bet he started stewing about his whole life, thinking about his old girl-friends. That's what I did when I got divorced. I even called up some of them." He laughed sadly. "'Course it would have been better if I'd called them sober."

"And April *was* an old girlfriend, more or less." My hands were freezing even with the clunky gloves. I took them off and held my hands near the heater. "It makes sense."

"Plus," said Mike, "even if it didn't work out the first time, Fred's rich now. Maybe he thought if he found her he could buy her back."

Maybe he could have. April loved to shop, Ginger said. I stared at a sepia-colored portrait on the far wall, trying to de-cipher it. Or was it a portrait? Maybe a landscape. "I wonder what Ivan told him."

"Whatever he told Terry, I guess. Frankly, I don't care if April's dead." His voice was bitter. "What if she wasn't and Terry found her and married *her?* I never would have gone to see him then."

"You never did anyway." Shit. I wanted to bite my tongue. "I'm sorry."

"You don't have to apologize," he said. "It's true. Now all I can do to make up for it is try and find out who killed him."

"Look," I said, pushing myself because I was fading, dim as the room, the events of the day closing in on me. "How about this? Terry was killed not long after Fred showed up at Ivan's. So maybe Fred said something, maybe not even on purpose, that focused Ivan onto Terry."

"Like what?"

Something both Fred and Terry knew, something threat-ening to Ivan? Something April had told them? But tiredness, and some of Mike's pain, his tension, had crept into my bones. I couldn't think anymore, I just wanted to go to sleep. And then, maybe brought on by my fatigue, in the darkness around me, among the dim shapes of covered chairs on the rose-patterned rug in Mike's grandparent's house, a strange thought entered my mind. I dismissed it. "I don't know," I said wearily.

I WOKE UP in a narrow bed, under an ancient sleeping bag with Barneys printed on it. On the bedside table, a lamp shaped like a rocket. A rocket? Then I remembered; Sam's room, when he slept over. Sam-sized jeans and T-shirts hung from the hooks on one wall. An electric heater like the one in the grandparents' house glowed red in a corner.

I'd had this idea in their house last night, what was it? I closed my eyes tighter, to block out the sun, shining bright through the window.

Sun. I had to leave by ten at the latest to pick up my stuff at the motel. I came to suddenly, thoroughly awake, and looked at my watch: ten after nine. I threw back the Barney sleeping bag and jumped up. I was already dressed except for my shoes. I walked out to the main room.

The place was reasonably neat but the rays of the sun picked up layers of dust on everything. In a little bathroom off the big room, I washed my face, avoiding my reflection in the speckled mirror over the sink. Everything I'd brought was at the motel so I brushed my teeth with Mike's toothpaste and my fingers. In the kitchen area, clean dishes were stacked in the drainer. There was coffee brewed and a box of doughnuts. I drank some of the coffee, put on my coat, grabbed one of the sticky doughnuts and my purse and went outside.

Over by the big shabby house, Mike was in the driveway behind my rental car, shoveling snow. I trudged over, munching on the doughnut. He was wearing rubber boots, a tan down jacket, and a red hat with ear flaps. His nose was red too. He looked up when I got close and stopped shoveling.

"I went out early." His breath made clouds in the frigid air and I could see a little patch of stubble on his chin, that he'd missed, shaving. "The roads are clear, and so's the driveway now, pretty much."

"Thanks." I stared past his shoulder at the basketball hoop on the garage. The net was half gone, the rest frayed, ancient. I thought of Fred, *boomity, boomity, boom.*

"Heather has to know the truth," I said. "That it's you and not Fred who wants to see her. I assume you still want to meet with her."

"Of course. Give me a day and time and I'll fly back down there."

"I'll work on that. And I thought I'd talk to this ex-bartender from where April worked. Tod Hines."

"Look, it could be all off base, you know, this stuff with April. It might not have anything to do with Terry's murder." He was backtracking fast from our conversation last night. "Check out the bartender, sure, but stay away from that Fowler guy." He looked at me meaningfully. "And Heather doesn't need to know we're doing this investigation."

"But she might be able to help."

"As far as I'm concerned she's not in the clear yet. Let me decide after I meet her."

"Whatever." I looked at my watch. "I should get going. Give me the number here, just in case your cell phone screws up."

He told me and I wrote it down. I opened the rental car door and got in. "Bye. Say hi to Sam."

I closed the door, but Mike didn't seem to be finished. I rolled down the window.

"Ever since Terry died," he said, "I've had this idea, that he was somehow speaking to me from beyond: get it together, Mike, wake up and change your life." He kicked at a mound of snow. "But now everything seems so complicated. I couldn't sleep last night, horrible thoughts kept popping into my head. I don't know where it's going, this whole thing, but, I mean, it's between me and you, no one else. Okay?"

"Absolutely."

A breeze came up and snow skittered across the driveway in little drifts.

"Look." Mike leaned wearily on the shovel. His nose was bright red and the arms of his down jacket were dusted with snow. "Even if Terry was sleeping with every woman in town, I don't want to hear about it. I just want to know who killed him. That's all I care about, only that. I loved him."

His eyes shone with unshed tears. He wiped at them with one gloved hand. Suddenly, I felt terribly sorry for him.

I DROVE TO THE Wayside Motel, showered fast, put on some makeup and my other set of clothes, checked out with the little white-haired lady, and took off for the airport. I thought about Mike and the way he lived, I thought about Mike and Terry.

The snow sparkled under the bright sun. All the shabby little houses close to the road were muffled under snow. Snow covered the white polyester chairs on the porches, shrouded the sticks that would be lilacs and forsythia in the spring. In one front yard, a snowman in a baseball cap, with a carrot nose, leered at me with coal-black teeth. A kid's bike lay on its side by the cleared driveway, snow along the handlebars, red banners stiff, pedals frozen: dead for the winter.

Arizona

THIRTY-ONE

I FLEW BACK from Ohio to Arizona, from winter into spring. Thanks to the time difference, it was still afternoon when I got into Tucson. In the terminal, couples embraced, children babbled. Carrying my overnight bag, I walked through a horde of people in shorts and tank tops, wearing my black turtleneck, my big black coat over my arm, like a bride of Frankenstein.

Outside, the palm trees stretched high toward the sky, the air was balmy. I thought of Craig, saying goodbye. I took the shuttle to the long-term parking lot, got in my car and headed for the I-10 freeway.

My driving was edgy, part of me still in Ohio, looking for patches of ice. It was cooler but not cold as I drove into Cochise County and took the Benson exit, headed for home. Home. No job and a possible serial-killer counselor maybe out to get me. I drove through Benson, past the Dairy Queen and the Horseshoe Café, in a kind of fog, thinking this: I would have talk to Dr. Ivan Fowler.

Or turn it all over to Flynn. Flynn interrogating Dr. Fowler. It was a delicious thought if (nice dream) Flynn would only let me sit in. But unless I wanted to tell Flynn about his harassment of Heather, interrogate Dr. Fowler about what? April? I haven't seen her for twenty years, he would say.

In St. David, I must have passed the elementary school and Church of Latter-Day Saints, so familiar I didn't notice them. *Dr. Fowler, why didn't April care what anyone thought? What made her so dangerous to herself?* I drove out of St. David, across the San Pedro River where the road curved through a sandstone mesa. *Dr. Fowler, did you kill her?* I blinked, and suddenly I'd gone thirty miles without noticing and was headed out of Tombstone. Ivan Fowler wasn't going to answer any of those questions.

But he would have some story about April. Whether it was true or not, I wanted to hear it.

To keep myself alert and to stop thinking I accelerated to eighty-five miles an hour on a long straight stretch of Highway 90, drove over the Mule Mountains and through the Mule Pass Tunnel. On the other side, as if I'd been gone for weeks instead of a couple of days, the cottonwoods lining Tombstone Canyon had begun to bud out. It wasn't quite spring yet, a false spring, but soon the air would be full of cottonwood fluff. Daffodils bloomed in the yards of the renovated miners' shacks and the fennel that grew in the drainage ditches scented the air with licorice.

In my house, on the kitchen counter by the stove where he was never allowed, Big Foot glowered at me. Except for the kitchen door, the dining chairs were still under doorknobs, silverware columns on the windows. How long was I going to live like this?

In the bathroom, the black silk sweater I'd worn to the opening hung on the door hook so now there would be a little bump in the knit where the hook had been. Next to the sink, the Street Wear color stick in Rita Red that had turned me into a Goth lay uncapped and dried out.

Time to get back to reality.

My answering machine was blinking. Four messages; three hang-ups and one actual message. "Hi, Chloe, it's Lee, Lee Thomas. I'm sorry I missed you. I'll be in San Diego for a week. I'll call when I get back."

Damn. Lee Thomas, who had a lot of influence, whose husband had been a judge, who could go to bat for me with Melvin Huber, maybe help me get my job back, and I'd missed her.

I checked the caller ID, found Lee's call, a series of calls from my old friend Unavailable, some of those probably from Mike, maybe some from Ivan, a call from Lourdes, from Larry, whom I'd asked to find out about Ivan from his partner, Nelson.

I made a pot of coffee. Drinking coffee is something the average person shouldn't do under stressful conditions; the adrenaline coursing through your body does enough without adding caffeine. Me, I was toughened up. Bodies fell around me like leaves in autumn, while I remained standing tall.

Clinging to this new and reassuring persona, I punched in Larry's number.

"You asked Nelson about Ivan Fowler?" I said when I reached him.

"Yeah. He's here now, talk to him yourself."

"Chloe? This Fowler guy? You were thinking about therapy with him?" Nelson sounded dubious. "He's pretty cutting edge."

"Oh? Why does that not sound like a recommendation?"

"Cutting edge is *good*. I mean, sometimes. I mean, it all depends." Nelson was practically stuttering in his attempt to remain strictly nonjudgmental.

"Depends on what?"

"The personality of the client, the skill of the therapist."

"Nelson," I said, "this is me, Chloe, and this conversation is just between the two of us."

"Well, okay, my impression is he's kind of a megalomaniac—operates on theories and works them out on the client. Don't get me wrong—it can be the way to real breakthroughs. Sometimes it works brilliantly."

"And other times?"

"You know those clinical trials they do with terminal patients? They try some new drug or treatment, and some of them get better, a few may even heal, but the rest, well, they go ahead and die, maybe even sooner than they would have without the treatment."

"You don't mean that literally, of course." I laughed. "Presumably none of Dr. Fowler's clients have died from his therapy."

Nelson laughed too, a little uncertainly. "Not that I know of."

We hung up. It hit me then, so obvious. Hadn't Ivan offered me therapy? I could beg off an actual session, but I could ask for referrals, his advice and *expertise*. The ideal way to approach him—go for his ego, soften him up; then in some nonthreatening way bring up April. It scared me, just thinking of it.

In spite of caffeine and adrenaline, I felt weary to the bone. Jet lag. It was only five-thirty, too early for bed. Pushing myself, I called Diana and Peter French where Heather had said she'd be staying. I didn't want to try to persuade her to talk to Mike over the phone, but I thought we could arrange to meet.

"Hello," said a male voice.

"Peter?" Peter pounding at the drunk cowboy with his fists. Presumably the man survived or surely Peter would be in jail.

"Yeah."

"This is Chloe Newcombe. Is Heather there?"

"Why?" His voice was stony.

"Come on, give me a break. Didn't she tell you it was okay for me to talk to her?"

He snickered then, as if relenting. "We kept running out of hot water, she could never get a bath. So she went home."

"Is that a good idea?" I said, in alarm.

"She'll be okay. Damien's keeping an eye on her."

Damien again. At least I knew where she was. I could drive out to the house in the morning before she had time to go anywhere. I went into the bedroom and lay down to rest for fifteen minutes. When I woke up it was dark. I fell back to sleep, in my house in Old Dudley where people renovated their old houses, sawing and hammering day and night.

Hammering mostly. Not hammering, knocking, someone was knocking at my kitchen door. And I hadn't put the chair back under the knob. I woke up enough to stagger to the kitchen, where I grabbed a steak knife, flicked on the outside light and peered through the window.

Standing in the carport, in his leather jacket and running shoes, holding a padded manila envelope, was Flynn. I put the steak knife in the closest drawer and opened the door.

FLYNN BLINKED when I turned on the kitchen lights, like some nocturnal animal caught unawares. Under the jacket he wore a red T-shirt with D.A.R.E. on it. Subtle. But he looked different somehow, more vulnerable, then I realized why: in the flattering kitchen light, his chin looked smooth as a child's—he'd just shaved. For a moment, I was touched. Why should we be enemies? We both wanted the same thing.

He looked around. "What the hell?" he said accusingly. "You've been sitting here in the *dark?*"

I bridled, instinctively. "There's a law against *that* now?"

Flynn took half a step back, his uneasy eyes shifting away from mine, into the dining room to the table, bereft of chairs. "What's this?"

"Never *mind,*" I said.

He walked past the counter into the other room, clicking on lights.

I followed him as far as the dining room table.

"Is that what it looks like?" He strode to one of the windows. *"Silverware?"* He looked at the door. "Silverware and *chairs.*" He began to laugh. "Looks like you got your own—" He laughed some more, uncontrollably. "Your own—" Hee, hee, hee. Hee, hee, hee. *"Security system."*

He doubled over, clutching his stomach.

"Laugh all you like," I said darkly, stung. "It's not like law enforcement has been providing any protection."

Flynn straightened, pulled up his D.A.R.E. T-shirt and wiped his eyes. Then he came back to the table. His face was red, eyes sparkling with leftover tears from his laughter. "Where you been?"

"What do you mean?"

"Car hasn't been in the driveway for a couple of days."

I stared at him. How did he know that? "I guess things were getting to me," I said. "I needed to get away. What's it to you?" My voice rose, a little anxiously. "What are you doing here anyway?"

"God, you're a suspicious woman." Flynn looked at me thoughtfully. "Maybe the most suspicious woman I've ever met." He held up the padded envelope. "I brought you a present." He opened it and slid the contents out onto the table triumphantly. My gun.

He stood looking at me, preening, like a peacock; such an egomaniac. But still.

"My God, what a relief," I said, overcome. "Thank you. Thank you so much."

"No big deal." His tone was modest.

I picked up the gun. It looked different somehow, cleaner. "Where on earth did you find it?"

Flynn's face turned to stone. "It doesn't matter. People make mistakes, people can be real assholes. Let's leave it at that, okay?"

"*People.*" I stared at him for a moment, as a horrible idea dawned on me. "Like who? *You?* You took my gun after all, didn't you?"

"What the hell are you talking about?"

"You took it, had the lab check it out, and it wasn't the gun that killed Terry, so now you think you can just return it to me, no questions asked," I said scathingly. "The big hero."

"Bullshit! I don't operate that way!" Flynn exploded, pounding the table with his fist. "It would be completely unprofessional!"

He wasn't going to intimidate me. "But you do," I shouted back. "You haul me in for questioning! You don't care who sees it! I lost my job because of it, not that you care, you're just doing *your* job. That's *professional?*"

We glared at each other, standing at the table, chairs gone, doing duty as a security system.

Flynn's jaw worked. "You'd be in a better position to talk," he said, "if you didn't run around with married men."

He turned on his heel and walked away, through the kitchen.

"He didn't *tell* me—" I called fiercely after him.

Out the door.

"—he was married," I finished.

THIRTY-TWO

THE NEXT MORNING early so I would have plenty of time to go to Tucson later, I drove out to Prophecy. I didn't call ahead. The blue Volvo was still in the same spot, but this time Terry's red pickup was parked next to it. I parked a ways down on the street on the off chance Heather would hide if she knew it was me; the woman who'd been harassing her to meet Fred. An image of Fred, the real Fred, subduing the basketball, came to my mind.

I got out of the car and walked down the street to the gate. The cottonwoods along the river were a soft green blur.

I heard Heather's voice as I reached the open gate. "Look," she said. "Worms! Lots of them!"

"That's good?" said Damien dubiously. He was standing in the front yard, sideways to me, holding a pansy clump of palest lavender.

"It's very good, you dodo." Heather's voice was unguarded, as affectionate as a caress.

She was down on her hands and knees, in jeans and a faded navy blue sweatshirt, by the flower border to the right of the porch steps. A blue bandanna was tied round her head, and she was filling in the dirt around another pansy clump with a spade. The rich earthy smell of fresh manure filled the air.

"'The worms crawl in, the worms crawl out,'" she sang.

"'The worms play pinochle—'" Damien spotted me suddenly and stopped.

Leave them alone, said all my instincts. Go home, dig in your own garden. "Hello," I said reluctantly.

Annoyance, exasperation flitted across Damien's beautiful face. He had a smudge of dirt on one cheek, more smudges on his faded jeans and black T-shirt.

"Oh, Chloe, hi," Heather said distractedly, patting earth around the pansy.

"It looks like you've decided to come home," I said.

"Well, I had to, sometime." She paused. "And Terry's here, if he's anywhere. Yesterday, I was doing the dishes in the kitchen. And I saw him, out the window. He was standing there"—her voice lilted up—"smiling at me. For a minute I felt so happy. Then he melted away."

"Ready for the last one?" said Damien loudly.

Heather planted the pansy Damien gave her, then sat back on her heels, looking up at me. "Why are you here?" she asked. "Wait, don't tell me." She sighed. "It's about talking to Fred, isn't it?"

"No," I said. "I owe you an apology. Frankly, I wouldn't blame you if you never talked to Fred."

"You wouldn't?" Heather stood up, dusting off her hands on her jeans. Her face was radiant. "You don't have to apologize for anything, if you're not going to try to get me to see Fred. Did you hear that?" she said to Damien.

"Then why *is* she here?" he said suspiciously.

Heather turned back to me, smiling, more relaxed than I'd ever seen her. "I'm going to put the kettle on for tea. Would you like some, Chloe? Damien?"

"Not me. I'm *working*." Damien picked up a shovel lying by the path, raised it high over a bag of manure and plunged it down.

HEATHER PUT A KETTLE on and set two yellow mugs on the table. Except for a couple of bowls by the sink, the kitchen was spotless, every surface free of dust and grime. She must have come home and had a cleaning frenzy.

"The man who asked me to set up a meeting?" I said. "It wasn't Fred. He said he was and I believed him."

"What?" She looked astounded. "Then who was it?"

"An old friend of Terry's. I'm sure Terry's talked about him." I paused. "Mike O'Reilly."

Heather blinked. "Mike O'Reilly." Her voice was too light, as if from lack of air. "Oh, my God, Mike O'Reilly." She turned away from me abruptly, opened a cupboard, found two teabags. She turned back to the table, put them in the mugs. Her hands were shaking.

I felt cold. The letter. She knew about the letter, maybe even had read it and saw Mike as a threat. Had he been right all along?

"Are you okay?" I looked her full in the face, trying to gauge her reaction.

She smiled awkwardly. "Hearing Mike's name kind of threw me. Spooky, like meeting a ghost, because Terry talked about him so much."

Maybe that was all it was, a little bit of Terry resurrected when I mentioned Mike.

"Terry always wanted him to come visit," Heather went on, "but he said you'd need a bomb to rouse Mike."

"Terry's death pretty much did that. He'd still really like to see you. He'll fly out again if you'll agree to a meeting."

Heather's eyes drifted away from mine, glancing around the kitchen as if looking for a safe place to rest. "I know I should," she said without conviction. "Terry cared about him. But it will be so hard meeting him now." She looked tired. "Just give me a little more time, okay?"

I felt tired too. It was no use; she was too slippery, too hard to get a hold of.

Then two things happened at once. The teakettle whistled, I jumped, and from outside, Damien's voice called faintly over the noise of the kettle, "Heather!"

The teakettle screamed on, a rising crescendo, then stopped as Heather pulled it off the stove.

"Heather!!" Damien's voice was loud now, urgent.

I followed her down the hall and out the door.

"Damien? What's the matter?" Heather said.

"I was digging up the other bed." His face was blank, stunned, as he stood by the flower bed on the other side of the porch steps, still holding the shovel. "I wanted to surprise you. I thought it would be like the other bed, hard and full of caliche, but I started digging and the dirt was really soft. Then—" He stopped.

Heather looked impatient. "Then *what?*"

"Come here."

I followed Heather down the porch steps. Damien drove the shovel into the dirt and brought it up again. *"Look."*

He shook the shovel lightly, clods of dirt fell away, and then we saw it, innocuous looking as it lay on the shovel, smeared with soil and grime—a gun.

Guilt-ridden for no good reason, but guilt-ridden all the same, for a second I was certain the gun Flynn had returned to me was a dummy, and this one lying on the shovel was mine, planted there by Flynn, or *someone,* to incriminate me.

But this one was clearly smaller.

"For heaven's sake," said Heather. She leaned down and put out her hand. "So *that's* where it's been."

"Don't touch it!" I said, coming to my senses.

But Heather was already holding it, barrel pointed away from her, wiping it gingerly on the dry grass. She let go of it, looking up at me. "Why not? It's just an old gun that belonged to Terry's father."

"I remember now," Damien chimed in. "Terry showed it to me last summer."

Heather had told Flynn, hadn't she? That she didn't own a gun, or Terry either. She had, I was certain.

"It's been missing for a while," said Heather as if in answer to my unspoken question. "I never liked having it around. Terry must have buried it here."

In the *soft* dirt?

I took a deep breath. "Don't touch it again. Not with your bare hands," I said to her. "What you need to do is put it in some kind of plastic bag. It has to be turned over to Flynn."

Damien snorted sardonically. "Probably doesn't even shoot anymore. I remember he told us—" His voice faltered, his eyes far away somewhere. He shrugged. "It's just a stupid old gun."

"Us?" I said. "You said 'he told us.'"

"Me. He told me."

"You need to give it to Flynn anyway. Just in case." I didn't want to touch it and besides I could hardly confiscate it myself.

"I guess you'll tell him," Damien said to me.

"Why would I have to?" I said. "I'm sure *you* will."

"Of course we will," said Damien.

"I feel sick," said Heather suddenly. She turned and walked away into the house.

Damien looked at me angrily. He hadn't known the gun was there or he wouldn't have gone digging, unthinkingly calling for Heather and me when he found it. But now he'd had time to think.

"Who was with you," I said, "when Terry showed you the gun?"

Damien looked away from me. "My grandfather. Who cares? And now Heather's all upset. You should just leave."

So I did. I walked out the gate and down to my car, got in and sat there for a moment, thinking of Heather's reaction when I'd mentioned Mike O'Reilly. *"Spooky, like meeting a ghost."*

Heather had gone for the gun right away, wiping it on the grass, destroying her prints and any prints that might be under them. Had she done it unthinkingly, or with a motive? It wouldn't matter if it had Heather's prints on it. It was Terry's gun. Probably didn't even shoot anymore.

Damien knew something he wasn't telling. What?

From here, I could see behind the house. In the backyard someone, Heather and Damien probably, had dug up a big rectangle of dirt for a garden. In the sun, the dried-out grasses that surrounded the workshop had a golden sheen; the broken glass glittered. Somewhere a bird twittered, a dog barked. A trick of the morning light or maybe just my own adrenaline made the shop seem closer than I remembered it, as if it were slowly inching closer and closer to the house.

I turned on the ignition and started the car.

THIRTY-THREE

I PARKED DOWN THE STREET but close enough that I could see Ivan Fowler's spiffy lime-green Volkswagen and the front door to his stucco office with the red-tiled roof. It was almost noon, lunchtime for the doctor. Sally would probably be with him. I didn't know how I'd handle that.

Maybe I should have asked Heather to give me the gun, but thank God I hadn't. It wasn't like I'd been wearing gloves, and the last thing I wanted to do was give Flynn a gun with my fingerprints on it. My purse lay beside me on the seat, heavy with my gun. Waiting for Dr. Fowler, I took Flynn's card out of my wallet and laid it on the passenger seat. If Ivan killed me, the cops would find it and notify Flynn. Then he would be sorry.

What a jerk Flynn was, I thought, longingly. I stared moodily at the door to the office, the big window with the curtains you could see out of but not in. Dr. Ivan Fowler walked out. Alone.

I saw him but for a moment it didn't register. Then it did and I got out of my car. I walked toward him, a little off balance but surely, here in the Tucson sunshine, so hot, so bright, I would be safe from any harm he might do me. I should have been planning how I would handle this instead of obsessing about Flynn. I reached him as he stood by the Volkswagen.

"Dr. Fowler," I said.

He looked up questioningly and without recognition, keys in one hand. The sun glinted off his trendy round glasses. "Yes?"

He was wearing a brilliant blue shirt, yellow tie. In broad

daylight, he looked older than I remembered; the exuberant brown curls more dimmed with gray.

"I'm Chloe Newcombe," I said. "Do you remember? You called me, offered me counseling. I was in town and I thought I'd look you up."

"Ah, yes." His face blanked out to neutral and benign: the look of a professional therapist. "The crusading victim advocate." But he must be surprised to see me, had to be. "How can I help you?"

"I've thought about counseling. I know you're the best, Dr. Fowler, absolutely the best. But I can't drive to Tucson all the time. I thought you could give me a referral, someone closer to where I live."

"In Cochise County?" His voice was tinged ever so slightly with contempt. "These rural counties, not much there." He looked at me with suspicion. "But in your job, you must know the therapists. Surely you make referrals all the time?"

Of course I did. This wasn't going to fly. "Yes." I smiled weakly. "But I thought maybe you'd have some added insight."

He gazed at me for a moment, letting my words sink under their own weight.

"Miss Newcombe," he said impatiently, "I'm feeling a little…manipulated here. Your entire modus operandi seems to be deception but, you know, honesty really is the best policy. Maybe we could put our heads together and come up with the real reason why you're here in, say—" He stretched out his arm, and glanced at a gold watch. "Five minutes?"

Creep. Suddenly, I didn't care, what the hell. All I wanted was to get him off guard, wanted, if only for a second, some kind of honest reaction that I could assess. "Maybe we could start with everything you know," I said, "about a certain person."

"And who would that be?"

"April Matasky."

There was a silence, so loud it seemed to ring in my ears, blocking out the perpetual noise of Tucson city traffic. Ivan looked at me, dark shadows in his eyes, no trace left of his benign smile. He seemed to age visibly—closer to fifty than forty. Maybe getting tired of it all: day after day, the whiny patients with their repetitious and insignificant complaints.

"Miss Newcombe, I'm appalled," he said at last. "What has happened to your professionalism? You're asking me to discuss a former client. I don't think so. That's it. Goodbye." He aimed the remote control on his key chain at the car and the locks clicked. He opened the car door.

"Even if she's dead?" I said.

He didn't react, just got in the car. I thought he would drive off, but the window slid silently down.

"Look," he said, "you're clearly obsessive-compulsive. I suggest again that you *do* seek therapy. Get yourself back on an even keel. If you go on without treatment, you could cause real harm and not only to yourself but to others. Please think about it. Goodbye."

I watched, speechless, as the window slid up, his profile, as he started the car, remote behind the glass.

I WAS ON AN even keel, I thought defensively as I parked the car, slightly askew, at a slot at the Tucson Mall. Inside, the mall was cool and full of senior citizens walking vigorously. I found Power Nutrition on the first level near Dillard's.

Amazing how people still suffered aches and pains, impotence, memory loss, and sleepless nights, when all they had to do was come to Power Nutrition. The bright lights in the store hid nothing, except maybe the proven efficacy of the supplements and vitamins in the bottles and boxes that lined the metal and glass shelves.

Halfway down an aisle, a brunette in a white jacket was stacking even more bottles on a shelf. She looked up when she saw me.

"Hi!" She had deep dimples and an impossibly clear complexion. "Just so you know, our entire stock of vitamins is twenty percent off, today only. It's our green light special."

"Your what?"

Her face colored slightly. "Green light special. You know how Kmart used to have a blue light special? Well, we have a green light one. You know, *green,*" she prompted. *"Nature."*

"Nature, of course. Actually I'm looking for Tod Hines."

She smiled. "The green light special was Tod's idea. He's the manager. Down there." She pointed.

I walked to the back. I don't know what I'd expected Tod Hines would look like, but nothing as ordinary as the man I saw, fortyish, brown hair in a decent haircut, white jacket, wearing glasses with thin black frames. He was sitting behind a counter on a stool, at a computer.

"Tod Hines?" I said.

"That's me." Behind the glasses, his eyes were brown and pleasant. "Betsy told you about our green light special? Twenty percent off all our vitamins, and they're guaranteed one hundred percent natural."

His white coat and manner said doctor but of course he wasn't really a doctor, he just played one in a health and nutrition store.

"One hundred percent natural," I said. "In keeping with the green light?"

He looked concerned. "Too hokey?"

"I'm not the one to say. I've never been too involved in vitamins. I wanted to ask you about someone I think you once knew."

"Sure. It's a slow day, anyway." He pushed the glasses up on his nose. "Shoot."

"April Matasky."

He looked surprised. His arm went higher and he ran his fingers back through his hair. "Wow. Haven't heard *that* name in a long time. But what—You're a friend of April's?"

"No. I talked to Ginger."

"Ginger." His warm eyes cooled a bit. *"She's* a friend of yours?"

"Not really. I just met her."

"Fed you full of crap, I bet." Tod stood up and removed his glasses and his white coat. Underneath he wore a navy blue Ralph Lauren polo. "Look, I got a thing about raspberry Orange Juliuses. I feel like one now and I run this place. What say we each get one, sit somewhere and talk."

"GINGER, THE DRAMA QUEEN," said Tod scathingly. "That's what April and I used to call her. I don't know what she told you, but I'd take it with a grain of salt. She's full of shit. Always was."

"But she and April were friends. They were living together."

"April got stuck is all," Tod said. "She needed a place to stay. She was always bitching to me about Ginger, how she liked to run people's lives for them."

Or at least, handle their makeup. I sipped at my Orange Julius, thinking about Ginger. A woman with a baby in a stroller walked by and two teenage girls in identical outfits, black tops and khakis. "She told me April vanished," I said.

Tod snorted. "That's what she told everybody. She even filed a missing persons report. Place like Ace's, people didn't talk to cops. I sure didn't. April would have been really pissed if I had. They would have told Ginger and she didn't like Ginger knowing too much."

"What are you saying?"

He took the lid off his Orange Julius, drained it. "April didn't *vanish*. I know where she went."

My mouth fell open. "You *know* where she went? Where?"

"Ohio."

"Ohio? *No.*" I stared at him. "You've got it mixed up. That was earlier, before she vanished."

"You're thinking of the first time. She went off with this guy to Ohio *twice.*"

"*Twice?*"

He nodded. "I saw them. They waited till her shift was over then the three of them left together."

"Three of them?"

"Yeah. This guy Fred she went off with before, and his brother. I was tending bar that night and they came in. You should have seen her face when she saw them. Lit up like she was six years old." He smiled. "Funny girl, April."

"You're mistaken," I said. "April never went back to Ohio." But I was confused, floundering. Had she? Unbeknownst to Mike? How could that be? "I mean—did she call you? Send you a letter, a card, from there. Or from anywhere?"

"Naw." Tod's eyes veered off mine. He brushed at his immaculate navy blue polo. "We were just bartending friends." He paused uncertainly. "What? You know something I don't?"

"Just enough to tell you she didn't run off with those guys. Tod, she left all her clothes, *everything*."

He shrugged. "Easy come, easy go. Maybe she didn't go to Ohio. Maybe she wanted a total change. Took off to be alone, away from all the people who knew better than she did how she should run her life." Doubt clouded his brown eyes. He scratched his head. "Shit. I don't know. It was so long ago. I just did what I thought April would want me to."

I SAT IN THE MALL for a long time, with my empty Orange Julius cup, watching the people go by and thinking, Tod, what did I know about him? In Ginger's words, a real asshole? Or was Ginger, in Tod's words, an interfering, dramatizing bitch? It didn't matter, because while their interpretations differed, the basic fact they told me was the same—April had vanished and no one really knew where.

Vanished the same night Fred and Terry showed up at Ace's.

Ivan, the brilliant therapist, cold and manipulative. Terry wouldn't know that side of him, six years ago, when he came out West. He'd only know what April had told him. Terry's mother had just died—"*he was a little off his rocker,*" Mike's words. Was Terry thinking about his whole life, the way people do when someone they love is lost, the way Mike was doing now?

Thinking about what had happened to April? Fred and Terry and April. *"You should have seen her face when she saw them. Lit up like she was six years old."* Lit up, not for Fred, I bet, but for Terry.

Two brothers, competitive, always feuding; one woman alone, with no brakes. Who left the bar with Fred and Terry and was never seen again.

What could have gone wrong? April's face, lit up, not for Fred but for Terry; all that jealousy from Fred and Terry's childhood erupting into a physical fight. What had April done, a free spirit, dangerous, laughed, egged them on? Had they turned on her suddenly in some kind of fraternal bonding ritual? *What if Terry had gone to see Ivan to confess?*

Was this the secret Terry wanted to tell me on that bench in Mexico? That something had happened that night? Something had happened, April had ended up dead and they'd panicked and concealed it. It, meaning her body.

THIRTY-FOUR

IT WAS LATE by the time I crossed into Cochise County and I was hungry, so I turned off at the Sierra Vista exit and when I got there stopped at a Kentucky Fried Chicken. The desert night was cold, though spring was close, but inside the restaurant was very warm, well past the dinner hour and nearly deserted. I ordered a two-piece breast and wing meal from a young girl and listened to the teenage employees whooping it up in the kitchen, as I waited for my order. When it came, I carried my tray to a window booth.

Salt and grease, the ultimate comfort foods. Outside on Fry Boulevard, the cars and trucks kept moving by at a steady pace. All around me, the bright lights cast reflections. On the window glass a ghostly version of myself looked back at me. A woman eating alone in a fast-food restaurant like some contemporary version of a Hopper painting.

A woman alone. I was tired, so tired, and it seemed to me in my exhaustion that there was no safety anywhere for a woman alone, hypervigilant, always on the lookout; easy prey. Fred and Terry and April. Gun heavy in my purse, I walked out of the restaurant to my car.

There were so many questions. If Terry had confessed something about April to Ivan, why didn't Ivan go to the police? Why did Fred go see Ivan, all the way from Ohio shortly before Terry's death? What was it Ivan had said to me, *"If you go on without treatment, you could cause real harm and not only to yourself but to others."* Jeez. Ivan was somehow involved too.

I headed for home thinking all this, through the tangle of

lights and traffic on Fry Boulevard and into the desert, down the long dark stretch to the turnoff, and then over the mountains through the Mule Pass Tunnel.

It was only on the last stretch up the hill to my house that the implications of my confrontation with Ivan dawned on me. I saw now the way he'd goaded me, roused me to anger, to truth. *"Miss Newcombe, I'm appalled,"* he'd said. *"What has happened to your professionalism? You're asking me to discuss a former client."* *"Even if she's dead,"* I'd said. He knew that I knew.

Shaky, I got out of my car, went through the carport to my door that I only locked when I was at home. I opened it and walked inside to my dark kitchen. My feet crunched underfoot. Everything, everything felt wrong. I flicked on the light to chaos.

The curtains were torn from the kitchen windows, the floor strewn with sugar, coffee grounds, Cheerios, pots and pans, and the contents of half my kitchen drawers. And something else, rage; shimmering rage hovered in the air. I began to cry.

GUN IN HAND, I tore through the house, opening closet doors, to make sure no one was still there hiding out. At least the damage seemed to be limited to the kitchen. Idiot, idiot, idiot, I thought, as I dragged the dining room chairs back under the doorknobs, arranged the silverware. Just because Flynn had returned my gun, I thought I was safe?

Call Flynn, tell him everything. Like what? My kitchen was out of his jurisdiction, he'd just tell me to call Dudley PD. And Flynn wasn't going to investigate an ancient murder without a body and out of his jurisdiction. Heather was too scared of Ivan to be any help. If it *was* Ivan who'd trashed my kitchen.

Mike was back in Ohio, in his house, listening to music probably and feeling sad, while I took all the chances. Goddamnit, I sniffled to myself, I wasn't going to go this alone. I thought of Heather's reaction when I'd mentioned Mike. Why?

Did she know about Terry and April and was she afraid Mike knew too? But he and Heather had to get together sometime whether she was ready or not. I got my purse, found his number, and punched it in.

"Hello." Mike, voice fuzzy. In the background I heard Neil Young, on the edge of a feather. Expecting to fly.

"Wake up," I said coldly. "It's Chloe."

"Chloe. Jeez. What time is it?"

"Late." I sniffed, walking through the kitchen to the bathroom for a Kleenex, feet crunching underfoot.

"You sound funny. Like you have a bad cold."

I laughed scathingly. "Someone trashed my house is all."

"What? Who?"

"Someone who doesn't want me investigating, I guess. I talked to the bartender guy, from Ace's. Fred and Terry showed up there the night April vanished."

"No kidding." Mike's voice was a little breathless. "They just missed her. Pretty tough luck for them, huh."

How obtuse could you get? "They didn't miss her," I said. *"She left with them."* I flicked on the bathroom light.

"What are you saying?" Mike asked.

WHORE was written on my bathroom mirror in Chocolate Rose lipstick. The tube lay in the toilet. I stared at it dully. I wanted this to end as soon as possible no matter who got hurt.

"Face reality, Mike. April left the bar that night with Fred and your best friend Terry and was never seen again. You figure it out. You need to get out here just as fast as you can. Tomorrow."

THIRTY-FIVE

MIKE'S PLANE WOULDN'T get in until three. I was up half the night cleaning and the rest sitting bolt upright in bed holding my gun. The next morning I called Heather.

"Chloe. Hi." Her voice sounded wan, tired. I thought of her planting the pansies with Damien, almost happy, until I showed up. "Is this about the gun?"

The gun. I'd forgotten all about the gun.

"Damien gave it to Peter," she said. "He's going to take care of it."

"Actually, it's not about the gun," I said. "Heather, listen. Mike O'Reilly's flying in today."

"Mike?" Her voice was despairing.

I wasn't going to let her make excuses this time. "I thought we'd come out there tomorrow morning," I said firmly. "Look, it's okay. You and Mike are on the same side, Heather. He loved Terry, you loved Terry. There's nothing to worry about."

Nothing to worry about.

I couldn't focus on anything most of the day and by six I was pacing the floor. All I could think to do was to tell Mike everything I knew and I basically already had. If Heather didn't know already she would have to be told. Why destroy someone's illusions? But I kept thinking about April, dead. Blond and wild and flirtatious. Did that make her evil? Did that mean she deserved to die?

Six-fifteen. Where was Mike?

A throwaway person, so young to become nothing more

than old bones in the desert, strewn about by coyotes. Instead of a headstone, only rocks and cactus to mark her grave as if she'd never existed. But she had. Relatives could be dredged up, people who remembered her as a child, as a teenager. I wanted there to be something more, some kind of investigation, some final answers, to define the trajectory of her short life.

Six-thirty. Seven o'clock. The phone rang.

"Hello."

"Chloe," said Mike. "I'm checked into the Copper Queen. I'll meet you in the restaurant."

THE HOTEL WAS only a few blocks away. I put on a warm jacket and walked down, in the chilly evening. It was dark by now and lights were on in the little miners' houses, televisions flickered. In some of the yards, under the streetlights, I could see California poppies and bright orange calendulas in bloom.

The Copper Queen is a six-story nineteenth-century building, with a fancy paint job. I went up the steps. Pansies were blooming in the boxes that lined the porch. It was the middle of the week, and the lobby was empty except for a bald man behind the desk, reading Kant's *The Critique of Pure Reason*.

The restaurant was mostly empty, too, and dark except for little lamps that made arcs of light on the white tablecloths. An elderly couple in sweats sat at a table in the center. By the door to the kitchen, a young Hispanic waitress held a tray as she leaned against the wall, in the act of yawning.

Then I saw Mike in a corner by the window. I went over and sat across from him. He was eating a large steak. Even in the weak light from the shaded lamp, I could see bags under his eyes and his brown wool sweater had a rip where the ribbing of the crew neck met the body of the sweater. He wasn't pretending to be Fred, supersalesman, anymore.

"That's the biggest steak I've ever seen in my life," I said lightly, to ease my tension.

Mike's jaw clamped.

The waitress came over with a menu.

My stomach lurched. "Nothing, thank you," I said.

Mike put down his fork as if weary of eating. "You don't *know* anything."

There was a long silence.

"Foil," said Mike suddenly. "You don't cook baked potatoes in foil if you know what you're doing." He took the foil off, and mashed the potato on what was left of his steak. "I've never in my life, the whole time I've known him, seen Terry do something that could be construed as violent."

"Oh, *please,*" I said.

"This is all such *bullshit.*" Mike clanged his fork on the rim of the plate. "I *never* liked her," he said vehemently. "See-through blouses, where's that at?"

He pushed his plate away. "I told you, didn't I?" His voice rose. "I told you all I wanted to know was who killed Terry, nothing else."

"Ivan's in on this somehow," I said. "And maybe Heather knows and is trying to protect Terry. We're going out to her house first thing in the morning to talk to her. And we'll get her to file a harassment complaint against Ivan. She can hide out afterward. Flynn, the investigator, can question Ivan. At least try to get him off the streets."

Mike looked at me stone-faced.

But my mind was full of an image of Terry, lighthearted, green-eyed Terry, and Fred, dimmed by shadows; carrying April's body, her flesh heavy with death; digging a grave somewhere in the desert.

"It's all I can come up with at the moment," I said. "Terry's dead, I think he was killed because he *needed* all this to come out."

Mike sighed, weary.

"There's one other possibility," I said. "This could turn out better than I think."

"What's that?"

"We'll discuss it with Heather."

THIRTY-SIX

THE BREEZE FROM last night had turned into wind and driven all the clouds from the sky, leaving it a chilly vacant blue. Gusts tore at the mesquite trees along the side of the road. Out in the desert a dust devil whirled. Wind whistled through chinks in the windows of Mike's rental car. We turned at Meeks's Mercantile. The sign on the door said open. It was 8:05.

"Maybe we should stop here. Pick something up for Heather," Mike said. "Juice maybe. Yeah. People can always use juice."

He turned into the parking lot. I waited in the car till he came out, carrying a brown paper bag, his head bent against the wind.

We drove down the road.

"Just small talk, at first," I said. "Keep it nice and easy till everyone's relaxed."

Mike sighed nervously.

The red truck and the blue Volvo were both parked at Heather's. Mike pulled in behind the truck and stopped, and opened his door.

DUST FROM THE ROAD blew in my face as we entered the gate. The pansies Heather had planted a few days ago bobbed their heads frantically. The bag of manure lay beside the other bed, where Damien had found the gun, the meaningless gun. I went ahead of Mike and knocked on the porch door, opened it and went through. Mike followed, the porch door banging behind him. I knocked on the inner door.

"Hello? Heather?" I called. "It's Chloe." I knocked again. "Heather?"

No one answered.

"She's not here," said Mike in exasperation. "She's not here because you told her we were coming and she's skipped out. Goddamnit, Chloe."

"The truck's here," I said. "And the car. She's around here somewhere. Maybe she's not up yet." I opened the door.

The wind blew all around the house but inside it was silent, eerily silent. I stepped inside the hall, a bubble of anxiety swelling in my chest. *"Heather?"*

Why hadn't I warned her when I called her yesterday, told her about my trashed kitchen after I'd talked to Ivan? What if something had happened to her? For a dizzy second I saw how I could have done everything differently, kept no secrets, squelched my ego, turned it all over to Flynn.

"Come on," I said to Mike.

We walked down the hall to the living room, with its potted ferns and faded rag rugs on the satiny wood floor, the incredible collages. Dust motes still danced in the sun that came through long windows. Mike stood bemused looking in at the room.

"Heather!" I called again.

The kitchen was empty. The hands of the Mickey Mouse clock swept round and round. A half-empty cup of tea sat on the table, cold when I touched it. I walked across the kitchen and opened the studio door. Empty. The bubble in my chest felt bigger. I went back to the kitchen and bumped into Mike.

"Do something," I said to him urgently. *"Look."*

He blinked in a fog, holding the brown paper bag with the orange juice. He set the bag on the table. "Calm down," he said, "she's probably—"

I brushed past him down the hall, opening doors, a neat little bedroom and another big one, a bed slept in, not made.

"Chloe," called Mike.

"What?"

"Come here."

Mike stood by the kitchen window looking out. I came up beside him.

Outside near Terry's workshop was the rectangle of dirt, dug up for what looked like a vegetable garden. Dust blew all around in the wind. Stakes had been driven along the perimeter. In big sunglasses, baggy jeans, and baggy sweatshirt, wind tugging at a bandanna tied around her mouth, staple gun in hand, trying to attach a coil of chicken wire to one of the stakes, was Heather.

"That's her, I presume," said Mike sardonically.

"Yes." I giggled. "What you can see of her." I giggled again, weak, silly, with relief.

I tapped on the window, to get her attention.

She looked over, and waved us out to the back. The wind gusted then, the chicken wire bounded out of her grip, wrapping itself round her legs, tripping her up. She sat down abruptly on the ground.

I GIGGLED AGAIN as we went outside.

"Xanax," Mike said to me. "That's what you need." He bounded over to Heather, nervousness gone, confidence restored at my expense.

"Hi, Heather, I'm Mike O'Reilly," he said breezily, looking down at her. "Let me."

He took the staple gun out of her hand, grabbed a coil of the wire and stapled it into the stake, once, twice, three times, pulled the wire taut and walked to the next stake.

Heather stood up clumsily, dusting off her jeans. Her bandanna had come loose. I stood beside her, near the workshop, glass glittering, dust blowing, watching Mike in his element as he went round the plot, manfully battling the wire, stapling it into the stakes.

"See," I said. "He's not so bad."

"I never said he was." Heather's voice was sad. "Good old helpful Mike."

Mike finished, threw down the staple gun, and walked toward us. "What you going to put in here anyway," he said, "lettuce?"

Heather pulled the bandanna off her face, shook it free of dust. Her bangs flopped over her sunglasses, filmed with more dust. "Not today, that's for sure," she said.

"Wait." Mike stood stock-still, staring at Heather. "Say that again."

Heather took off the sunglasses, cleaning them on her sweatshirt bottom, looking up at Mike. "Not today," she said.

"Shit!" said Mike, suddenly exploding. "Shit, shit, shit. No wonder Terry didn't stay in touch much. He couldn't bring himself to tell me. He thought I'd be pissed."

He threw back his head, looking up at the sky. "Jesus Christ." Suddenly he whooped. "He didn't do it!" He whooped again. "Thank you, God, thank you. He didn't do it after all."

"What is he *talking* about?" Heather said to me.

"I'm not sure," I said. "Help us out here, Mike. Who didn't do what?"

He threw out his hands. "Terry didn't kill April."

"How the hell do you know that?" I said.

"Because she isn't dead."

"Oh, yes she is," said Heather. "She's dead as dead can be, but Terry didn't kill her." Her mouth twitched. "I did."

"You always were a bitch, April," said Mike.

He turned on his heel and strode away.

THIRTY-SEVEN

"A BITCH," SAID HEATHER. "He called me a bitch."

"You were April," I said, still stunned, as Heather and I walked inside to the kitchen, out of the wind, and yet I'd had an intimation of this, days ago in Mike's grandparent's house. *"Why?"*

"It was a way to break out of my rigid personality. It was Ivan's idea. My ex—he used to be my therapist. The ultimate role play." She rolled her eyes and went over to the window, peered out. "Mike's still walking."

"Don't worry," I said. "It's just how he deals with things."

She giggled. "He's such a dodo."

"So Ivan told you how to act, in this ultimate role play?"

"Not exactly." She turned toward me. "April was my first collage. I made her up out of bits and pieces of girls I knew in high school, bleached hair, sexy clothes, and suddenly she turned into a real person—April Matasky from San Diego."

"Pretty extreme," I said. "Wasn't she a little self-destructive?"

"No. Well, maybe. But it was really fun being her, at least for a while." Her eyes gleamed. "All these guys started coming on to me, the kind that had never noticed me before, and I was invincible. I didn't give a damn." She glanced out the window again. "Ooh, Mike's almost at the river."

"I followed your trail," I said accusingly, wanting her attention. "All the way from Ace's to Ohio and back again. Then you up and vanished the same night Fred and Terry showed up at Ace's. What happened?"

"I fell in love with Terry in Ohio. When he showed up at

Ace's with Fred, suddenly I lost the knack of being April. I didn't think he'd love me back if I was me," she said sadly. "She was magic and I wasn't."

"There's all kinds of magic," I said.

"Well, I didn't have any that night. None. I felt too vulnerable to deal with anything. I had them drop me off a block from my parents' house. I left everything behind and went home to my parents, just plain old Heather again."

"Heather's *fine*," I said. "She's talented, creative. Terry married her, didn't he?"

"I don't know." Heather sighed. "Sometimes I think he married the ghost of April."

"But why the hell," I said, "did you marry Ivan?"

She looked defensive. "He seemed so nice, so caring. But he kept pushing and pushing me to go back to being April. When I wouldn't, he started being awful. When I left him he said, 'Who else would want an ugly girl like you?' I guess his ego couldn't take it."

It still couldn't, I thought. Still searching for April, seducing his receptionists and dumping them.

"Even after we got divorced," Heather said, "he wouldn't leave me alone."

I pounced. "What about *now?*"

"Sometimes." Heather brushed at her bangs. "God."

"What if he killed Terry?"

"Ivan wouldn't kill anyone," said Heather shakily. "He's too subtle, he'd rather torture them." Her voice rose. "When this is all over, I'll move away. Somewhere he can't find me."

"He sounds like a killer to me," I said. "How can it be over if you won't tell the cops about him? You need to tell *Flynn*. And you need to get a restraining order."

"*No*," said Heather, despairingly. "They don't *work*."

"They can," I said urgently. "If Ivan killed Terry, Flynn can figure out a way to trap him, a wire or a recorder, or something. Build a case, slowly."

"No." Heather turned back to the window, as if to shut me out. *"Mike.* He's coming back. He hates me. Oh, God." Her voice trembled.

"I don't think I'm ready to have it out with him right now."

I wanted to stay, work on persuading her, but Mike would just make things worse. "I'll head him off," I said, reluctantly.

"Would you? Please?" She bit her lip. "I feel bad about Mike. Always wanting to be like Terry. But everything rolled off Terry, and everything stuck to Mike." She sighed. "He always had to be so…so, I don't know—real!"

MIKE DROVE DOWN the road to the highway. The wind blew through the chinks in the windows, but the silence inside the car was stifling. Why should I say anything? I wasn't the one who'd walked off in a huff to the river.

Mike turned onto the highway and sped up.

"Goddamnit!" he said suddenly. "Look what you did, with your theories. You actually had me believing Terry was a *murderer*. Terry, my best friend. And we wasted all that time."

"We have a good suspect," I said. "Ivan. He's still harassing Heather, she told me."

"Ivan? Are you kidding? Can't you see what's right in front of you? Heather killed Terry."

"How can you say that?" I yelped.

"He cheated on her, had affairs. You told me so yourself."

"Not for at least a year. And it doesn't mean she killed him anyway."

"Oh, no? *April* would have. She never loved anyone but herself. You think Heather's not April because she has a different name? Hah! She's an *actress,* Chloe. And think of the anguish, the public humiliation, being cheated on and lied to. We're talking about feelings here." He banged on the steering wheel. *"Passion!"*

"Calm down," I said.

"Not only that, Chloe, you know what?"

"What?"

"You were there when that woman got shot by her husband, what was her name?"

I turned my head away, to the window. "Evangeline."

"I think you're biased in favor of Heather because you feel responsible for Evangeline. So you fixate on Heather, as if Terry were abusing her like that woman's husband was."

"Cheating on someone *is* abusive," I said.

"Give up, Chloe, okay? Just give it up."

For some reason, I saw Craig right then, I saw him quite clearly, poling down the Amazon in a long boat, like a scene from *Aguirre: The Wrath of God*. I saw piranhas too, nibbling at the surface of the water.

"You're biased too," I said, "because you slept with Heather when she was April. You know what? I bet you had a secret crush on her. That's why you're being such a shit."

The car swerved. "I can't believe you said that." Mike's voice was outraged. "How stupid can you get. She's not even pretty."

"Oh, *grow up,*" I said in exasperation.

"I'm dropping you off," said Mike. "And I'm going to see that Flynn guy and tell him everything I know. We'll work together."

"Well, good luck," I said, "working with Flynn."

"I've had it with you, Chloe," he said through his teeth. "You're *fired.*"

THIRTY-EIGHT

FIRED AGAIN. SO WHAT. THAT didn't mean I was quitting. Back home I made a pot of coffee, drank two cups and paced the floor. I was full of energy, raring to go. Mike was going to talk to Flynn, turn him against Heather; I had to talk to her, prepare her, persuade her to tell about Ivan. I drove back out to Prophecy.

Mercifully the wind had died down. It was sunny and springlike, with a faint fuzz of green on the borders of the blacktop. But at Heather's there was no truck parked next to the old blue Volvo. Damn. I parked and got out.

The pansies were perky in the flower bed where Heather and Damien had planted them. Through the porch windows I saw the flare of red geraniums. Our domestic world goes on for a while longer when our lives fall apart around us. I went down the path and knocked at the door just in case. I called her name but no one answered. The key might still be under the doormat, but I didn't even look.

I walked around the side of the house to the back, to the rectangle of dirt, where Mike in his last moments of usefulness had stapled chicken wire to the stakes along the perimeter. The big cottonwoods along the river were soft as clouds.

Terry's workshop was fuzzed around the edges with green, like the highway. The door to the shop was open, padlock dangling from the hasp. It had been closed, earlier that morning, I was sure. *"Don't get too close,"* Brandon, Damien's grandfather, had said, *"the structure's not too stable."*

Damien. He knew something. What? The gun didn't seem

so meaningless anymore. Heather said he'd turned it over to
Peter French. Had he? I looked over at the Blofeld house. No
old VW, no motorcycle.

I walked over to the door of the workshop, and looked in.
Sunlight came down in shafts though the window, shining onto
a big Skil saw as if it were some kind of altar. Tools hung in
neat rows on a pegboard along one wall that was partially
blackened with soot. Next to it, incongruous in the shop setting, where you might have expected to find a lurid girlie cal-
endar, was one of Heather's collages; vibrant, alive.

It seemed to me, in spite of everything, Terry really had
loved Heather, just not enough. *"I have been faithful to thee,
Cynara, in my fashion."*

A cot near the back was turned over on its edge. It must be
the cot where Terry had been sleeping. I held my breath and
saw him clear as day, measuring the space for my bookcase. I
could feel his reassuring presence. What a lie.

Nothing moved in the big sunny room, nothing seemed tot-
tery; no creaking boards about to fall. I stepped inside for a better look. Terry's playhouse. He played at being a good
carpenter, played at being married. Poor old Fred, building an
empire, when he could have been having fun like Terry. Then
something did move, in the shadows to one side of the door.

A man stepped out in front of me, a man who must have
been there all along; quiet, motionless, while I was thinking
about Terry and Fred.

"What a waste, huh?" said Howard Meeks. "What a terrible waste."

"For pity's sake," he said. "I didn't mean to startle you."
There was soot in his pale red hair, and soot blurred his pink-
rimmed glasses as if he'd been rummaging through the ashes.
"You was in the store, not too long ago."

I nodded. "I'm Chloe," I said. My heart was still beating a

little fast from the shock. "A friend of Heather's. What are you doing here?"

"I left something, before Terry was killed. Put it on his workbench. Didn't have the heart to ask Heather about it before, but I decided it was time and then—she wasn't home." He scratched his head. "I thought—well, it won't hurt to have a look around."

He must have looked for whatever it was really hard. There was soot on his brown shirt too, and on his denim pants. You couldn't call them jeans, exactly.

"What was it?" I asked.

"A videotape." He took off his glasses, blew on them. In the bright light that came through the windows, his blue eyes, which I'd remembered as mild and benign, now seemed vacant. "Just a little old video like we rent out, but this one's got Brother Louis on it. Healing folks."

"Oh?" I said. The video I'd found in the trash. The strange blurred vision of another world, where Howard lived. I didn't have the nerve to tell him it was at my house. I could drop it off at the store the next time I came out here.

"Brother Louis was a real healer," said Howard, "a healer of the body, and a healer of the mind too. The mind can be very, very sick while the body appears perfectly healthy." Behind the glasses, his eyes shone with a supernatural sweetness.

"Sickness," I said, remembering the video. "Or the devil."

"It's all called 'sickness' nowadays," said Howard. "People are too afraid of that other word. People don't believe in the Kingdom of God anymore, think it's too hard. But it's easy. Just believe one thing, just one, and it leads you to all the rest."

"Ah," I said.

He went on, almost dreamily, "Sometimes that sickness of the mind, that devil, takes over the body and it perishes, but sometimes it infects other minds, pure minds even, and causes great suffering. I watched little Heather suffering for a long time. He wasn't a good husband." Howard spat on the ground. "Little Heather would go away and she'd be there."

"Who?"

"Don't know." He looked mysterious. "I saw her sometimes when I was out walking my dog, going into the workshop, back to me, big old hat on. Never heard her car, not once. I know all the cars."

"The night of the murder? Did you see her then?"

"No." He shook his head. "It was too cold for me and Buddy to be out that night. I hadn't seen her for a while before either, or I would have told the investigator."

"Maybe she was just a friend," I said.

"I don't think so." He stared past me, for a moment. His eyes were moist, as if with tears. He took out his sooty handkerchief and blew his nose. "I don't hold with gossip so people think I'm blind, but I see what goes on," he said thickly. "Terry was so blessed too. God gave him gifts." His voice rose. He looked a little demented. "I *tried,* I always tried to offer Heather assistance."

Suddenly I was really spooked. Had he killed Terry to save Heather from suffering? Howard was staring at me. Afraid he might see this thought dawning in my eyes, I looked ostentatiously at my watch. "My goodness, I'm late."

I walked backward, away from Howard, wanting to reach my car. He followed.

"I'm so *late,*" I said, half running to my car. I got in.

Howard hammered on the window. "Wait!" he said.

"Have to go!" I yelled. I backed and started down the road.

I COULD SEE Howard in the rearview mirror as I drove away, standing by the house, scratching his head. He looked like a skinny old redheaded crane. The farther away I got the less threatening he seemed. I mean, why would he have to do anything—it would all come out anyway on Judgment Day. Poor guy. I should have told him I had his precious video.

How could he believe what he did? About devils and suffering and the healing of the sick. *"Just believe one thing, just one, and it leads you to all the rest."* April was dead and Terry and Fred had killed her. It was only then that I began processing what Howard had told me. Howard the gatekeeper. A woman, coming to Terry's shop? Who? According to Peter and Diana, Terry hadn't been unfaithful for at least a year.

Did Heather know?

Up ahead was Meeks's Mercantile, a motorcycle parked in front.

As I slowed for the turn, Damien came out of the store. Damien. I braked, pulled in next to the motorcycle, got out of my car.

He was in the act of uncapping a bottle of water, but stopped when he saw me.

"Hi," I said. "Heather told me you turned the gun over to Peter French. So I guess he gave it to Flynn?"

Damien went back to opening the bottle, throwing the cap on the ground. "Flynn's picking it up today." He upended the bottle and drank about half of it. He wiped his mouth and shrugged lackadaisically, his eyes far away. "I mean I *think* today."

I didn't believe him. "You told me someone was with you last summer when Terry showed you the gun. Who was it?"

Damien backed away a little. "Told you that too. My grandfather."

He was hiding something, I could sense it. I didn't know what to ask, the right questions. I said, feeling my way, "When someone is murdered, it changes the person who does it. It makes them dangerous, even to themselves. They have to be caught."

Damien drained the bottle and tossed it. He walked over to his motorcycle and got on. "Not if the person they kill deserves it."

I stared at him. The sun shone down on his dark hair and eyelashes, his beautiful blue eyes, as he started the motorcycle. Damien, Heather's friend. Damien, the poet: *"I thought I could save her, I don't know why."*

My mind veered crazily. I felt a little sick.

Damien roared away. *Had* he given the gun to Peter French? The gun that Heather had wiped so carefully on the grass? I needed to know.

THIRTY-NINE

I DROVE DOWN the gulch past the art galleries, the shabby wooden miners' houses, the spiffy remodels, and parked by the long flight of steps that led up to 32 Zacatacas. The pile of bricks was still there. I got out of my car and climbed up the cement steps with the iron railing that meandered up the hill, through rabbitbrush, pyracantha, spiky ocotillo.

And somewhere someone was still practicing their guitar, the same chords over and over.

I stopped at the rust-colored gate of free-form geometric designs. I could imagine Peter welding that gate, maybe taking a few days, making a nice gate for Diana.

"Hello?" I called and opened the gate. "Peter? Diana?"

The door and all the windows of the adobe house were open. They were casement windows, *"magic casements, opening on the foam of perilous seas."* Keats. That was what a liberal arts education did to you.

"Hello," I called again.

No one answered, no one came from the house; a small house with a door opening onto each room, bedroom, living room, and kitchen. I peered inside each room, in case the gun was just lying out in the open, waiting to be given to Flynn. Given to Flynn? Or disposed of?

The hell with just looking. I glanced down the stairs, saw no one. I started with the bedroom, Flynn had said, hadn't he, most likely place for a gun, bedroom; bedside table or—I stopped in my tracks. Flynn, the cop. It was Peter who'd stolen my gun, I'd bet on it. A cop once too, he'd known where to look. Had he been so pissed that it wasn't the right gun that he'd come back and trashed my kitchen?

I opened all the drawers, looked under the mattress. Nothing.

I passed the living room, not as promising, went into the kitchen with lots of drawers; dried herbs hanging, pans and plates on the counter, big cast-iron frying pan set to dry on a stove burner, daffodils in the brown jar. Lots of drawers, untidy and full of junk, but no gun. Then I saw another door, one I hadn't noticed last time, open, leading to a room off the kitchen, dark, without windows. But I could make out a sewing machine on a card table, big sewing basket beside it on the floor.

I went in, grabbed the sewing basket, carried it out to the kitchen, took off the lid and felt inside. Ouch. Needles, pins jabbed at my fingers. It was like stroking a porcupine. And saw, not a gun but something familiar. A walnut half, polished to a dark sheen, like the one Terry had given me that night at the restaurant in Mexico. I turned it over. "Diana" was inscribed on the edge. *"I don't have too many,"* he'd said, *"just for special people."*

Oh, well. Easy come, easy go. I put it back and saw, at the bottom of the sewing basket, another one. As if in a dream, I turned that one over. "Chloe" was inscribed on the flat edge. I hadn't seen it for ages, had thrown it into the junk drawer in my kitchen. How—

"Chloe!"

I jumped.

"I saw your car." Diana stood at the kitchen door, her blond hair tied back with the blue and gold Indian paisley scarf she'd worn at the art opening.

She stepped into the kitchen. The paisley scarf gave her an exotic look, as though a beautiful butterfly had perched on her head. "What are you doing with my sewing basket?"

"I lost a button." Guiltily I closed my hand around the walnut half. "I was looking for a safety pin."

Then suddenly understanding swept over me. Howard knew everyone's cars, he knew when strangers drove down the road.

"I'm used to the regulars, they go in and out and I don't even notice." Diana was a regular, Heather's best friend. I knew who had trashed my kitchen, written WHORE on my bathroom mirror: knew the meaning of the two walnut halves, hidden in her sewing basket.

Outside birds chirped, stopped. A shadow drifted past the kitchen window, sun going behind a cloud, coming out again.

"And I found this." I opened my hand, showed her the walnut. "Terry gave it to me, just like he gave one to you. You had an affair with Terry, didn't you?"

Diana looked stunned. There was a silence. Guitar chords drifted into the room. "Yes." She sat down on a rush-bottomed chair. "I'm tired of all this. So what if I did?"

"Why, Diana? *Why?*"

"He hypnotized me, turned me against Heather." She looked at me in despair. "He said things about her, that she was an actress who fooled everybody, that he could never ever trust her. He said she was having an affair with *Damien.*"

"You *believed* him?"

"Yes. I felt so *sorry* for him." She put her hands over her face. "Anyone could see it wasn't true. Me especially. She was my best friend." She moaned. "He told me he was going to leave her, then he couldn't do it. He said it was all over between us, last fall, right before Heather and I took a trip to Mexico."

There was a silence. Down the hill, someone called for a child. Nearby a small animal rustled the bushes.

"Actually, it was a relief," she said. "I got my life back. And my best friend. He said he was going to be faithful to Heather from that day on. And that was that. End of story." She smiled weakly.

"Not quite," I said. "Peter told you he'd seen Terry with a strange woman in Mexico. That must have been a shock."

The smile left her face. "I was so *disgusted!*" Diana stood up suddenly, face red with anger. "He'd lied about being faithful to Heather! I'd been just like all those others he didn't really care about. He turned me into nobody and, even worse, he was doing that to Heather over and over. It kept going round and round in my head, how Heather must feel. In his own mellow way, Terry was evil."

"What about Peter?" I said, goading her. "Does he know?"

"Peter? The prison guard?" Diana erupted in rage, pushing at a pile of plates, knocking them to the floor. "No, no, no! He was so *sure* it was you, like he *needed* it to be you. What? You think you're blameless?" She knocked the jar of daffodils off the table, then stopped breathless, out of steam. "You're as bad as me."

"Does Peter know Terry showed you and Damien the gun, last summer?" I said, undeterred. "The gun in his workshop?"

"Damien said he wouldn't— So what? The hell with everything!" Diana spun round her kitchen, a blond Valkyrie in some overwrought opera, knocking a pan off the counter, a big brown teapot. "So what if Terry showed me the gun." She smacked at the dried herbs hanging from the ceiling. They crumbled into bits and drifted to the floor.

"You drove out to Terry's when Heather was at the poetry reading," I said. "You knew where to find the gun."

She put her hands over her ears. "Will you just shut up. You can't prove anything." Under the butterfly scarf her face was defiant. "Besides, it's the best thing that could have happened. Heather will miss Terry for a while, but then she'll start to heal. She'll—"

"No! That's enough!" Peter French strode into the kitchen. "You lying bitch!!"

Diana screamed.

Time stopped.

FOR WHAT SEEMED LIKE eons, no one moved in the wrecked kitchen. Outside the guitar strummed on witlessly. A fly beat itself against a window. *The stillness in the room.* Then Diana backed away from Peter, toward the sewing room, crushing daffodils underfoot.

He didn't follow, his face vacant. "I loved you so much." He gave a kind of sob. "You were my princess."

Suddenly I wanted to see Flynn now more than anyone else in the world. With Flynn around I would never have to lock my doors again. With Flynn around—It was not the time to think like this. Surreptitiously I skirted the kitchen.

"I love you too." Diana's hands were shaking, her face pale, drained of blood. "It was a mistake, is all. The worst mistake of my life."

I reached the door to the living room.

"You always did everything right," said Peter. "I thought you were perfect."

"Look, Peter, we need to sit down, talk." Her voice was reasonable, as if she'd talked to him like this many times before. "There's so many things you don't—"

Suddenly he howled. "Goddamn you to hell." He leaped toward her, pushing her back against the wall, his hands going to her throat. "You deceitful bitch!"

She screamed again.

No one noticed me. I could leave now, save myself. But he was strangling her, she wasn't screaming anymore, her eyes bulging, face contorted, the butterfly scarf like a sick joke. He was going to kill her right in front of me, like he might have killed the cowboy if someone hadn't called the cops. I had to do something.

I came up behind him, pummeling him with my fists. It was like beating on a stone wall. I backed away, frantic; slipping on the wet floor, stumbling over pans, teapot shards. And saw the cast-iron pan on the stove. I grabbed it, raised it high, and brought it down on Peter's head. It broke his hold for a second, but his hands came up again. God, I didn't want to have to kill him, but I swung the pan again, as Diana coughed and coughed, slumping to the floor.

"Stop!! Police!!"

I turned wildly, pan held high, ready for action, and there at the door was Flynn, beautiful Flynn.

FORTY

"THERE'S SOMETHING I WANT to tell you," said Mike. "But first, congratulations on getting your job back. When do you go back to work?"

"Monday morning." I sighed. Monday was law and motion day, the busiest day of the week. Did I have an intact pair of panty hose? I didn't feel quite ready, had lost my edge. A job was like electricity; something you didn't notice till you lost it.

"That's great," said Mike. "They changed their minds, just like that?"

"Not just like that. I pulled some strings. I have a friend who's the widow of a Superior Court judge. She helped. And it helped that I'm not a murder suspect anymore."

He laughed. "I never for a moment thought you might have killed Terry."

"No, you were too busy focusing on Heather. But Flynn thought so."

"Jeez. He's kind of a scary guy."

"He gave me a hard time for a while but he's not so bad as I once thought. He's coming over to my house later today to put in a security system for me in exchange for dinner." I smiled. "Kind of to make up, I guess."

The morning was already warm. We were sitting on the terrace at the Copper Queen amid pots of pansies, near a big sago palm. Tourists ambled in the street below, taking their time, blocking the cars. Mike's rental was parked a little ways farther down, his carry-on bag beside him on the terrace.

"I feel sorry for the husband. Pete? That's his name?" said Mike. "Poor guy."

Poor guy indeed. But he was sticking by Diana. Oddly enough, so was Heather; visiting her in jail, bringing her things. It would take a year at least before it went to trial, if it went to trial at all. But I had faith in Flynn, there was no way she wasn't going to serve a whole lot of time. I could see her in prison, organizing the other inmates, setting up shows, Felony Art by Women.

"All the stuff that's happened," said Mike, shaking his head, "the years that have gone by, and what always keeps coming back is that summer twenty years ago. The time we drove over to Clifton, me and Fred and Terry and April. Remember I told you about that?"

"When April was wearing the famous see-through blouse."

Mike smiled. "That blouse was something. Blue with kind of glittery threads in it. From India. The girls in Ohio didn't wear blouses like that. She wasn't that pretty, she was something different than that, absolutely, totally alive."

He closed his eyes and held his face up to the sun. He was clean shaven and his hair had grown past the awkward stage, revealing a hint of a curl, kind of unaffected arty. He looked good, better than I'd ever seen him. He even had a faint tan.

"It was one of those hot muggy nights," he went on. "We went to this bar, Dutch's, and the air-conditioning wasn't working, so it was hot but the band was even hotter. Heavy metal kind of stuff. We were all pretty drunk. Everybody except me and Terry asked April to dance. Me and Terry were looking around the bar every which way except at her. You ever notice sometimes, how the guys that are the most interested, look like they're paying the least attention?"

"What about Fred? What was he doing?"

Mike laughed. "He was left pretty much high and dry. Every time he tried to dance with her someone would cut in."

"You told me you were all drunk," I said. "I'm surprised you remember so much."

"I remember everything," said Mike fervently. "I was still innocent then. Looking back, I can see it was one of the best times of my life." He tilted back his chair and gazed down thoughtfully at the tourists going by. "I didn't realize how significant it was, when it was happening." Then he grinned. "Guess that's 'cause I was living in the moment, huh?"

"Living in the moment. Sounds like Terry." I looked over at him. "But you said you had something to tell me?"

"My plans." Mike tilted his chair forward again and rested his elbows on the table. "First I'm going back to Ohio and take care of a few things. Spend some quality with Sam. Then—" He stopped.

I waited. "Then?" I asked finally.

"Then I'm taking a trip." He paused. "I'm going to Paris for a couple of weeks."

"What?" I laughed. *"Paris?"*

He looked offended. "What's wrong with that? You act like I'm some kind of hick. You think I've never heard of Paris?"

"You're going there all by yourself?"

"No." His face reddened. "Actually, Heather's coming with me. She's flying to Cincinnati to meet me in ten days and we'll leave from there. She's had such a rough time. It's the least I can do for Terry."

"For Terry," I stated.

"That's right, for Terry." He looked at me accusingly. "Don't say it. Don't you dare."

"I told you so."

"I don't care."

I thought of Flynn. We would probably get into an argument within ten minutes of his arrival at my house. I didn't have any better sense than Mike, but I didn't care either.

Mike stood up.

He picked up the carry-on and looked down at me. "You can say what you want. I know we're probably just spirits floating through space, but sometimes I think my whole life since that time in Clifton has been leading up to this."

He looked at his watch. "Got to go."

"Have a good trip," I said. "Both of them."

I watched as he went through the restaurant. Heather in Paris. She wouldn't be visiting Diana in jail anymore. A thought went through my mind: Heather and Diana, best friends. Then the thought passed, quick as a flash of light.

Mike came out from the front door, went down the steps to the street, and passed below me.

"*Au revoir,*" he said over his shoulder. Who did he think he was going to Paris with anyway? Heather, or April?

"Be careful," I called after him; I couldn't help it.

I watched him go down the street. He was still innocent.

A street spirit.

(fade out)

HARLEQUIN®
INTRIGUE®
WE'LL LEAVE YOU BREATHLESS!

If you've been looking for thrilling tales of
contemporary passion and sensuous love stories
with taut, edge-of-the-seat suspense—then
you'll love Harlequin Intrigue!

Every month, you'll meet six new heroes
who are guaranteed to make your spine tingle
and your pulse pound. With them you'll enter
into the exciting world of Harlequin Intrigue—
where your life is on the line
and so is your heart!

THAT'S INTRIGUE—
ROMANTIC SUSPENSE
AT ITS BEST!

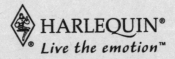

HARLEQUIN®
Presents

The world's bestselling romance series...
The series that brings you your favorite authors,
month after month:

Helen Bianchin...Emma Darcy
Lynne Graham...Penny Jordan
Miranda Lee...Sandra Marton
Anne Mather...Carole Mortimer
Susan Napier...Michelle Reid

and many more uniquely talented authors!

Wealthy, powerful, gorgeous men...
Women who have feelings just like your own...
The stories you love, set in exotic, glamorous locations...

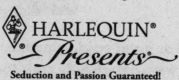

HARLEQUIN®
Presents

Seduction and Passion Guaranteed!

www.eHarlequin.com

HPDIR104

eHARLEQUIN.com

The Ultimate Destination for Women's Fiction

For **FREE online reading,** visit
www.eHarlequin.com now and enjoy:

Online Reads
Read **Daily** and **Weekly** chapters from
our Internet-exclusive stories by your
favorite authors.

Interactive Novels
Cast your vote to help decide how these
stories unfold...then stay tuned!

Quick Reads
For shorter romantic reads, try our
collection of Poems, Toasts, & More!

Online Read Library
Miss one of our online reads?
Come here to catch up!

Reading Groups
Discuss, share and rave with other
community members!

For great reading online,
visit www.eHarlequin.com today!

INTONL04R